About the Author

Liz Allen was born in Dublin in 1969. She wrote her first newspaper article at the age of 15, whilst still at school. She has worked on several national newspapers in Dublin as crime correspondent and her career took her into the depths of the Irish underworld and the judicial system. She was also called by the State to give evidence against several high-profile gangland figures.

In 2001 she left journalism to become a full-time writer. She lives in Dalkey, Co. Dublin, with her husband, Andrew, and their daughters, Elise and Anna.

Praise for Liz Allen and *Last to Know*:

'This well-researched crime thriller turns the spotlight on a world that most of us will be grateful never to visit'   *Irish Independent*

'Gritty and engrossing'   *Irish World*

'A terrific read . . . the plot sweeps along, never missing a beat . . . we might even have a Minette Walters in the making here. More, please'
Irish Times Weekend Review

'Deftly plotted, the book bristles with the pace of a good news story . . . It would be a crime not to read it'
. . . d on Sunday

D0645769

Also by Liz Allen

Last to Know

LIZ ALLEN

The Set-Up

HODDER

First published in Great Britain in 2005 by Hodder and Stoughton
A division of Hodder Headline
First published in paperback in 2005 by Hodder and Stoughton

A Hodder paperback

1

A CIP catalogue record for this title
is available from the British Library

ISBN 0 340 82928 1

Typeset in Plantin by
Palimpsest Book Production Limited,
Polmont, Stirlingshire
Printed and bound in Great Britain by
Clays Ltd, St Ives plc

Hodder Headline's policy is to use papers that are natural,
renewable and recyclable products and made from wood
grown in sustainable forests. The logging and manufacturing
processes are expected to conform to the environmental
regulations of the country of origin

Hodder and Stoughton Ltd
A division of Hodder Headline
338 Euston Road
London NW1 3BH

PROLOGUE

For the first time in her life, Kate Waters was terrified. She was trapped, along with the other missing women. They were in a basement, just minutes from where police were investigating the disappearances. But the police had absolutely no idea where the women were. Nor did they know that Kate, central to the whole investigation, was among the trapped.

The best investigators in the Irish police force were on the case. Their hunt had taken them to within a stone's throw of the place where the women were being held. Unfortunately, the officers had no idea that they were so close. Kate was aware of this and it frightened her. She knew that they had no reason to search this place. And although they knew her captor, they had no idea that he was the man behind the abductions, and they certainly did not think that he lived here. That thought petrified Kate.

A rancid smell of sweat and stale urine permeated the dingy room. Three other women lay listlessly on the cold slate floor. She could see that two of them were breathing, their chests heaving slowly up and down like in the simulated slow-motion scenes they show on television to try to frighten motorists with the consequences of speeding.

Kate wasn't sure about the third woman, whose face had been kicked in, in a fit of aggression, by their deranged captor just hours earlier. Blood had congealed on the woman's chin and three of her teeth dangled from the nerves which attached them to her gums. The woman's body was bruised severely. Her hair was matted with blood and she was emaciated. She looked like something out of a horror movie. But this was the real thing, not celluloid fiction. This was really happening to Kate Waters and her fellow hostages.

The profiler now knew that she had been part of their scheme all along, that she had been used by sadistic figures out to seek revenge. She had learned so much about the whole plot over the past twenty-four hours and she would not have believed it possible that so many of those she had trusted were involved.

One thing troubled her more than anything:

where was the man she had thought she could trust most? Why had he not come to rescue her? Did he not care that she was missing now? Or, even more chilling, did he know that she was among the captured?

She shivered, a cold fear working its way violently down her spine. She wrapped her manacled arms tightly around her huddled body, as an horrific thought enveloped her mind.

Yes, indeed, where was Timmy Vaughan, the detective who had appointed her to the case? She thought he knew where she was. But why had he failed to come to the rescue?

'Please God,' she prayed. 'Please don't let him be part of it too.'

I

Dublin, March 2004

Number One disappeared after a night out in the city with her girlfriends. She was young, successful and beautiful.

Number Two disappeared after leaving the ultra-modern office complex where she worked, at the end of another day's work which ran into darkness. She was young, successful and beautiful.

Number Three disappeared after disembarking from a flight following a business trip to New York. She was also young, successful and beautiful.

It was four months since the first disappearance and only now had they called Kate Waters, the specialist crime-solver. She knew that most of them resented her being there. They had waited weeks before relenting. And now . . . now it was like an admission of failure that they needed outside help. Not that they put it like that. When she worked with the police, she rarely got credit from them.

A lateral overview of the situation. That's what they called it.

'We are conducting a review of the cases and you might like to come and hear what we have gathered so far.' That's how they put it to her. Well, they all spoke the same language. They needed her help. She knew it and they knew it. But they would never come out and say so. It was just a question of pride.

Still, they were paying her fifteen hundred pounds a day for her services. They needed her help.

They should have called her in much earlier, but from past experience she knew what they had been doing. They'd been following police procedure, doing everything by the book, trying to get a lead on a case when what they really needed was outside help. Given the pattern that had emerged so far, it was hardly your run-of-the-mill crime.

When Number One was reported missing, they took it as just that. A missing woman. Perhaps she had a fight with her rich boyfriend? Perhaps she'd a fight with her parents? A Missing Person's report was blithely filed on the police computer system and nobody lost any sleep over it.

When Number Two went missing, the same thought process was invoked and the same procedure was followed. There were hundreds of similar cases each year. Most of the MPs, as police forces refer to missing person's cases, turned up a few days or, at worst, weeks later. There was usually some domestic or love-life strife as explanation.

But when Number Three went missing, some bright spark in the Missing Person's Bureau at police headquarters, where all of the information on MPs was stored in the database, suddenly made the tenuous connection.

The bright spark normally logged the details of the month's disappearances on the last Friday of each month. And it had been on the last Friday of the third month, that a pattern was noticed.

The disappearances were grouped in order by gender, age, address, physical attributes and profession. The bright spark was a member of the force but he did not work as a regular cop – he was a trained computer programmer who had taken an extra night course in the subject because he figured it was the way to advance in the job. Office politics, he was not good at. In computers, he excelled.

His brief was not to find parallels between the MPs. That was the job of the officers in the individual policing divisions in which the MPs lived.

It was also the job of the officers who operated the TRACE system, the operation that was put into place by the top brass in the late nineties after a string of young women went missing. It was a big deal and had cost the force a fortune. Everybody was still waiting on a result.

The bright spark who made the first links had an analytical mind. He had devised a program with a flag system. It was pretty basic really, but the way he told it made it clear he wanted them to think it was rocket science.

'I ran my program on an Intel Chip 1.6 giga-hertz processor. There are certain characteristics which are bound to be recurring, such as eye colour and gender, so that's your basic informa-tion which the program just digests and pays little attention to. However the flag system is more intel-ligent than that. The flag system is colour-coded. We have blue flags for MPs whose profiles do not match any of the others within the database. The blue means cold.'

'Gosh, thanks, Einstein,' Kate said to herself. 'This guy must think we were all born yesterday.'

Bright Spark did not appear to notice the look of resigned boredom on the faces of some of those gathered in the room. He ploughed on, too vain to even contemplate that he was boring the others.

'Black means there are similarities and it might be worth cross-referencing cases. For instance, a case will flag black if the characteristics of the MPs are different, but they might live in the same area or work in the same business. Nine times out of ten, though, the black flag similarities are just that. Coincidental similarities.'

As he uttered the last two words his eyes scanned the people in front of him, stopping briefly to be sure they were paying attention. Control freak.

Then a look of enthusiasm came over him. He was full of energy and anticipation. He must be coming to red . . . Wow!

Kate sat back in her chair and crossed her arms.

'Now a red flag is a different story altogether. A red flag means a series of similarities which are just too numerous to ignore. A red flag pops up when two or more MPs have close or almost identical traits, be it physically, professionally or education-ally. Or say, for instance, when the circumstances surrounding their disappearances are very similar. In this case, several of the strands apply.'

As he uttered his last sentence, there was a collective shuffle. Those who had been sitting back getting bored with Basic Computers I suddenly sat up straighter. Others had pens poised.

But he wasn't letting them off the hook that easily. He was intent upon dazzling them with his superior knowledge before revealing how he had reached his conclusions.

'As you all know, the MPB office is seen more as an administrative centre,' he said, clearly not happy about the fact. 'But I have been working with computer experts on a Natural Language Searching program. It's based on two types of data, structured and unstructured. The structured data searches on the basis of specifics, such as dates, phone numbers, car registrations, physical attributes, et cetera. The unstructured data is based on information that cannot be specifically categorized into any particular field. For instance, it will search for variances of red cars, such as burgundy, cherry, cerise . . . Now the extension of this Natural Language Searching is what we refer to as Fuzzy Logic. That means that there might be some logic to the data supplied, but the lines might be a little blurred. Basically, it conducts an intelligent search based on fuzzy data provided by people who are not one hundred per cent sure of their facts.'

Bright Spark paused, as he prepared to click on his Power Point presentation. 'Jesus Christ,' somebody further down the table sniggered, 'he thinks he's Bill Gates.' There was a low rumble.

Certainly, Kate had never seen anyone do a presentation on Power Point at Irish police headquarters before. It just wasn't that kind of a force. No wonder he didn't fit in.

'Number One. Sophie Andrews. Age, twenty-nine. A software engineer with computer giant Intel. Salary of a basic seventy grand a year plus expenses. Hails from the seaside town of Howth in north Dublin, but now lives in a penthouse apartment in one of those developments overlooking the sea in Blackrock in south Dublin. She went into the city centre four months ago for drinks and dinner in Ocean Bar and hasn't been seen since leaving Renards nightclub in the early hours of the morning. She had a pass for the club's Private Members' Bar and was well known on the social scene there. Her friends have reported that she said that she was tired and they walked her to the club's front door. The doormen remember saying goodnight to her and said that she told them she was walking to St Stephen's Green for a taxi.'

Bright Spark was turning out to be useful after all. It would have taken a specialist like Kate hours to glean this amount of information. She looked at the gathering of men in the room. Most of them resented the fact that she was in their midst at all. But, unlike Bright Spark, that resentment was nothing to do with the fact that she didn't fit in. It was more a case that most of the investigators didn't want her there for no other reason than because she wasn't one of theirs.

Privately, she had been told that they resented an outsider being brought in on their cases. Tough. Deep down, they knew they needed her.

'Number Two. Andrina Power. Age, twenty-nine. Rising star in the Mergers and Acquisitions division of the esteemed law firm Longwood Hayes Fitzsimons. Salary of seventy-five thousand a year plus bonuses. Originally from Dalkey on the south side, but now living in one of those swish ware-house conversion-style apartments in our very own Left Bank, Temple Bar. Frequently worked late in her offices at the Irish Financial Services Centre and was last seen leaving those said offices at 10.50 p.m. three months ago.'

'Where is this guy going?' she asked herself, as Ken Jones prepared to load a third slide for the last MP. He had not drawn any parallels between the first two. What was all this stuff about red flags? She wondered if she was the only person in the room thinking he was just an egomaniac on a day out away from his dingy office and his grimy computer screen.

'Number Three. Nikki Kane. Age, twenty-nine.

Second-in-command in the event management company named No Boundaries. Salary last year was a basic of eighty thousand and she took home another twenty in bonuses. Originally from a big pile in the embassy belt in Ballsbridge, but now lives in her mews on a site owned by daddy on the very exclusive Raglan Road in the same area. Last seen after stepping from the Arrivals hall at Dublin Airport following a connecting flight from London after a flight from New York.'

Jones could see that they were all waiting with bated breath for the similarities he had been going on about in his flag system earlier.

'Gentlemen, as these Missing Person inquiries were all handled by different stations, there has been, hitherto, no correlation of the facts available to you.'

From the look of admonition on his face, it was clear that Jones was critical of the way in which the three different police stations had handled the inquiries so far. He looked disapprovingly at the gathered officers as he spoke. His criticism might have been justified, but he should have kept it to himself. He just didn't know how to play the game.

Kate noted that he hadn't involved her. She was the only woman in the room. Maybe he would have addressed her if she were a cop. She wasn't going to lose any sleep over it.

There were uncomfortable stirrings in seats. These guys were detectives. They didn't like being told how to do their jobs by bespectacled computer nerds. Disgruntled looks flew about the room. Jones had better not so much as park on a double yellow.

'At face value, I'm sure you have all guessed that they have two things in common. All three women are aged twenty-nine and all three are successful.'

'Wow, Jones, thanks for giving us some credit,' somebody shouted out.

There was a collective howl of laughter that helped lighten the atmosphere a bit.

Jones continued as if there had been no interruption. 'But there are more similarities than that. Since my computer program made the connection between these three disappearances, you all now know that each of the women disappeared on a Friday night.'

They were beginning to take him a bit more seriously now. They were thinking, OK, maybe we have a sliver of something in common here.

'As you all know, our internal police computer system does not have the capacity to circulate photographic bulletins and as none of these women's disappearances had been categorized as high priority, until my discovery – until now, no cross-referencing has been done. Those of you in each of the three separate police stations will know what your MP looks like, but perhaps it might help all of you if you were to take a look at the photographs of the missing women from the other stations.'

Jones paused and opened a folder. There was a sense that he might be on to something good here. He passed copies of photographs of all three women around the table. 'I have also been working on a Facial Recognition program. We don't have those facilities here yet either.' Another look of disapproval on his face.

'In a nutshell, it is very similar to fingerprint and ballistic identification. I won't bore all of you with the science of it, but suffice to say, based on a series of characteristics, it reduces an image through a mathematical equation to a recognizable form. Because it is based on mathematics, that equation is constant. I took all of the physical characteristics which each of the three investigating teams listed pertaining to their missing women and created computer-generated images then used facial recognition to get to where we are now.'

There was complete silence.

Then the penny dropped. Everybody present immediately realized that all three women were almost identical in appearance. There was a common link all right – only the finest in the force had failed to realize it.

Detectives from each of the three stations started the damage-limitation exercise. 'But we had no reason to suspect that there was anything untoward,' said somebody from the Sophie Andrews inquiry.

'For Chrissake, this could still be very circumstantial evidence. We could be jumping the gun big-time here,' somebody from the Andrina Power team butted in.

'Come on, Jones, we all know how many bullshit MPs reports there are each year. Why should these, in isolation I might add, have been any different?' somebody from the Nikki Kane inquiry team barked. 'We don't even have any physical evidence to suggest that crimes have been committed.'

Which is exactly where a specialist like Kate came in.

2

Although Kate was not a police officer, she frequently did the job of a detective. So she did not hold it against the detectives for being stand-offish with her. She accepted that it was only natural human behaviour.

As she often asked herself: 'How would you feel if some outsider came into your field of expertise, with no qualifications in your line of work, and started doing your job?'

She admitted that her vanity would suffer. She would not be a happy camper if an outsider came in and not only did her job, but actually succeeded in solving major problems for her and her colleagues. She knew how it would make her look: inadequate and incompetent.

But she was also mature enough to know, even though she was only thirty-four – a baby in the minds of some of the detectives she dealt with – that sometimes what was called for to solve a big problem was an outside perspective. Or indeed, as they told her when they called her, 'a lateral overview' of the situation.

She could offer more than an outside perspective, however. She was a professional in her own field. She was frequently called upon to give evidence in court cases. But she was always quick to point out that she was not a professional witness, like certain psychologists who regularly took the stand in favour of the State's cases, no matter what the circumstances. They were known within the professions as 'witnesses for hire' and they were generally looked down upon by their more selective colleagues.

Kate had no interest in the celebrity aspect of the notoriety attached to being the public figure she had become. The media christened her 'Cracker', likening her to Fitz in the British criminal profiler drama. The similarities certainly weren't physical.

Although she was frequently invited to help solve crimes, she did not regard herself as a cop, though many did. Nor was she a psychoanalyst, because she did not delve into the depths of people's personalities. In fact, she rarely got to meet any of the criminals she helped to identify.

Kate Waters was a qualified psychologist and

practising anthropologist, now with the title of consultant crime profiler added to her curriculum vitae.

As she was quoted in one of the few newspaper interviews she ever granted: 'My love and passion is for the aetiology of human behaviour. I am intensely interested in what makes the human mind behave the way it does. Society is on a constant search for a reason as to why some people do the things they do. I, along with thousands of other colleagues worldwide, am there to try and find some of the answers.'

She came to prominence four years earlier, with an academic paper entitled 'Crime Times; The Make-up of the New Criminal and the Societal Factors Contributing to His Actions'. In researching it, she had been the only Irish academic ever granted access to the environs of the FBI's elite Behavioural Science Unit.

In her endeavours to break new ground regarding the causes of crime and the prime stimulants for recidivist perpetrators of serious crimes, she had chosen three well-known Irish criminals and used the BSU's profiling methods to profile the offenders and pinpoint the motivating factors behind their activities.

Kate's approach had certainly been a novel one

as far as Irish academia was concerned and when the Irish media got hold of the medical journal in which the synopsis of her thesis was published, she became an overnight sensation. The media loved writing about people profilers, such was the insatiable appetite for crime-related stories in Ireland. Kate felt that the interest in her area was mainly to do with voyeurism, hence her reluctance to grant interviews. It made her an even more prized asset.

After her study gained her such acclaim, prison governors, probation workers and certain judges started referring to her work and before long, the Irish police force decided to experiment with using a profiler on certain high-profile crimes. She was the woman they called. Now she was at the top of her game.

Which was why she was now sitting in a conference room at police headquarters in Dublin with thirteen men.

Her main stumbling block in dealing with detectives was always the same; all were trained to look for evidence. A gun, a knife, a weapon, a motive. Telephone records, bank statements, a warm engine in a car. A broken window; was it broken from the inside like the suspect says, or was it broken from the outside? Child's play to the forensics guys.

Kate was all too aware that the pressure from the public was on detectives more than ever, because advances in forensics brought DNA into common vocabulary. Gunpowder under the nails up to seventy-two hours after a gun has been fired. A strand of hair from a meticulously cleaned crime scene. Semen from a rape victim. Saliva taken from the rim of a once-used glass. The tools of crime-solving were becoming so refined that the public had come to expect immediate answers. The pressure was always on the crime-solvers to provide those answers.

In this instance, they had no evidence to work with. Without physical evidence, they were lost. The detectives made it clear that this was the only reason Waters was there.

Timmy Vaughan was the lead detective on the case. He was a typical weather-beaten cop with a passion for policing. Not just any type of policing; his was a passion for solving serious crimes. He had worked in Fraud, Domestic Violence and Sexual Assault, Drugs, Vice, and currently, the National Bureau of Criminal Investigations – home to the so-called crème de la crème of Irish detectives.

Vaughan was the man who called Waters in on the investigation. He was probably the least sceptical of her because she had worked with him previously, on two rape cases, three murders and a big white-collar scam which, it turned out thanks to Waters' deductions, was being perpetrated by the complainant who had devised an elaborate plot to pin the whole thing on a colleague and abscond with the proceeds. Six million of them, to be precise.

Nonetheless, Waters understood that Vaughan had his professional pride and, in front of his colleagues, he wasn't going to treat her with any deference. Not now at any rate.

'So, Cracker,' he said, 'as far as we can see, we may not even have a crime here at all. We are just having this conference because Jones's computer was flashing a red flag and the powers-that-be in Computer Section say that when we get a red flag, we have to at least look at it.'

Vaughan didn't like Bright Spark Jones and made no bones about it; if it was up to him, he would wait until he had a crime scene.

But, from past experience, Waters knew that Vaughan wouldn't even have been in the room had he not believed that there *might* be a case. He just wasn't going to give any credit to Ken Jones.

He was standing at the opposite end of the room to Jones. A subtle but effective point. He gestured with a sweep of his arm, as if addressing his colleagues, but excluding Jones. Jones did not count as far as Vaughan was concerned and that was plain for all to see.

Vaughan didn't look at Waters either, but she was the one he was really talking to. He knew it. She knew it.

'We have got to look at this in the cold light of day. Three women go missing. All are high fliers. All are beautiful. All go missing on the last Friday of the month. So what? At least one pensioner a week dies in my division. We're not exactly running to the local GP centre looking for the next Harold Shipman.'

At six foot tall and with a mane of jet-black hair, Vaughan was an imposing figure. He had the attention of each of the men. They all nodded silently in agreement. None of them wanted to admit that they may have overlooked the commission of a series of abductions. Or worse. Though nobody had mentioned the murder word yet.

'The fact of the matter is that these women are *missing*. That is the only *fact* we are dealing with at this point in time. Sure, there is also the coincidence that they all look strikingly similar. But apart from that we have nothing to go on. *Z-I-L-C-H*.' He spelled the word out for emphasis. To discredit smart-ass Jones.

Vaughan, his hands stuck stubbornly in the pockets of his worn-out chinos, waited for somebody to speak, waited for Waters to speak. He knew it. She knew it. Tough! She wasn't playing his game. She remained quiet. If this was the way he was going to treat her, then she could play hard-ball too.

Maybe ten seconds passed. The silence grew uneasy. Not for Waters. For Vaughan. She knew he'd get his own back later. But she was not going to offer a theory unless asked. The words from his phone call still rang in her ears: 'You might like to come and hear what we have gathered so far . . .'

Eventually, he was left with no option but to *ask* her opinion. Of course there was nothing deferential about it. But Kate Waters didn't really go for deference anyway.

'I suppose Cracker here has some read on the situation that us mere mortals haven't considered in the line of duty? Come on, Freud, what do *you* think we are missing. What's the explanation behind all of this?' More chuckles followed.

If Vaughan was hoping she would come out with some long-winded answer about disorganized social offenders and conclusions based on a series of scant propositions; something that would leave them all thinking she was full of bull and should scurry back to her dust-laden text books, he'd be disappointed. She had learned how to handle detectives the first time they worked together.

'You're wrong,' she said.

Vaughan looked taken aback. She had challenged him publicly and the chemistry was in full flow now. Both loved a challenge. How many of the men in the room could see what was really going on, she wondered. How many were aware of the previous history between her and Vaughan? In fact all of them knew. The story was legendary in Irish policing circles.

The hands came out of Vaughan's chinos and he performed a sweeping gesture, like a proud maestro encouraging an audience to congratulate his brilliant orchestra. Waters took the cue. It was the closest she was going to get to an invitation to elaborate. She could only be so cruel.

'You say that you may not even have a crime here, but in my professional opinion you certainly have. What you don't have is the type of crime scene you are used to working with. But you do have the signature of a crime. Look at the evidence.'

Vaughan merely raised a cynical eyebrow. He still wasn't buying her theory. What did she have to back it up? Certainly not evidence.

But Kate was not to be deterred: 'You *do* have

evidence, Detective Vaughan. It's just not the kind of physical evidence that you're used to.'

Vaughan threw her a sarcastic look. She had just insulted his intelligence and professional opinion by telling him that his approach was too basic, but there was no time for pussy-footing around as far as Kate was concerned. Work was work.

'Even if we were to take your first five points: they are the same age; they are all missing; they are all high fliers in their chosen careers; they are all beautiful; and they all disappeared on a Friday – only the most unsceptical person in the universe would not seriously question the commonalities. I can see why you want to look at this thing as an overall series of coincidences. But if you atomize it – and this is just on the face value of what Ken has given us so far – there are far too many of them for you to discard this as three separate MP cases and nothing more. When you pool the resources of the three separate investigation teams together, you will find *some* common link between all three.' She paused a minute before adding: 'It's my understanding this has not been done hitherto.'

The implied criticism did not go down well.

Kate let her analysis sink in a minute. She wanted to make them work to prove her wrong.

There was more disgruntled shuffling. They

would work like mad on it now, for if there was one thing Kate knew about detectives, it was that they hated anybody else telling them how to do the job. Basic psychology again.

'But without doubt –' she paused a beat – 'there is a common link and that link will lead you to the reason for the disappearance of these women.'

Waters was about to step onto the precipice now, but she had a gut feeling. 'I would say that the person responsible for the disappearance of these women is a man. He will probably be in his early to mid thirties, with a good job and a poor social life.'

'That could be half the people at this table,' Vaughan offered, 'except for the bit about the good job! With us it's the other way around, a poor job and a great social life!' His men laughed in unison.

Kate gave Vaughan a wry smile, but continued: 'He needs respect and he needs the trappings of success, but he has such a problem personality that the only way he can get those things is by exerting control over these women, after he has somehow managed to lure them into his confidence.'

They were all engrossed now. They were buying in, albeit grudgingly, to her scenario. After all, it was the only one they had. And most of them were thinking the same thing: what harm did it do to consider it?

'I would say that he is not a socially communicative person, but, at the same time, is involved in communication with others for his job. He probably had a bad role model in his father and either has no family or, if he does, has cut himself off from them. Most importantly of all, this guy is a loner. He is not flashy and he is not in a stable relationship. People don't wonder where he is after work on a Friday night. Finally, I would say that he is a good-looking guy. Otherwise, how else would such a sad loser end up attracting the attention of these women? We're not even talking about average-looking women here, gentlemen. We're talking about *really* attractive women.'

A few of the men nodded in agreement. It was clear to Kate that some of the younger men would probably kill for a date with one of these girls. She let them have their knowing looks, before continuing.

'Our culprit obviously has a type. Long black hair, big brown eyes and about five foot eight in height.'

As she finished her last sentence, a chill ran through her veins. Kate had just described her own physical appearance.

3

Barbados, November 2003

Sophie Andrews threw her head back in laughter. Her eyes were sparkling, her hair glistened and her body was tanned honey gold. Her long legs stretched fully on the luxuriously padded lounger she occupied. She was a happy woman. She was in love.

She still couldn't quite believe she had come with him. It had been such a wild thing to do, just up and leave everything. She hadn't told a living soul. That had been his idea, of course. It added to the intrigue of their relationship. It was so risqué! It felt like she had eloped – though without the marriage. But if things kept going the way they were, she would have no problem accepting if he popped the question. This was the life!

She felt bad about having lied to her friends

about her reasons for wanting to leave Renards nightclub before them, but they would understand why when they met him. He had suggested the rendezvous time. 'Three o'clock in the morning and tell nobody,' he had said. It had only whetted her appetite.

He had collected her from their pre-arranged meeting point in the tiny laneway linking Molesworth Street to Nassau Street. His driver had been so deferential, addressing him as 'sir' and never once speaking out of turn as he drove the gleaming black S500 Mercedes to the airport. Jonathon was obviously a very powerful man.

She had baulked when they pulled up to the private hangar. 'What are we doing here, Jonathon?' she had asked. 'Why aren't we at the main terminal?'

He had put an index finger to her lips and told her to shush. She had practically melted at the look he gave her. He was the first man around whom she literally could not control herself. She wanted, wanted, wanted, every minute she was with him.

He had leaned over and licked her lips then. It was just the slightest brush with the tip of his tongue along the outline of her mouth. She would have gone anywhere with him.

*　　*　　*

Sophie had first met him four weeks earlier at the taxi rank in St Stephen's Green. Her friends, Kathy, Evelyn and Janet had all scored lucky on their usual Friday-night trip to Renards and she had insisted they each go their separate ways, saying that she would take a taxi home.

He had seen her two weeks earlier in Renards. It was the most exclusive nightclub in Dublin and you had to be a known face, or be very expensively dressed, to get into the Private Members' Bar. She was the woman who was turning all the guys down. Nobody was good enough for her, it seemed to him. That's where the challenge lay for him.

But he hadn't approached her in Renards that first night. He did not go in for rejection. He waited and established that she went to the club regularly and that she always took a taxi home. If his plan was to work, he had to be certain nobody was waiting for her at the other end.

Two weeks later, as she had approached the long queue at the taxi rank, he had quickened his pace and reached it before her.

It wasn't uncommon to wait for over an hour for a taxi in Dublin city after midnight at the weekend. That was what he had counted on. Fifty minutes later, he was at the top of the queue. It had been fifteen minutes since the last cab pulled up. It was bitterly cold and pouring from the heavens. Typical Irish weather.

They began chatting, after she muttered something about the lack of taxis. 'I'm going to Blackrock. If you are going anywhere near there, feel free to share the ride. Who knows how long it will be before the next one comes?' he'd said.

Sophie mentally gauged the situation. It would be more sensible to wait, but that's where she was headed too and sure wouldn't the taxi driver be there for her security? She accepted the kind gesture for what she felt it was, a kind gesture.

He gave the driver his address first. She did the geographical calculations in her head. His place came first.

They began talking. Sophie first. He had stayed silent until she talked and she had liked that, been surprised even that he wasn't trying to hit on her. He was in business, he had told her, nothing else. But from the expensive cashmere coat and the Italian suit he was wearing, she figured it must have been very lucrative business.

When the cab pulled up at his house, she immediately thought the driver must have stopped at the wrong place. He was too young to own a place like this. But when she saw him press the zapper to open an electronically controlled set of high wrought-iron gates, she realized that the house was indeed his.

'Randall Lodge' it said on each of the high pillars positioned either side of the gates. She adored old houses. She had grown up in one herself by the sea in Howth, on the other side of the city, but now that she was out in the world on her own, she could never hope to live in such splendour. Property prices in Dublin were amongst the highest in Europe and she had resigned herself to living in her modern apartment for as long as she was single at least. Not that she was ungrateful for it. Her property developer father had purchased it for her when she secured her highly paid job at Intel. 'It's your start on the ladder, love,' he had told her.

The journey had taken only fifteen minutes, but during that time, he had certainly managed to put Sophie at ease. He had been so relaxed and, unlike many of the guys she seemed to encounter these days, he did not fit the pushy category. Perhaps that was what drew her to him, the fact that he could not be accused of trying to schmooze her. He was simply confident in himself. He wasn't arrogant, but he came across as being almost unconcerned about her.

She didn't know quite what had come over her when she heard herself accepting his offer of a brandy. Uncharacteristic was not the word for it. An educated twenty-nine-year-old woman should know better, she had told herself, but there was something about him that inspired trust. And if she was really honest with herself she would concede that the wealth helped a little too. It was so difficult to find a guy in Dublin who had the whole package – the looks, the charisma, the personality and the success. She wasn't getting any younger and many had accused her of being too choosy. Well, maybe the wait had been worth it?

Randall Lodge was a three-storey house over a basement, running to four thousand square feet. Despite its large size, it had a warm and inviting feel. It had clearly had the touch of an interior designer, she had thought to herself as she sat in the drawing room and admired how he had chosen to incorporate stunning minimalism with the original old feel of the house. She loved the simple linen curtains that draped elegantly against the white walls, bare of the usual gilt-edged mirrors and heavy frames that tended to be overused in old houses.

The modern artwork against the white looked amazing. It was exactly what she would have done.

He came into the room with a tray and two long-stemmed Villeroy and Bosch champagne flutes. 'I know I said brandy, but I prefer to celebrate life,' he had said as he filled the glasses, then waited for the bubbles to calm before filling each to three-quarters full. It was her favourite drink.

He saw her admiring the two rectangular side tables, which stood at either end of the couch and were used to hold stunning linen-shaded silver lamps. 'They are actually wine-coolers, believe it or not. The lids of the tables lift out and the wine is stored in the box beneath. Wine should never be stored in the kitchen, but it should be stored in wood, as opposed to metal wine racks. Wood maintains the temperature better and doesn't unbalance the body,' he told her.

Sophie hadn't wanted to appear too impressed. She changed the subject to his business. 'So what type of business do you do exactly?'

'I'm a venture capitalist,' he had responded. 'People who have good ideas, *very* good ideas, for investment projects, come to me with their proposals. If I think they've got a winner, I fund their projects, or more frequently, organize teams of investors to fund them.'

Sophie was into computers. Ask her anything about advanced mathematics and she would blind you with science. But the world of business baffled her.

'So how do you make money if the idea belongs to somebody else?' she had asked.

Jonathon Hunt had laughed at that. 'Money breeds money, sweetheart. Very often, the people with the best business ideas don't have two pennies to rub together. That's why people like me exist. When I am finished with them, they are usually worth several million more than they were to begin with and I get a huge chunk of their profits. Without the likes of me, they would never get their projects off the ground in the first place. It's a mutually beneficial relationship.'

The next few weeks passed her by like a hurricane. That first night, she had ended up talking to him for two hours, before he put her in a taxi and asked if he could call her again. He did not even attempt to kiss her that night. That was a first for Sophie. It left her wanting to see him as soon as possible.

But he did kiss her four nights later, on their second date, and on each subsequent date – always over a candlelit dinner in the best and cosiest of restaurants – and his sensuous mouth and hands always left her wanting so much more. A tingling sensation had filled her each day since their first meeting.

Four weeks after that first night at the taxi rank, Sophie was ensconced in the house he had rented for them in Barbados. From her position on her lounger on the deck, she was just feet away from the warm waters of the beautiful Caribbean Sea. Every minute of her trip with him so far had been nail-biting and pleasurable. From the shock of being taken on a private jet, to the passionate kissing as he had told her to lie back in the fully reclining cream leather seat whilst he fed her strawberries and champagne – mouth to mouth – she felt that she was living a fantasy.

She had been lost for words when she walked into Windy Villa. It was right in what was known as the Garden on St James's Beach. They were on the west coast of the small island, winter home to the rich and famous.

From the outside, it looked like a quaint little beach house, but once you looked from the shaded driveway through the wooden louvre shutters covering the windows, it was like seeing paradise. Two maids had come to greet them at the front door. Marcia, the cook and Elizabeth, the housekeeper, stood back proudly as they watched Sophie take in the stunning views.

The huge lounge was decorated in cool colours; the walls just a shade deeper than white and the couches a subtle pale blue. But what really took her breath away was the view through the wall-to-wall French doors to a deck that housed a swimming pool to one side and a huge bathing area to the front, from where it became obvious that the deck was actually perched high up on stilts above its own private beach.

Sophie was speechless. She'd thought she was doing well in the world, but this place was beyond her wildest dreams. She had never imagined herself in a place like this.

Taking her by the hand, Jonathon whispered in her ear: 'You think this is stunning, wait until you see the view from upstairs.'

Along the upstairs hallway, he pointed to a bedroom. 'I never go in there when I come here, even though there are three double bedrooms. This is the only room I use.' He led her into the most beautiful bedroom she had ever seen. It had French doors which looked onto a tiny balcony and, again, that spectacular view. And a huge antique four-poster bed stood in the centre of the room.

She had not slept with him yet. She wanted him to take her in that bed, but she knew that part of the excitement she felt about him was connected to the fact that he was deliberately keeping her at bay, teasing her. It was certainly working because there was no other man she could think of with whom she would have contemplated escaping to paradise after only four weeks. And certainly not without a word to anybody.

She had walked into the huge en suite to throw cold water on her face when he appeared behind her in the mirror. 'Take your clothes off,' he murmured. Sophie could feel herself throbbing as she looked at his reflection. He was so close there was no room for manoeuvre. 'Finally,' she said to herself, 'this is it.'

But Jonathon Hunt was clearly a master of the build-up. 'The maids have unpacked my bags. I took the liberty of shopping for you. Put your bikini on. We're going for a swim. I think you need to cool down.'

He had said it all in a whisper into her right ear and she hadn't been able to take her eyes off him as he spoke. The desire was too much. She thought she was going to die.

4

Dublin, March 2004

Timmy Vaughan and Kate Waters left the conference room in Harcourt Square separately, each
having maintained the sideshow of mutual resentment, and met up at Elephant and Castle in
Temple Bar. Timmy didn't want to be seen
hanging out with Cracker, lest it give his colleagues
the impression that he gave any credence to her
theories. Kate Waters played along because it was
part of the game they had always played. And she
enjoyed his company, even if things between them
were complicated, to say the least of it.

She looked on enviously as he tucked into his
big basket of chicken wings. He was totally focused
as he licked off the sticky sauce, then discarded
each one like a greedy child who couldn't wait to
get to the next sweet.

She was totally focused on them too, but she

was on a diet. Even though she was five foot eight in her stockinged feet, she had to watch her weight. Vaughan knew this and laughed as she took another forkful of her mushroom, spring onion and sour cream omelette. It was probably just as fattening as the wings, but it sounded healthier.

'Only thirteen left to go,' Vaughan teased in between bites.

Kate knew. She had counted the twelve he had eaten so far in an effort to speed up the torture. There were twenty-five in the basket. On previous occasions they had counted to ensure equal distribution and there was always a fight over who would get the last one.

'You can have the twenty-fifth, Waters,' he said teasingly.

'Just hurry up and eat before I resign from the case.'

'You're not on the case, Waters. You were just invited to hear the overview of the situation.'

'Yeah. Whatever.'

The problem with this case was that it was all over the place. They were both aware of that, though, in fairness, it was down to the system rather than the failure of the detectives. But they were the ones who would pay the price for not having been more alert to the shortcomings in the system. It was always the same and everybody involved knew that if the media got hold of the details, management would hang the investigating officers out to dry.

There were three different aspects to Missing Person's cases and Kate suspected that this was why it took so long before links were drawn between the three women.

In the old days, there had been a forty-eight-hour rule. A Missing Person's report was filled out at the police station in the area where the person went missing and only after forty-eight hours had passed was the case considered active. Even then, unless the circumstances were suspicious, people didn't become unduly worried.

But in 2002, the Crime Policy and Administration branch at police headquarters in Phoenix Park, or 'The Park', as the officers referred to their administrative headquarters, devised a new system of dealing with MP cases. Vaughan had handed her a copy of the document outlining it.

The big bold writing at the top of the official-looking document read:

THIS IS A CONFIDENTIAL DOCUMENT FOR USE ONLY BY MEMBERS OF AN GARDA SIOCHANA.

Waters raised a cynical eyebrow. 'So I *am* on the case?'

'Oh shut up, Waters, and get on with it. This is the stuff you need to understand if you're interested in finding out what we are dealing with here.'

The first part of the document cautioned, again in bold writing, that **accurate assessment** of the seriousness of the circumstances of the disappearance was 'paramount to ensure appropriate action'.

MP cases were now being classified into one of three categories, A, B or C, and as she studied the document, Kate immediately knew that this was the reason nobody had been overly concerned about the missing women, in isolation.

Category A was simple enough. Immediate action was needed if the MP was considered to be at serious risk by virtue of suspicious circumstances, being aged under twelve, suffering from an intellectual or physical disability, possibly abducted, a possible suicide risk or in need of dire medical attention.

There were a whole load of other bullet points outlining Category A situations, but only one of them caught her eye. It was the one that referred to 'persons who are missing for no apparent reason or whose circumstances have recently undergone radical changes (social, family difficulties, etc.) and who have not taken any personal effects with them'.

'Our women clearly don't fit into any of these categories, so immediately they were bumped down the priority scale,' Vaughan said.

Her brow furrowed quizzically. 'Didn't you say in the conference that all of them disappeared in only the clothes they were wearing? Wouldn't that qualify them for inclusion?'

'Yes, you're right to assume that they should have been included. But when Ken Jones made the link last week, none of them was being treated as a suspicious case because the initial inquiries learned from relatives that each woman had taken her passport with her. That would imply wilful intent.'

Vaughan moved on to Category B.

'These are people, who cannot immediately be classified as high risk or who have probably disappeared of their own volition. For instance, they could be between the ages of twelve and eighteen, still legal minors, and have had run-ins with the police before. In cases like this, we are encouraged to take pro-active involvement, but not to become too worried about them.'

As she looked down at the confidential document, it became clear to Waters why none of the
missing-women cases had been given a high level
of attention. Category C read: 'Disappearances
where there is no apparent threat of danger to
either the Missing Person or the public. For
instance, persons aged eighteen or over, who have
decided to start a new life.'

In isolation, each of these women might have
decided to throw in the towel and live on a desert
island, but the collective similarities regarding their
disappearances and physical profiles meant that
this could not be the case.

They were nearing the end of a very palatable
Faustino V and Vaughan was in full flow now.

'This system is only the tip of the bloody
iceberg,' he said. 'What happens when each report
is filed is that an *incident* is created on our PULSE
computer system. The officers dealing with these
incidents just log them as MPs and they are not
given high priority on the system unless they fit
Category A. So no All Stations' Bulletin was
attached to any of our three cases, and therefore
none of us knew about the other missing women.'

Waters knew about the Missing Person's Bureau
at headquarters in The Park and wondered why
no link had been made when the second woman,

Andrina Power, went missing. Vaughan was ahead of her.

'The Missing Person's Bureau at HQ is, by and large, just an administrative centre. Sure, it has links to Interpol and a host of other international policing agencies, but it is really more of a collating centre than anything else. It doesn't have an investigative role in the same way that officers on the ground do, so unless it was a high-alert case, the staff there wouldn't have noticed the similarities.'

She asked him about the TRACE computer system. It had been widely publicized in the media since its introduction. 'Why didn't TRACE pick it up, at least when Power went missing?'

Vaughan looked her straight in the eye, the frustration growing on his face: 'That's the whole bloody problem with the system I have outlined to you here. All MP cases go straight to TRACE via the MPB files. TRACE is a fantastic system because it contains a register of all sex offenders dating back to 1981. It contains the names of the people, particularly men, who missing women have been in contact with prior to their disappearances. It contains details of possible suspects and all suspected abductors and sexual deviants. It also has a search and cross-reference capability of sex offenders and their victims.'

'So what was the problem?'

'The TRACE system is bloody great when you define a particular set of search criteria. You simply tell the computer what you are looking for and it comes back with the information within seconds. But, as you heard from know-all Jones, it has no facial-recognition capabilities. Bottom line is that if we hadn't followed the damn ABC categories in the first place we would probably have looked more seriously at these cases from the outset. But we didn't and now we are up the creek without a paddle and three months behind the times.'

Waters felt sorry for Vaughan. He was a good cop, a thorough cop, prevented from doing his job by the system. A series of crimes had been committed here. She firmly believed that and she hoped she was right, because she had just stuck her neck out in front of a sizeable number of Dublin's detectives.

Waters looked him in the eyes. He looked down. He couldn't look her in the eyes for very long. She knew why. He knew why. Their history told a big story.

'You may not have any physical evidence yet, Timmy,' Kate said. She always referred to him publicly as Vaughan. But when they were alone, he was Timmy. 'But you do have something much more solid than a simple lead. You have three possible crime scenes. Not just one,' she said for emphasis. 'And not just two. You have three possible crime scenes. It's just not the type of evidence you normally work with. Which is where I come in.'

He looked a bit more hopeful when he spoke again.

'We need to go over their homes again, over everything, and I mean *everything*. There is something there, some clue, be it in their phone records or receipts or computers or diaries that will lead us to a reason for these disappearances and I would put money on it that that reason is a man. We just need to work hard at finding the common link, and now that you are on the case, I hope to jaysus that we will find it sooner rather than later.'

Much later, she sat in the coach house she called home, in front of a blazing fire. She prayed that she had been right in her assessment that there was a common link and that the common link would be a man with the characteristics she had outlined.

Part of it was professional pride. But another part of her wanted to be right because of Timmy.

She had caused him problems once before –
although she knew that he didn't blame her for
what had happened as a result of their *friendship*.
She didn't want to cause him problems again.

5

His father had always been big on respect. He knew the proverb by heart. It had been quoted to him often enough during his childhood, as his father had attempted to toughen him up.

Now the proverb served as his screen saver. He lived by the dictum.

He could still remember some of the scenes at home. He could remember them vividly, as if they'd happened yesterday.

'Come on, son. Be a man. Stand up for yourself. Why do you let them get to you?'

He could picture the drawing room on the first floor, looking out over the park. As a child, he had had it all; the stable home, the well-to-do parents, the first-class education in the best boys' school in the country. He had wanted for nothing. Nothing but respect.

At first it would be a friendly man-to-man chat. 'So, son,' his father would inquire as he fiddled with the watch chain hanging from the breast pocket of his bespoke suit, 'you have another excellent academic report, I see.'

'Yes, Father. Thank you.'

'So how are things coming along on the social side of things now?'

The teenager would stammer then. He lived in fear of his father's interrogations.

'Fi-fi-fine than-thank-ke-ke you, Father.'

His father's eyes would narrow to a squint.

'Really?' he would ask. 'So where is the proof then?'

And the teenager's failure to provide proof of any friendships would lead to the taunts.

'You are nothing if you do not have friends, boy. Nothing! You are nothing without respect and without friends you do not have respect. Do you hear me, son? Do you hear me? Write it down one hundred times. Write it down now,' his father would shout.

The boy would walk to the blackboard. His father had installed it at the bay window so that the boy would be forced to look out at all of the other children playing in the park and witness what he was missing.

HE THAT HAS LOST HIS CREDIT IS DEAD TO THE WORLD.

HE THAT HAS LOST HIS CREDIT IS DEAD
TO THE WORLD.
HE THAT HAS LOST HIS CREDIT IS DEAD
TO THE WORLD.

On and on he would go until he reached one
hundred lines.

It always took him at least an hour. His father
insisted that he draw perfectly straight lines. If the
lines were not straight, he was sent to the special
room as punishment. He had been going there
since the age of thirteen.

If the lines were straight and his father was
happy with them, they would go on to phase two
of the interrogation/lecture process.

'Now, son, tell me what this proverb means,'
his father would ask him as he sipped his post-
dinner brandy.

'It means that I must have the respect of others,'
the boy would answer, close to trembling.

'And how do you go about getting respect, son?'

'I must have friends, Father. And I must be
brilliant at what I do in order to gain their respect.
Once I gain the respect of a few, I will gain the
respect of many.'

'And what are you without friends and respect,
son?'

'I am nothing, Father. I am worthless. I have no place in the world, Father.'

'Very good, son. Now put that knowledge to use. Show me that you are NOT A FAILURE,' his father would bark, his eyes blazing with a potent mixture of fury and contempt.

The boy would know that he would be given one month's grace and if he did not have a friend home from school by the last Friday of the month, he would go through the same humiliation again.

And so the experiences of his childhood left an indelible print on the boy's personality.

He had never quite managed to make the friendships he so craved. He couldn't quite understand why. Maybe he tried too hard. Or had it been because he had always known that he possessed a superior intellect and somehow intimidated those around him?

These days, he didn't try at all. At least not in his everyday life. But when it came to women, he was different. He had watched his father with his mother. The man had never been anxious around her. He had always been self-assured. He had always made his wife work for his respect and, on the rare occasions he wanted to dole it out, affection.

'It doesn't do to let women know that you are

in any way keen,' his father had once told him during one of his monthly lectures. 'The way to lure them in is to feign indifference, son. Women love that. Especially well-bred women. Educated women are the only ones who have the intelligence to understand the subtleties of a man's complex personality and the empirical fact that a man must take control.'

Now he sat in his office and contemplated what he had achieved so far. He was brilliant, so he must be well on the way to achieving the respect of his peers.

As for the women? They were just a tool in an elaborate game. Nonetheless, he had each of them in his control. Each of them would do anything for him. It had been so easy. They were attracted to his wealth and his power. He had not had to bribe them, but he had taken control. Even more satisfying, he knew each of them liked him, not for the wealth he possessed, but just for his personality. Each of them had told him that in her own different way.

His father had been right all along. It was amazing what one could achieve when one had the ability to command respect.

6

'That poncey little prick'd better not fuck this up on us. He's like a bleedin' power freak, the way he's goin' on. He'd better not land me in it or he's a fuckin' dead man.'

Mickser Cummins was one of the most vicious criminals on the Dublin crime scene. He had a 'rep' which instilled fear in every up-and-coming thug on the scene and left most of his 'equals' on the same scene regarding him cautiously from a very safe distance.

At forty-eight and with more money than he could probably hope to spend, despite his flash lifestyle, he had built a reputation through sheer violence.

His nickname was 'Spiller' because his favourite method of pissing off the police was to masturbate in whatever police station they managed to haul him into for questioning. They never got to keep him in for very long, but he always left his mark against the wall – literally.

As far as the cops were concerned, Spiller Cummins was pure scum. An out-and-out knacker with not an ounce of human decency. As far as the other big-time 'crims' on the scene were concerned, he was a thieving, double-crossing, fearless, uncontrollable psychopath. They loathed the way he constantly aggravated the law, causing them to come down harder on the gangland crims. But drawing attention to his antics was Spiller's favourite pastime. He just couldn't help boasting about his accomplishments in his chosen 'profession' – thuggery and violence.

'Why the fuck hasn't he been in touch with us yet? I want to know what the bleedin' hell is goin' on. What's he doin' with those women anyway? The scummy little bastard is gettin' them all to himself. I tell ye, lads, when he gets them back here I'm goin' to have some fun with them. I've always wanted a threesome of look-alikes. And these three are like bleedin' triplets. The only way I've ever achieved that effect before is when I've been stoned!'

His 'boys' laughed, but Spiller was deadly serious. He intended to have some fun with these women, after he was finished pissing off the cops and watching them chasing their tails for months.

What was really annoying Spiller Cummins now was the lack of any media attention. He was really peeved about it because it was part of his grand plan to ruin Timmy Vaughan and show the pig who had the real power.

'Fuck's sakes, lads. We're dealin' with a bunch of bleedin' imbeciles here. They can't even spot a fuckin' pattern and they call themselves detectives. Fuckin' cowboys, that's what they are. A bunch of bleedin' losers.'

Spiller Cummins' crew all nodded in unison. They were gathered around a huge circular table which he had commissioned from one of the top furniture designers in Dublin. Its gleaming mirrored surface was held in place by a thick gilt-edged gold pedestal. The designer, who was more used to working on less flamboyant pieces, had tried to talk Cummins out of the mirrored surface, at least. But Cummins had insisted. He wanted the surface to ensure that he didn't lose any coke when snorting, although he hadn't told the designer this. Instead, he had handed her a brown paper bag containing twelve grand and told her to 'just get it done, love'.

As usual with Spiller Cummins' orders, they were followed to the letter and in double-quick time.

His crew consisted of Knocker Griffin, so named because he knocked people off, or shot them in the major organs to be precise. So far, he had four fatalities and eleven counts of GBH to his credit, although he had not been fingered for a single incident.

Then there was Breaker Daly, a huge body builder who specialized in breaking bones, particularly ankles and noses, which he found inflicted the most pain. He usually plied his talents on victims *before* Griffin got to work and if his violent antics failed to reap results, Knocker was sent to finish off the job.

The remaining member of Spiller Cummins' crew was No Knickers Grimes, a rampant sex fiend who liked to inflict painful anal sex on Spiller's targets, specifically men. He didn't go in for women at all. That was Spiller's kind of thing. Very often, if it had been decided that Knocker was going to finish off a victim, No Knickers would be given a while with him first, just to provide the guy with a memory of Spiller's crew which he could take to the grave, or, more likely, to hell. The presence of Knocker and Breaker on Spiller's team certainly frightened the hell out of the toughest of crims on the Dublin gangland scene, but it was the threat of an encounter with No

Knickers that terrified the opposition most. His reputation as a relentless deviant capable of the most public displays of sexual savagery was enough to frighten most other thugs into submitting to whatever Spiller and company wanted.

Knocker, Breaker and No Knickers had been with Spiller Cummins for the past fifteen years and they bore the scars to prove it. They had fought their way up from the mean streets of Dublin's inner city through more turf wars than there were heroin addicts and they were now at the pinnacle of their careers.

They had started out specializing in 'blags', or armed hold-ups as the police called them, and from there moved on to prostitution rings and car-ringing scams, and from there to credit-card fraud. And latterly, drugs.

Spiller and his associates had made a fortune through internet credit-card-fraud scams and for the past six years had been concentrating solely on the drugs trade. Their main contacts were in north Africa, Morocco and Northern Europe, Holland to be precise. They had a fantastic distribution network, which had been going swimmingly until eight months ago. Then there was a major cock-up in their distribution channels.

When their carrier was apprehended at Dublin

Docks, a contact had informed the gang and
Spiller had seen to it that the young carrier said
nothing by politely phoning the carrier's solicitor
– who was also the gang's solicitor – on his mobile
as they sat in Store Street Garda Station and asking
him to pass on a message to the carrier.

'Tell him not to worry,' he had told the solicitor. 'I want you to be sure to let him know that
I am keeping an eye on his wife and kids. It's
important to us that he knows that.'

The solicitor understood the message clearly
and so did the twenty-eight-year-old carrier, who
was mad about his super-skinny, peroxide-haired,
platform-wearing wife and the three kids they had
had before he finally married her. He just adored
Tiffany, Cassandra and Kylie, and whatever his
own propensity for violence on the scene, he would
never let anything bad happen to his kids.

But despite the carrier's loyalty, Cummins had
still lost his Dutch and north African distribution
lines and he was now branching out into this business with the women, in order to exact revenge.

Cummins had congratulated himself on his plan
on more than one occasion over the past four
months. He had needed something that would be
serious enough and high-profile enough to
demand the attentions of the best in the force.

Yet, at the same time, he had needed something that was in no way associated – in the minds of 'the filth' – with gangland activities.

He had a single objective – to make Timmy Vaughan's life absolute hell, to cause him so many problems that he would be ridiculed within the force and lose his livelihood.

Spiller Cummins wanted revenge for all of the millions Timmy had cost him by intercepting his drugs distribution line, and boy, had he devised a fabulous way to get it. The man would be the laughing-stock of the criminal community and a disgrace to the force by the time he was finished with him. He would lose his precious career, just as Cummins almost had.

And the beauty of the whole scheme was that nobody would ever dream of linking it to Cummins or his ilk. They would all be too busy hanging Vaughan out to dry for his mishandling of the investigation – from his post at the National Bureau of Criminal Investigations, to where he had been posted as the top cop after his bust on Cummins' network – to even look in his direction. It was a beautiful plan.

The idea had come to him one day when he was reading the *Irish Sun*. Actually, he had been studying the huge-breasted Page Three bird and wondering if she was Irish – and he had seen a teaser for a feature further on in the paper regarding various missing-women investigations which were baffling police throughout the country.

'Why not get the big cunt Vaughan in on the act with a spectacular series of abductions and see where we go from there?' he mused, and the idea put out its first roots.

Cummins didn't normally go in for 'outside help', but he had known that he would have to if this plan were to work. Which was where Jonathon Hunt came in.

They had watched Hunt for quite some time before deciding to use him. He had been a perfect choice: a loner, but educated and good-looking. He didn't appear to have a friend in the world and that's what had made him the perfect man for the job. It had been so easy for them to befriend him. The guy was a bleedin' loser who, as Cummins had told his crew in assuring them of his cooperation, needed all the friends he could get.

Knocker was effectively Cummins' right-hand man and he was also the one most capable of affecting a posh accent. Not even Cummins knew this, but Knocker had, in fact, been to elocution lessons. When the business had begun to really take off, Knocker had found himself with all of his new-found wealth and the material trappings which accompanied it, but he still hadn't felt like a 'real' monied person.

The thing about Knocker was that even though he was a hard-core criminal, who associated with similar-minded thugs, he liked a bit of class and he certainly liked to think he had a bit of class himself. The convertible Mercedes SL, the Gucci shades and the Armani jeans and shirts were all very well and good, but Knocker had still felt like a piece of shite with his harsh north-inner-city accent. He had picked up the telephone one day and rung the Muriel Smith School of Voice Coaching.

When Knocker had turned up in the school's Grafton Street offices for his first assessment, he had been furious to discover that he was being put in with a group of seven-year-olds from a posh south-side school. The receptionist had baulked when he had angrily asked if she was 'taking the piss' and the upshot was that he had paid a total of two grand for one month's intensive voice coaching – or, as Muriel Smith had privately described it, voice alteration. Now, you'd think he'd been born with a silver spoon in his mouth.

After a few weeks spent tailing Hunt to and from his office, Knocker had engineered a minor car crash – Cummins had promised him a spanking-new SL for his troubles. One thing led to another and Knocker arranged to meet Hunt for a drink the following evening, telling him that he accepted full responsibility for the prang and would rather settle the bill privately so as not to suffer a hit on his no-claims bonus.

They hit it off like a house on fire and within weeks they were regularly socializing in the best bars and restaurants Dublin had to offer. Hunt was having a blast.

Knocker was fed up of hearing his new friend's tales of woe about how difficult he found it to make friends and how much he despised some of the people who worked for him. Knocker couldn't see anyone taking orders from Hunt, but the way Hunt told it, he ran the whole bloody place!

Then Knocker dropped his bombshell, a bombshell he knew would appeal to Hunt's sense of superiority and outrage at not being treated with sufficient respect. When Knocker also threatened to end their cosy new friendship, it was a done deal.

Hunt became the gang's frontman and the trap was set for the disappearance of three women.

Hunt had no knowledge of the true motivation behind the elaborate plan. As far as he was concerned, it was merely designed to show the cops that they were less intelligent than they were given credit for, and as this coincided with his own view, he assumed his new friend Griffin had devised it to demonstrate his own superior intellect. As far as Hunt was concerned, he had finally met a kindred spirit.

Cummins' mobile phone rang and Hunt's number flashed up on the screen. 'Where the fuck have you been, son?' he said to Hunt.

It was a long time since anybody had referred to him as 'son', but the memory of his father addressing him thus sent shivers down his spine. Still, Hunt said nothing to Cummins. He was beginning to get the measure of the man and he didn't like what he saw.

'It's done. The ball is rolling. They will be on their computers searching for sex fiends and possible abductors for the next six months, Mr Cummins. They will never link it to you.'

Cummins' reply was short: 'About fuckin' time too. Bring them back to me when the time is right, son. Otherwise, enjoy them while you have them.'

Hunt intended to. He didn't get this kind of respect and attention from women very often.

7

Los Angeles, December 2003

Andrina Power was in pain. Serious pain. But still she didn't stop him. He had cast a spell over her and she was powerless to stop him.

The suite at the Four Seasons in Los Angeles had left her breathless. Not to mention his method of transporting her there. His own private jet. She was used to the five-star treatment in her position at Longwood Hayes Fitzsimons. Mergers and Acquisitions was big business and her law firm handled deals running into hundreds of millions. But the top-class treatment she was familiar with at work was merely a by-product of the business she worked in. It certainly wasn't just for her.

Everything Jonathon Hunt did was designed to give her optimum pleasure. Yet he made it all seem so effortless. That's what drew her to him more and more with each minute they spent together. His manner was relaxed and confident, but it left her in no doubt that he was in total control.

He was certainly in total control now. As soon as the bellboy had departed the sumptuous suite, having unpacked Jonathon's Louis Vuitton case – containing his own clothing and four stunning and perfect-fitting size ten slip dresses which he had chosen on Andrina's behalf and without her knowledge – he had set the scene for the rest of their stay.

She had been about to walk out to the terrace to take in the view over the glistening pool, when he had put an arm around her waist and pulled her back to him.

He pressed her body against the wall-mounted mirror and moved himself in front of her. He was so close that she could feel his heart beating as his chest brushed hers, and the excitement in her own body intensified as she felt his penis touching her.

'Jesus Christ. Take me now. Take me before I go crazy,' she murmured, her head buried in his shoulder.

He ran his fingers roughly through her mane of black hair and tilted her head to look into his eyes, eyes which were piercing and green and bright and boring into her now.

'No,' he said, putting a hand down and pressing it against her pelvis. 'No. We do what I say, when I say it. We do some exploring first. I will take you to new heights. Just do as I say and you will feel the true power of surrender.'

At that point, she would have done anything for him. Or let him do anything to her. Which was exactly what he was doing now, three days later.

He had taken on the role of her boss and she was to call him sir. If he asked a question, the answer had to be 'yes, sir' or 'no, sir'. If he taught her something new or reprimanded her for not fulfilling his wishes correctly, she had to respond with a 'thank you, sir'.

'Never ever close your mouth in my presence. Always have it ready and open for me,' he had told her during one of their sessions. And twenty-nine-year-old Andrina Power, successful lawyer and a woman who could never have been described as subservient, obeyed. Her anticipation of what he would do to her next was so great that she had become utterly acquiescent to his every instruction.

During their sessions, he forbade her to talk, unless he asked her a question or demanded thanks for his instructions to her. Their game had become progressively more outrageous, but Andrina just could not bring herself to give it up.

This morning, he had placed a dog collar around her neck. He then lay back on the bed and ordered her to kneel by his side.

'Tell me what you are now. Tell me what you are,' he demanded, his stern eyes never wavering from hers.

Andrina couldn't answer. She knew what he wanted her to say, but felt it was a step too far.

'Tell me or you will be punished,' he told her, his penis stiffening.

Tears came to Andrina's big brown eyes. This had begun as an erotic game and there had been no sex on an equal footing between them. She was beginning to fear of it.

As the tears streamed down her face, he sat up in the bed and pushed her forward on all fours. From the bedside locker he then took the belt he had been using on her and hit her with it. Hard. The more she cried, the harder he hit her.

'Please, Jonathon. Stop it. This has gone far enough,' she begged.

'You know the rules in this room,' he shouted at her. 'Where is your respect?'

She moved to stand up, but he caught her by the hair and leapt from the bed, fury burning in his eyes. It was possibly even contempt, she thought.

She made to lurch away from him, but it was futile. He jerked her back with the lead and breathed into her ear that it was time she learned about the 'special room'.

She submitted, thinking that if she played along, she might get him back on a more even keel.

He led her into the huge walk-in wardrobe and removed the portable luggage rack from a shelf.

'Bend over it,' he ordered.

And when she did, he removed a second, similar rack and lifted the bottom half of her body onto it.

'What are you doing, Jonathon? For God's sakes, this is going too far.'

He spanked her hard. 'You must be taught respect. I thought you had it, but clearly you do not respect me. You must be taught respect.'

Taking a pair of stockings from the shelf, he used them to tie each of her ankles firmly to the rack. He then opened a drawer and removed two pairs of silver handcuffs and did the same thing with her wrists. Then he pulled the contraption out into the bedroom and placed it in front of the floor-to-ceiling mirror.

Andrina was horrified when she saw her spread-eagled image in the mirror. But she didn't speak. She was far too shocked and worried.

He walked behind the rack and straddled it, placing his entire weight on her buttocks, all the while looking at her in the mirror. She turned her head away in disgust.

His right hand came down hard on her leg. 'Look in the mirror and open your mouth, bitch,' he shouted. She did as he said.

He placed his hands on her shoulders and pressed his weight firmly onto her body. She thought he was going to take her like this. But he leaned down and whispered into her ear. 'Don't worry. I'm not going to touch you,' he told her. Then he got up, bandaged her mouth, dressed himself, placed the 'Do Not Disturb' sign on the outside of the door and left the room, reminding her, with the point of an index finger: 'He that has lost his credit is dead to the world. You must have respect, my girl.'

8

Dublin, March 2004

Kate Waters was not one to bear grudges. In fact it struck her that a weakness of the Irish police force was the insidiousness of the bitching within its ranks. If someone was regarded as being a bit different, he or she was excluded from the pack. Simultaneously that person's ideas or contributions were generally cast aside in favour of the opinions of more popular members.

It was a human foible which never ceased to amaze her. Apart from anything else, such futile behaviour often worked to the detriment of investigations.

Which was where Ken Jones came in. He may have been a bit of an oddball, totally oblivious to the effect his condescending behaviour had on others. But it was his work that had led the team to conclude that there were circumstances for an investigation. There was no getting away from that.

And so, it was Jones whom she arranged to meet first as she started her own exercise of gathering information on the case. Now, as she made her way to their rendezvous, she thought about how easy it was to underestimate others, even for Kate Waters.

'Ken. This is Kate Waters here. You may recall we met at the briefing session yesterday. I was wondering if you might be free for a further chat at some stage soon?' she had asked him.

'I'm a very busy man you know, Ms Waters. Generally speaking, I make my appointments a week in advance so as to keep on top of my schedule,' came the curt response.

As she listened to his pompous reply, Kate kicked herself for not having realized that a guy like Jones would never want to appear to be too available.

'So I guess I will just go ahead and work with the detectives on my analysis of these details then. Perhaps you could call me if you find yourself with a free hour or two,' she'd said, predicting an immediate reaction from Jones to the suggestion that the detectives might actually be of assistance to her. Her trick worked.

'Well, since I am the one who discovered the common links between these cases, I think it would be useless to go talking to the detectives. As it so happens, I could squeeze you in today, although I am very busy tomorrow and for the rest of the week.'

Funny thing, Kate thought to herself; if he was so busy in his job at the Missing Person's Bureau, how come he had the time to work on his flag system and his facial-recognition programs? Yeah. Sure, he was back-to-back with appointments . . . As if.

She had expected that he would summon her to his dusty little office at HQ to show off his exemplary computing skills and was surprised when he suggested a much more exotic meeting place, the Tea Rooms at the Clarence hotel on Dublin's south quays.

'We'll do lunch,' he said. 'I'll put it on my expenses.'

Now, as she walked through the doors into the discreet foyer, wondering if she would catch a glimpse of some famous actor or model friend of the rock band who owned the hotel, she acknowledged she had misjudged Jones. Never, in her wildest dreams, would she have put the computer nerd in these swish surroundings. And as for expenses . . . she knew from Vaughan that the only expenses detectives received were with the prior backing of their superiors and even then they were generally confined to paying inform-ants. The subsistence allowance they did receive for lunches and teas wouldn't even buy a Big Mac Meal.

Jones was already ensconced at one of the coveted centre-floor tables when she arrived. He sat facing the room, leaving Kate with no option but to sit opposite him, with no other view bar the one of his nerdy, know-all face.

Control freak, she thought to herself as she observed the empty tables which would have afforded her a similar view of the room to the one Jones would now enjoy throughout their meeting. It was an established fact in the field of behavioural science that a key way to take control of a situation, be it for a criminal mind or an investigative one, was to alienate your opponent from contact with others and force them to focus only on you.

Nonetheless, Kate was there to do business and she wasn't going to let Jones's control fetish disturb her primary objective; to get a fix on how he had come up with his theory that the three cases were somehow linked. As she approached the table, she forced a smile to her face. 'It's good to see you again so soon, Ken. Thanks for taking the time to meet,' she said.

'This is actually a bit of an inconvenience for me, but I suppose it's better for all concerned that you get the correct information. I mean, you are the one who is probably going to end up solving this crime,' he said, his disdain for the investigating detectives as apparent as it had been at yesterday's conference.

'Well, thank you for the vote of confidence, Ken, but for the record, I am only on this case in an advisory capacity. I guess you could call me a peripheral player.'

'Yes. Well, whatever. The fact is that a crime has been committed, as you so rightly pointed out yesterday, and only those of us on the so-called peripheries can do something about it,' Jones said.

He leaned forward, a conspiratorial look on his face as he continued: 'Look, I am not a cop and neither are you, but who guessed there was a crime here? These guys are *supposed* to be detectives, but none of them noticed anything. And what do they do when they are *told* that a crime has been committed? They call you! So, from where I'm sitting, it's you and me together in this.

Otherwise, these women will be dead before Vaughan and his band of merry men find them.'

Kate found it interesting that someone with so few life skills could be quite so arrogant. Jones obviously had very little going on in his life if he was capable of attaching such importance to his own role in this affair.

'So what exactly was it that drew you to establishing these tracking systems that led us to this position?' she said.

'It was very simple really. Within the MPB I am the acknowledged expert when it comes to cross-referencing data. My workload keeps me extremely busy and the demands the detectives put on me keep me even busier. However, I believe in always keeping an accurate record of my workload. One never knows when they might introduce performance-related pay and I can assure you, I would be the highest earner in my section.'

With every word that came out, Kate disliked the guy more and more.

'Anyway, I digress,' he said whilst clicking his fingers to instruct the wine waiter to pour Kate a glass of the wine he had ordered prior to her arrival. She didn't drink during the day, but Kate was not going to offend Jones's ego by informing him of the fact. She looked at the indignant wine waiter and thanked him profusely after he filled her glass.

'On the last Friday of each month, I catalogue all of the cases of my own accord and, most recently, I have begun to cross-reference them in order to refine our rather basic computing methods at HQ. I have felt for some time the need to introduce more sophisticated technology to enable these facilities to be at our disposal, but since the uniformed officers who run the force do not place any real emphasis on the intelligence of computers, I decided to go about setting up the system myself. It was as simple as that really.'

Kate wondered if, on the last Friday of the second month, when Andrina Power had been reported missing, Jones had not noticed any parallels between her disappearance and that of Sophie Andrews.

'Well, no, how could I have?' Jones replied defensively. 'She only went missing that night and I did my cataloguing and cross-referencing earlier that day. So no commonalities popped up on my screen until the following month. Even then, I was not aware of the Nikki Kane abduction because, again, I catalogued the MPs for that month on the day she went missing. I wasn't actually aware of her disappearance until the following month.'

Kate was playing unenthusiastically with her Caesar salad. She had hoped to glean further knowledge from Jones about other possible links between the three MPs; information which perhaps he may have held back from the team yesterday.

Jones seemed to sense her dilemma and offered to conduct a series of searches which, she knew from Vaughan, had not been offered to the investigating detectives.

'One of the things I could do for you is to initiate the Natural Language Searching system and use a combination of the fuzzy searching I talked about yesterday and a search known as "chaining",' he said.

Kate sat forward in her seat. Her face was just inches from Jones's and she realized that behind the spectacles he was actually an attractive guy. And he *was* being helpful. She wasn't quite sure why, but she suspected that he was one of those men who was much more comfortable around women than with his own male counterparts.

And who could blame him? He was, after all, working in the midst of a very cliquish organization; but was he to be condemned just because he was not *one of the lads*? She had every reason to sympathize.

'I can use fuzzy logic to put in commonalities such as boyfriends who may have had the same first names, or cars they drove which may have been different shades of the same colour, and then I can use the chaining to bring all of the characteristics together. It may be that deep down in there we may find some common link that has been overlooked. Basically the chaining will take the information input as fuzzy logic and will use that information to look outside the loop. It will be time-consuming, but it could reap some results.'

Kate was delighted with the offer. She knew that Vaughan was far too busy with coordinating the 'jobs' on this investigation – in police-speak, that meant assigning a number to each task he wanted the other detectives to conduct – to provide her with such analytical information which might help her draw a fuller picture of the person they were looking for.

But Jones's contribution to the case did not stop at computing. After another hour of computer-speak, he volunteered his own opinion on her thumbnail profile of the man behind the disappearances.

'Far be it from me, Miss Waters, to tell you your job, no more than you could tell me mine,' he said. 'But isn't there a fundamental flaw in yesterday's analysis of the perpetrator?'

Kate narrowed her own eyes in concentration now. Jones's eyebrows remained arched as he waited for her reply.

'I'd be more than willing to listen to your thoughts on it,' she said, through gritted teeth. Now she had an inkling of how the detectives must feel when she put her spin on their cases.

Once again, he leaned forward conspiratorially. 'Well, if this guy has managed to date all of these gorgeous women, perhaps he has a very good social life indeed? And if he has a good social life, he must have a good personality.'

He paused, to let his words sink in: 'I mean, he can't be attracting all of these women if he is not – how did you put it? – a socially communicative person.'

Kate Waters pushed aside her coffee cup. Ken Jones had given her food for thought, and the beauty of it was, he didn't even know it. She would not share her new lead with anybody, even Vaughan, for some time to come. Despite what they said about him, Jones had been very helpful indeed.

9

New York, January 2004

They sat in an intimate little restaurant-cum-bar in the style of the mid fifties. Bill's was the kind of Manhattan place she had imagined existed only in movies about New York. With the cute checked tablecloths on the candlelit tables along its back wall, the original oak-panelled bar and – the real draw of the place – the piano which hosted a different performer every night, belting out everything from Manhattan Transfer to Barry White to Sinatra, the basement was populated only by those in the know about the hidden treasures of the city. It certainly wasn't the kind of place you would ever find in a travel guide. This was quintessential New York and Nikki Kane was enjoying the thrilling ride.

'I can't believe I'm back here so soon. Why didn't you just tell me to stay here and you could have joined me? It would have saved me a lot of jet lag,' she asked her new beau, Jonathon Hunt.

The piercing green eyes gleamed as he answered: 'That would have ruined the surprise now. Wouldn't it, my darling?'

Well, she had to admit it had been one hell of a surprise.

She had just stepped off her connecting flight from New York, dying to see him after being away on business for five days, when she spotted him standing behind the arrivals barrier. He had embraced her with a lingering kiss, then took her hand and led her down a corridor to a part of Dublin Airport she never knew existed.

'Where are you taking me, Jonathon?' She was breathless with excitement.

'I'm taking you on the ride of your life, baby.'

As he led her into the private lounge, it was clear to Nikki that the ground staff knew Jonathon well. Seated in a circle of bucket seats were two pilots and a stewardess. They stood and greeted Jonathon and he casually told them to take Nikki's luggage to the plane. Then he led her outside the lounge to where a car waited to take them across the tarmac. Five minutes later she was boarding a private Lear jet.

On their journey across the ocean, she had

pondered the wisdom of what she was doing. At twenty-nine, she had had her fair share of suitors, but none of them had inspired such impulsiveness in her. She didn't buy into fairy tales, but she couldn't help thinking of Julia Roberts in *Pretty Woman*. She would have gone anywhere with him.

They had met just three weeks earlier at a blind-date charity ball which her company, No Boundaries, had organized at the Four Seasons in Dublin.

She was doing the rounds of the tables, ensuring that all the guests who bought tickets were having a great time, when she had noticed him sitting there, looking aloof and uninterested. They were always the ones to watch out for. The challenge of the chase. It got her every time.

He had been sitting with a friend at the Blonde Ambition table, aptly named because each of the six women had blonde hair, and she had noted that he did not seem overly impressed by the company. As the evening wound up he had bumped into her and the rest was now history.

Aldo, the manager of Bill's, approached their table. Now in his seventies, he was as much a part of the institution as the institution was a part of the real New York. Over the years, he had played host to statesmen and sportsmen and broadcasters and entertainers whose names were synonymous with the city. He was part of the reason people went to Bill's.

Jonathon, on one of his previous reconnaissance trips to the city, had made certain to get to know Aldo. 'So, Mr Hunt, how you doin'?' He asked in his thick New York accent. 'I'm glad ta see you have da company of such a stunnin' lady dis evenin'.'

Jonathon was pleased with the compliment. Nikki, dealing with maître d's and proprietors on an almost weekly basis as she went about planning events for her clients, recognized the roguish twinkle in Aldo's eyes. It was what summed up a good host for most people; respect mixed with a healthy dose of charm, always added to the ambience. Aldo was a master of the art.

Jonathon told him that the filet mignon was excellent, 'as usual', and complimented him on the full-bodied Barolo. He asked Aldo for the bill and ordered two sambuccas to round off the meal.

Nikki was already light-headed from a combination of jet lag – it was now only midnight in New York although it had been nine o'clock when he'd met her from her flight in Dublin – and the wine. Not to mention the champagne on the journey. But Jonathon didn't listen to her protestations.

Again, the penetrating look in the eyes as a voice, rich with promise, told her: 'This will perk you up, my sweet. You're going to need all your energy tonight.'

Her stomach somersaulted. She wasn't exactly a 'sleep on the first date' kind of girl, but she had wondered when their relationship would progress beyond those long, lingering, tantalizing kisses he'd teased her with so far.

They left Bill's and were met outside by the same driver who had collected them from JFK just a few hours earlier. Again, he was silent as he drove them across Manhattan to Fifth Avenue.

When they entered the doors of the Pierre, Nikki was blown away by the serene elegance of the building. The only sound to be heard was that of her heels on the pristine marble floor as they walked past the concierge – another deferential greeting to Mr Hunt – to an elevator leading to the suites.

Once inside, Nikki walked straight to the huge picture window which ran the full length of the room and afforded the most stunningly romantic views of Central Park and Fifth Avenue. The lights of the city danced in the darkness, creating a fairy-tale setting, and across the way, to her left, she could see the romantics leaving the equally famous Plaza Hotel and taking jarvey rides around the park. She felt as if she were on a movie set.

Her body tensed as Jonathon eased up behind her and removed the shawl from her shoulders to reveal the slashed v-back of the sleek Armani dress he'd given her in the plane on their journey over. She could feel his breath on her shoulders as he undid the zip, allowing the dress to fall to the ground and leaving her standing there in the black silk lingerie and suspenders he had also presented.

He took her hand and led her towards the queen-size bed.

'Finally,' she said, exhaling in anticipation of what was to come.

'Finally indeed,' he agreed. Again, the piercing green eyes penetrating her.

He laid her on the bed, then removed her stockings, using each to tie her arms to the posts of the four-poster. Kneeling over her body, he pressed his full weight down on her. She could feel his penis erect against her own throbbing pelvic bone.

'Jesus, Jonathon, this is too much. Take me now, for God's sake. Please take me now.'

He got up from the bed and looked at her

again. 'This is it,' she said to herself. 'It's going to happen now.'

But Jonathon Hunt stepped away and told her: 'I have already taken you, my dear. You just don't know it yet.'

He left the room and turned out the lights. His mission had been accomplished. Now it was time for the chase to begin.

IO

Dublin, March 2004

They were beginning at the beginning. 'No point in just taking what Jones has given us so far and working off these facts, lads. We've got to start anew at the very beginning,' Timmy told the team of men assembled in Sophie Andrews' penthouse apartment in Blackrock.

If there was one thing detectives hated it was the suggestion that they might have been less than thorough in their investigations. Professional pride led to a natural resentment of any suggestion that they had missed something. It was a macho thing common to detectives the world over. The Number One team, as they were referring to the Andrews' investigation, were not happy campers.

'Listen up, fellas. I know that you have all been through this place with a fine-tooth comb already, but the fact of the matter is, we have got to look at this now from a totally different perspective. We have got to look for links between all three women,' Timmy said.

Softening the blow a bit, he added: 'I don't have any magic wands here so I don't know what it is we are looking for either.' He paused, allowing the men to absorb his own admission that he had no jump on them. 'We are all in this together.'

The three detectives, Liam Cunningham, Paddy Daly and John Finnegan, knew that Vaughan was just placating them. Still, they appreciated the gesture.

Vaughan put his hands into his thick black hair and scratched his head. He looked like a man who had had little sleep and his colleagues knew that this was very probably the case. He had a reputation for sleeping, eating and breathing the job. Everybody knew that. And it wasn't as if the poor fella could go home and share his troubles with his wife. Everybody knew that too. You could keep nothing secret within the force.

His ruddy face scanned the room as he advised them: 'Everything, lads. Everything in this room needs a complete overhaul. There is a link in here somewhere to either the culprit in this case or our other two missing women. No matter how minuscule you think the evidence, take it, document it, bag it. You know the drill.'

He left the men to get to work and spent the rest of the day going through the same drill with the men from the Number Two and Number Three teams. Nothing would be left to chance this time.

It was two days later when Kate met up with Timmy. His weather-beaten face showed signs of exhaustion, the kind resulting not from late nights but from mental tension. She could see that his mind, working overtime on the taxing investigation, was taking a much greater toll than any number of late nights. He wore the pained expression of a troubled man.

They were in her home in Killiney. It was blustery outside. He rubbed his hands together as he stood before the crackling log fire. She handed him a Hennessey and he rolled the balloon glass in his hands before knocking the liquor back in one gulp. He shook his head and the colour immediately came to his cheeks. He felt warm again. Was it the brandy? Or was it just being in her presence? Kate Waters always had that effect on him.

It surprised him that he could still walk into her home and feel absolutely at ease. He had loved her dearly once, and now he wondered if he still loved her just as much. He had certainly had a job putting her to the back of his mind, but circumstances had forced him to. And then there was his wife, Laura, to think about. Whereas once he would have considered leaving Laura, who had turned into a woman very different from the woman he had married, fate had seen to it that he could not leave her now. He was a hostage to the situation and Kate had played a role in the events which had resulted in him being shackled to Laura for ever. None of it was Kate's fault, but he knew that she shouldered a huge part of the blame for what had happened.

He flopped into the oversized armchair beside the big stone fireplace and put his hand into his breast pocket, the place where all detectives stored their little black notebooks.

He took his out. The black cover was shiny from years of use and the words An Garda Siochana, the Gaelic name for the Irish police force, were barely legible on the front. Just like its owner, Vaughan's notebook had seen better days. He removed the elastic band which held it all together and flipped the pages until he got midway through.

'Now here's the thing,' he said, coming to the

first page of his notes. 'The lads on each of the teams have been through each of their homes again with a fine-tooth comb and they have come up with zilch. Zilch.' His frustration was written all over his troubled face.

He continued: 'They have done all of the pro forma stuff and more, and still nothing. Forensics has already eliminated all traces of alien substances – I mean hairs and fingerprints which don't belong to these women – in their homes, and matched them to non-suspects such as their regular visitors and families. Still nothing. We've got no crime scene here, Kate. I've got nothing to give you to go on.'

The disconsolate look on Vaughan's face was enough to prevent Kate from repeating her insistence that there was a crime scene. They just had to figure out how the evidence manifested itself.

Vaughan squeezed his chin with his right hand and looked at her. 'The more I think about this, the more I wonder if we haven't got it wrong, Kate. I mean not one clue has been left behind. It would take some machiavellian mind to achieve that at three scenes. I think these women may have gone to wherever it is they are voluntarily.'

Kate said nothing, but a smile came to her face. Vaughan did a double take as he watched her.

Just then, the realization hit him too. He got to the point before she had a chance to say 'exactly'.

'Surely not? We are dealing with three intelligent women here. There is no way that each of them would have just gone off without notifying somebody.'

'Unless they weren't given a choice,' Kate said.

'Then it wasn't voluntarily,' he said.

'No, Timmy, you're into semantics here.'

He raised a sceptical eyebrow in her direction.

'What I am saying is that they have been abducted, yes. But as far as they were concerned, they went with whomever it is voluntarily. The person they went with had other ideas and only when they got to wherever it is did they realize that they had effectively been abducted.'

Vaughan thought her theory implausible.

'No way, Kate. There is no way in this scenario that they could have been abducted without some scintilla of evidence being left behind. We wouldn't miss something like that.' The detective was back in defensive investigator mode now.

Kate took out some spreadsheets and placed them on the coffee table before them. Vaughan's eyes widened when he saw the name of the unit on the print-out. It read: Garda Siochana Missing Person's Bureau.

Vaughan's face flushed with anger: 'The little prick. What the hell has smart-boy Jones been doing passing information to you before informing the investigating team?' he snarled.

'Steady on, Timmy. It's not what you think. I met with him to ascertain if there were any other pieces of the jigsaw which hadn't been cross-referenced in his computer database and he came back to me with the same information we had at our conference.'

She paused a beat before adding: 'Only he presented it in a different way and it got me to thinking – laterally.'

Vaughan helped himself to another slug of Hennessey. He sat back and sipped it as she talked.

Kate thought that it was just like old times. He was still very comfortable in her home, still the same old Timmy, strong, persistent, belligerent even, tenacious as a dog with a bone. Even his chinos were all crumpled and frayed, just like in the old days. It was one of the things she loved about him, the lived-in feel. It had always been so easy to be around him. It still was.

'He took all of the data from the profile sheets we were given at the conference and he cross-referenced it. It contains precisely the same findings we were working with the other day. The only difference is that when you look at all of the facts cohesively, as opposed to looking for clues regarding each of the individual disappearances, you see a pattern. It's your biggest lead to date.'

'Go on,' Vaughan encouraged.

'OK, take Sophie Andrews, our first MP. We know the gen. about her circumstances. Great job, great house, great looking. Very responsible. Regarded as being as steady as the proverbial rock, yet she ups and disappears and there is nothing to say that there was even a hint of a struggle. Yet here is the thing.' Kate paused to make her point. 'She is said to be an absolute creature of habit. She did her shopping for the week every Thursday night in Marks & Spencer's food hall in Grafton Street. Has done so for the last two years, except when she was away on business, sick or on holiday. Yet on the Thursday before she went missing, no shopping.'

'It's hardly the crime of the century, Kate. Maybe something came up. I don't buy that as evidence of foul play,' Vaughan said, a surly look on his face.

Kate pressed on: 'No, in isolation, you are right, Timmy. But remember, I am now looking at your profiles as a cohesive unit and Andrina Power's apartment contains evidence which your men overlooked.'

Vaughan stood up and stuck his hands defiantly into the pockets of his chinos. Again displaying the stubborn policeman's streak. 'What did you deduce there then that my men and I missed?' he asked sarcastically.

'It's OK, Timmy, you're forgiven for missing this one. It's a woman's thing really. According to her diary, her period began on the day before she went missing. The receipts they found in her bathroom bin show that she bought a packet of Tampax on the way home from work on the Thursday. On the basis that two discarded tubes were found in her apartment and a further three were taken to work that day, we can deduce that she wasn't planning on being gone for very long. Otherwise, she would have taken the whole packet of twelve. But she didn't. She only took enough to see her through an average twelve-hour day.'

'Christ, Kate. That's a bit far-fetched, isn't it? I mean surely a posh firm like the one she works at has all sorts of machines in the ladies'? Maybe she stocked up at work?'

'Then why the three she took with her to the office? Why would she have bothered if she could have used the machines there?'

She could tell he wasn't really buying her theory, but he hadn't heard the best of it yet.

'OK, then we come to Nikki Kane. Equally gorgeous, intelligent and talented. Same MO as the other two; a creature of habit whose friends and family are all shocked by the lack of contact. Every Saturday, without fail – except when she was busy or on holiday, she went to the Riverview Club for a long work-out, a swim and a sauna. No show on the Saturday following her disappearance.'

Timmy had that *you can't be serious* look about him: 'You're telling me that because one didn't do her shopping, one didn't take enough tampons with her and one didn't turn up at her posh gym, we have a case of multiple abductions here? Sorry, babe, but I'm a policeman and I need a lot more evidence than that. This is all just circumstantial, Kate. We're back where we began, as far as I'm concerned. There's nothing solid enough for me to go on.'

Kate was becoming frustrated by his stubborn attitude.

'Listen, Timmy, you invited me into this to get a different take on the evidence you already had and that's what I am giving you, but your head is so far away from the lateral overview that you said you were conducting that you can't see the wood for the trees. My conclusion is just based on a series of propositions. If you want my involvement, you've got to take my observations seriously.'

Kate took her long black hair out of the chignon and let it fall about her face and drape down her shoulders. The action was symbolic of the frustration she was releasing from her system. He drove her mad sometimes!

'Otherwise, Timmy, I don't know why you've invited me to get involved in this thing.'

Immediately, he was seduced into a more temperate approach. 'OK, say we work off your conclusions, it doesn't exactly take us anywhere. Does it?' he asked, a conciliatory tone to his voice. The last thing he wanted to do was to lose her from this case. It felt so comforting to be around her – again.

'That's where you are wrong, Timmy. As I say, it's all about looking at things individually and then in aggregate. What, for instance, did your guys do when they went over the girls' mobile and house-phone records?'

'They checked the bloody numbers on the bills and nothing unusual came up. Everybody they rang is accounted for and out of the picture as far as suspects are concerned,' he said heatedly.

'That's the problem, Timmy; you are looking

at what is there as opposed to what's not there.'

Vaughan hadn't a clue where she was going with this. He told her so.

'Your people found no unusual phone calls, so you ruled telecommunications investigations out of the picture, so to speak. But the funny thing is, all three have something in common here which is very much a salient point.'

'Let me have it,' he said.

'Well, thanks to Jones's handiwork, I have in my possession a complete print-out of their telephone bills, the bills given to each of us at the briefing session. Now, I asked Jones to cross-reference their telephone records and hey, guess what?'

Timmy sat forward. If his men had missed something so obvious, the shit would hit the fan.

Kate continued: 'I know what you're thinking and the answer is no. None of the numbers they dialled correspond. But, more significantly, their records from the beginning of the year show extensive use of their mobile phones, yet in the weeks leading up to each girl's disappearance, not one of them made a call on their mobiles. What does that tell us, Timmy? Either someone didn't want them talking on their mobiles and told them not to do so, or someone gave them, for whatever reasons, new phones.'

He had to hand it to her. He could definitely smell a rat now. He took a few moments to absorb the scenario she had come up with. It was certainly a sinister and highly premeditated plan if it was true. Too sinister to be a simple case of missing women.

'So what we are saying is that somebody had enough influence on each of these women to somehow cajole them into not talking on their mobiles; ergo, he wanted to hide any communications he was having with them because he planned on taking things a step further. Add to that the fact that each woman would appear to have high-tailed it with him to wherever, quite voluntarily, and when they got there he prevented them from making contact.'

'That's right,' Kate said. 'That's definitely my read on it. So you see, whoever our perpetrator is, he has left part of himself at the scene. He was able to win the trust of three pretty smart women. He doesn't appear to have deviated from his MO with any of them, so he's probably got a control fetish. He has had total control over each of the three women, although they will not have seen it as such. We are definitely looking at an educated, fairly refined and confident individual here. We have a pretty good profile, Timmy. It's just a matter of targeting our man. What's your next step?'

Vaughan was in no doubt: 'Well, the first thing we are going to have to do is trawl through the mobile-phone companies to ascertain if any of our MPs set up new mobile accounts. Then we'll be on to the no-bill phones and that's another story altogether. Tracing a pay-as-you-go phone is about as easy as finding a needle in a haystack. We've already looked at their e-mail accounts and there was nothing unusual there, so the phone route is the only possible avenue for a new lead at the moment. You're right, Kate. We've got to be less one-dimensional about this. Thanks for all your help.'

Kate stood up from her chair as Timmy rose from his. She wanted to tell him to stay, just as he had many times before, but she couldn't. They both knew it could never work. But that didn't stop either of them wanting it to.

11

Kate sat at her desk in Trinity College with a mound of paperwork before her. It was ten o'clock and she had just finished marking a stack of student papers. Her classes were hugely popular and she was realistic enough to know that the attention foisted upon her by the media contributed to that popularity.

She came from a family of medical doctors – mother, father and two brothers – who had initially scorned her aspirations to delve into the world of criminal anthropology. Both parents and older brothers had been convinced that it was a soft-option academic path to take. But once the media paid attention, so did her family. She had a good relationship with them, but still resented them for not supporting her career. She resented it even more that they only began to take any real pride in her achievements *after* the media latched on to her.

Now, her mind wasn't really on the job. She was impatient to get to the mountain of other paperwork awaiting her inspection – fifteen years' worth of files on previous missing women.

She had a policy of not allowing her college work to take a back seat to the consultancy work she undertook for the police, but at the same time, these investigations were thrilling for her and she derived from them a level of excitement she knew she would never achieve in her day job. It was a tough balancing act, because her superiors at the college took great pride in her prominence. It gave the department cachet and that always helped with funding.

It was four days since she had seen Timmy and although she had since visited each of the missing girls' homes to get her own feel for the investigations, he hadn't accompanied her on any of the trips. Instead, he had sent Paddy Daly along, citing his own work pressures.

She knew that Timmy was in one of his huffs; trying to make his point by not making himself available. Honestly, the man was impossible, but he just couldn't seem to help his emotions getting in the way. She knew the feeling well.

'It's been three years, Timmy. I thought we had put all of this behind us,' she had said to him as he looked beseechingly into her eyes after their cosy evening in her coach house earlier in the week.

'Sure, Kate. You have put it behind you because it suits you to. But I know you have the same feelings for me as I do for you. Why do you choose to ignore them?'

'I don't choose to ignore any feelings, Timmy. And for the record, you don't know what I am feeling.' They'd stood shivering in her hallway, the door ajar, but Timmy had been reluctant to go.

Her remark got to him big-time. His handsome eyes bore into her and beneath the anger she could see much sadness. 'Oh that's below the belt. Why don't you just drive your dagger through my heart?' he had said, his eyes bleak and his voice on the verge of cracking.

She had tried to console him by putting a hand on his shoulder, but he had pushed her away angrily. 'Don't come at me with your bloody pity, Kate. Deal with your feelings. Deal with the issues here instead,' he shouted.

She took a step back and eyeballed him. Now she was angry too. 'You think you are the only one who has been hurt by what happened, Timmy. You think this is all about you. As usual. Well let me tell you that I suffered too. Not in the same was as you and your family, perhaps, but I suffered. I still suffer every day.'

She had tears in her eyes. She hated this discussion but it always reared its ugly head, no matter how hard they tried to avoid it. It was always simmering, just beneath the surface, ready to boil over into a cauldron of emotions.

This time it was he who comforted her. He stepped forward and pulled her to his big chest, stroking her long black hair gently. Abruptly she pulled away. It was too dangerous, too tempting. The desire to go back to where they were before was too great. She could handle most things, but she knew that she couldn't handle that.

She looked up at him, her huge brown eyes imploring him not to make it more difficult for her. 'Please, Timmy. Go. Go now. Why do you do this? Why do you get me involved if it's always going to be like this?'

'Because I have to, Kate. I need you. I need you now more than I ever did. Surely you understand that? I thought I didn't. I thought I was over you. But I'm not. Spending time with you has made me realize that I need you more than I ever did.'

But what Kate understood was that it could never be. It would never be. She couldn't allow it. She just couldn't live with the guilt. She told him they would talk again when she had more to report.

Kate snapped out of her troubled thoughts. It was time to get to work.

Jones had telephoned her yesterday morning to inquire about progress and when she had informed him about the search for the possible additional mobile phone records, he had dismissed the theory out of hand and suggested that she would be better served using her fine mind to draw comparisons between the old cases and the three new ones they were now investigating.

'I have to tell you that I am not authorized to give you these documents. In fact I downloaded them from the database without the permission of the superintendent in my section, so I would appreciate it if you would respect that confidence. However, I think that you are probably the best person to go through them and make a definitive decision on any commonalities and, as I am going on leave, I thought you should have them now.'

When he had arrived a few hours later, laden down with files, Kate was surprised by his enthusiasm. By giving her the documents relating to the previous missing women, it was as if he really believed that she was the only person who could solve this crime. She had almost phoned Timmy to tell him how helpful Jones was being, to get him to cut Jones some slack, to just try and understand him more. But she didn't. It might look like an excuse for getting in touch.

It was half-past two in the morning before she called it a night. She had been through four of the files and was already despondent. There were no similarities between any of these cases and the three they were currently investigating. Still, she would continue to trawl through the remaining files. It would take her days to do so and she worried that the time spent on this would be to the detriment of other leads.

As she closed the door to her office and started to turn the chunky key in the old lock, she thought she heard a creak along the corridor. She stood completely still, afraid to turn her head for fear of what she might see. A few seconds passed. She could hear nothing but the breeze outside. She pulled herself together and reprimanded herself for letting this case get to her. She wasn't normally a jumpy person. She reasoned that it was just the tiredness.

As she turned in the corridor to walk towards the exit door, Kate did not see the silhouette slip out of the stairwell and move towards her office.

12

Dublin, 1983

'Go to the top of the house and await your punishment,' the respected surgeon told his son.

The fifteen-year-old boy knew better than to object. To do so would only serve to heighten his father's fury.

The day had got off to a bad start. After school assembly, he had been called to the dean's office. Everybody at school knew that when a boy was called to Mr Sexton's rooms it meant trouble – with a capital T.

As far as the boy was concerned, there was only one other person who instilled fear in him besides his father and that was Dean Sexton. He quivered as he stood before him, hoping that he had not been rumbled.

'So, boy,' Dean Sexton peered through his round-framed spectacles, his eyes narrowing in a gesture of suspicion, 'it has come to the school's attention that you have made a lot of new friends lately.'

It was hardly the crime of the century. The boy said nothing.

'Don't come the innocent with me, boy. Everybody knows the reason for your sudden popularity. You have sullied your year and your reputation by your actions. What kind of a pathetic creature are you?' the dean had asked, a look of utter contempt in his eyes.

'I don't know what you mean, sir,' the boy replied.

'Then perhaps we should ask your father's opinion on the subject. I'm sure he would be very interested to hear what his son has been up to. *Bribery*,' the dean spat. 'What kind of a boy needs to coax people to befriend him?'

The boy started to try to deny the allegation, but before he had time to do so, the dean flung five copy books onto his desk as evidence of his accusations. He had indeed been rumbled.

'Please, Dean Sexton,' he said, his voice desperate, 'I'm begging you. Please don't tell my father. I only did it to please my father. He is insistent that I make friends and doing their work was the only way for me to do that. Please, sir, I'm begging you not to tell him.'

The dean was outraged. 'You don't seriously expect me to believe that, do you? This is preposterous. Wait until your father hears. Perhaps then we will get to the bottom of it.' He picked up the phone.

Now it was seven o'clock in the evening and the boy stood in the 'special room' at the top of the house waiting for his father. The small room had once been his nursery but was now stripped of all things reminiscent of the innocence of childhood. There were more sinister changes.

He stepped back in fear. He knew immediately why his father had installed the floor-to-ceiling mirror along one whole wall. It would mean even further humiliation. He contemplated running away and reporting his father to the authorities, but who would believe him? The word of a boy against an eminent surgeon. His father would say that he was only doing what any right-minded parent would do – teaching his son discipline and respect.

An hour later he heard the stairs creaking. He jumped up from the corner where he had huddled and stood in the centre of the room, sick with fear.

'So, you have disgraced me beyond belief,' his father said, disdain pouring from every syllable.

'*Buying friends. Bribing boys to become friends. What kind of a freak are you? Where is your respect? For yourself? For your family name? For your father?*'

'I'm sorry, Father. I didn't know what else to do. I can't seem to make friends. How else was I to please you?'

'This is not about pleasing me, you fool. This is about earning the respect of others. But clearly you know nothing of respect. You have no respect for yourself or for the rules of this house. For that you must be punished.'

He shivered as his father opened a brown suitcase. Out of the case he removed what looked like a long silver chain. It was a dog's lead.

'Kneel down,' his father commanded.

The boy did as he was told.

'Face the mirror and answer "yes, sir" when I tell you to do something,' his father instructed.

'Yes, sir,' he quivered in reply.

The hatred on his father's face was intense as he attached the lead to the boy's neck.

'You must be taught obedience, my boy. You must be taught in the strictest possible way.'

He glared expectantly at his son in the mirror until the boy remembered his earlier instruction and answered, 'Yes, sir.'

The boy's eyes then opened wide with shock

as his father started on the next stage of the operation. His father smirked as he saw the reaction
the straps elicited – it was just the response he
had hoped for.

Each of the black leather straps was cut perfectly
to size. His father ordered him to press his palms
to the floor and fastened two to his wrists and
two to his ankles. Then he nailed each strap firmly
to the floor.

'You behave like an animal, you will be treated
like an animal. Do you understand why you are
being punished in this way, son? Do you understand why I must treat you like a dog?'

'Yes, sir,' came the obedient reply.

Then his father took a seat in the corner of the
room and ordered his son to look him straight in
the eye, through the mirror.

'You may begin now,' he said.

For five hours, the boy repeated the instruction, as his father watched over him cowering to
the ground on all fours: 'He that has lost his credit
is dead to the world. He that has lost his credit
is dead to the world. He that has lost his credit
is dead to the world . . .'

He would never forget the impact his father
had upon him. Nor would he ever forget those
words. He lived by them now.

13

Dublin, March 2004

'So if we're right that somebody gave them each a new mobile phone and if we can get those numbers we might be able to put a finger on who they were communicating with in the weeks before they vanished.'

Timmy was in his chief super's office at Harcourt Square, making his case for an order to search each of the missing women's telephone records. His men had already checked the phone bills they found in their homes, but in order to get other bills from the phone companies, they needed a special warrant. It was all to do with privacy laws.

As usual with Donny Nolan, it was going to be a battle. He was of the political school where everything had to be played strictly by the book. Otherwise it might come back to haunt him and then his ambition of achieving the coveted rank of Assistant Commissioner would go down the tubes.

'I don't know about this, Vaughan. It's not like you have any actual proof that these women are victims of a crime. For all we know, each of them could have gone off of their own accord and then where would we be? We'd be getting sued left, right and centre for the invasion of privacy. That's where we would be.'

'I'm just trying to get the job done, boss. I think at this stage we can safely say that the evidence is more than circumstantial. My fellas have been as thorough as is humanly possible and this is the next logical step for us to take. We have justifiable cause here in taking this route,' Timmy said, knowing that before Nolan agreed to sign the form authorizing the telephone company to release details of the women's incoming and outgoing calls, he would have to be sure that his back was covered.

Nolan sat back in his big swivel chair. It was much more spacious than the crappy ones which Timmy and the other detectives got to sit in and it had arm rests too. Timmy reckoned the provision of better chairs for the senior officers was a deliberate management policy – most of the guys in the higher echelons of the force sat on their backsides all day and they had to be comfortable in their environment.

It was time for Timmy to put the boot in.

'I suppose the reality is, boss, that it's only a matter of time before the media gets hold of this and when they do, questions are going to be asked about how seriously we took these disappearances in the early days. I want to cover all the bases,' he said.

Nolan opened the right-hand drawer of his expansive desk and removed a form. Timmy stifled a smile when he saw the writing on the top. It said: Application for the discovery of incoming and outgoing calls subject to approval by the Commissioner of An Garda Siochana.

Timmy waited while Nolan signed and stamped the form and then got out of the office as quickly as possible before his boss had a chance to change his mind. He walked about ten feet down the narrow corridor to the conference room where his colleagues from each of the three investigating teams awaited him.

'OK, lads, we've got the green light. Let's get to work,' he said, waving the authorization form cheerfully in his right hand. 'Before tomorrow morning, we will have a full list of all incoming and outgoing calls to and from each of the women's phones. Remember, we are dealing with somebody who has well and truly covered their tracks here, so I suggest we focus on the unregistered numbers when they pop up. Something tells me the person we are dealing with knows exactly how these investigations work and, if I'm right, they'll have left us with slim pickings to work with.'

The message from Kate had come to Timmy's mobile earlier that morning, but he had wanted to get the more pressing business of the phone searches out of the way before ringing her back.

'Timmy, it's Kate here. Can you call me please? It's urgent.'

Her voice had sounded troubled and very emotional. Could she have changed her mind? He was filled with anxiety as he anticipated the possibility that she might want to let him into her life again.

She answered her mobile after two rings.

'Timmy, I've got a big problem on my hands. The files on the missing women, all of them, they are gone. I left them on my desk last night. When I got here this morning they were gone. Every last one of them is gone, including my notes.'

'Calm down, Kate. It's only three files. It could be a big problem for us if this gets out, but it's not the end of the world. Have you reported it to college security? How much damage has been done to your office?'

'No, Timmy, you don't understand. It's the files going back on *all* of the missing women, the files on the first investigations. They're gone. All of them.'

Timmy's hackles immediately went up. 'What in the hell were you doing with those files, Kate? They are confidential police documents. This is going to cause mayhem. Absolute mayhem . . .'

He went silent. Then it sunk in.

'Ah for Chrissake, Kate. Please don't tell me that devious little prat gave them to you.' It wasn't a question and anyway, Kate couldn't give him an answer. She had to respect the fact that Ken Jones had sworn her to confidentiality when he had passed the files to her.

She made no comment about Jones and confirmed that she hadn't informed college security. 'But the thing is, Timmy, when I was leaving the office last night – well, in the early hours of this morning actually – I thought I heard somebody in the corridor. Then I thought better of it. But my initial instincts were obviously correct. There was no forced entry and nothing else was touched.'

'Whoever did this knew what they were about, Kate.' As an afterthought he added, 'Have you told Jones yet?'

'No, but it's not for want of trying. He's off on holiday and he's not answering his mobile.'

Vaughan's first instinct was to drop Jones in it for going behind his back and giving files to Kate, but to do so would mean dropping Kate in it as well. Besides, it wasn't the done thing to turn on colleagues. Even a condescending know-all like Jones.

He considered the situation rationally. OK, the files Jones passed on to her were most likely duplicates of the originals anyway, but that was not the point. Sensitive police investigation details were now in the hands of God only knew who, and if that information got into the public domain there would be hell to pay.

Vaughan cursed Jones for not realizing that if the files got into the public domain, the investigating detectives would get the blame, not Jones.

'OK, Kate, here's what we are going to do. You keep quiet about this. We have got to keep the lid on it, so we are just going to have to pray that management or, God forbid, the press, don't get to hear. Those files were taken for a reason and we've just got to hope that whoever took them will contact us with their demands. If Donny Nolan hears about it, we're all for the guillotine.'

Kate was relieved. 'Thanks, Timmy, I knew I could count on you,' she said.

'Well, Kate, you're going to be counting on me a lot more now. I'm not leaving you alone after this. Somebody is watching you, and I'm going to see to it that nothing bad happens to you. Not on my watch.'

Kate was flabbergasted. What was he saying? Was he contemplating moving in with her? That must have been it. He could not legitimately organize police protection for her without explaining the reasons to his superiors, and then serious questions would be asked.

Kate's stomach churned at the thought of hurting, or even offending him. How could she tell him with any subtlety that his protection was not necessary?

'Thanks for the offer, Timmy, but I can look after myself. I think you're overreacting here,' she said hurriedly.

'Look, I know that you're questioning my motive for suggesting this, but you are wrong. This has nothing to do with us – other than the fact that I care about what happens to you. I'm not taking no for an answer and I'm not prepared to alert any of the other lads to what has happened, so it has to be me.'

'There's no need, Timmy,' she hesitated, before adding, 'honestly.'

There was a silence, while Timmy read between the lines. 'What are you saying here, Kate?'

'I am already being looked after. I already have somebody to watch over me.'

A silence hung in the air between them. Then Timmy asked her: 'Is it someone I know?'

Kate laughed nervously at his roundabout style of questioning: 'No, Timmy, it's not one of yours,' she answered.

She clearly wasn't going to elaborate on the identity of her mystery man. 'OK, Kate, have it your way. I guess if he's not one of mine, then he must be better. I always knew you'd never settle for an ordinary member of the force.'

Kate was stung by his words. How could such a hard-bitten cop be capable of such juvenile behaviour? It was like dealing with a spoilt child. Or, if she was honest with herself, a sore lover. Hadn't they agreed to put their past behind them?

She wanted to have things out with him, but Timmy slammed down the phone.

Kate suddenly felt very alone.

14

'I want revenge and I want it soon. I'm goin' to
make that bastard's life a complete and utter
misery. I'm goin' to get to him like no one ever
has before,' Spiller Cummins said, his eyes
squinting pure malice. 'Who the fuck says us
crims are stupid? The bleedin' pigs think we are.
They give us credit for fuck all, so they do. Well,
by the time I'm finished with them, they will be
handin' out degrees in intelligence to our lot. I'm
tellin' yez, lads, I won't fuckin' stop until that
bastard gets what's comin' to him. I'll see him
ruined before I die.'

Spiller's crew were sitting in the den of his
five-thousand-square-foot mansion in Howth in
north Dublin. A specialist UK firm had been
brought over to equip his pad with the latest
state-of-the-art security features, which consisted
of an abundance of CCTVs, motion sensors,
anti-bugging devices, bullet-proof glass and – the

pièce de résistance as far as Spiller was concerned – his Kevlar-insulated den. The place was so well protected that Saddam would have felt right at home, as Spiller so frequently pointed out. Then again, they had caught Saddam in the end and Spiller Cummins had no intention of being the subject of anyone's capture.

The heavy-duty security was not designed to protect him from the police. Spiller and his gang could handle them, no problem, with the arsenal of weapons they had buried both on site and at selected locations around the city. Indeed he was particularly proud of the ingenuity displayed by his crew when burying their 'pieces'. In one instance, they had chosen the nearby home of a well-known politician, where No Knickers Grimes, working there undercover as a gardener, had stashed three Kalashnikovs beneath the perfectly manicured flowerbeds. In another instance, they had chosen a graveyard, where some poor soul whose grave hadn't been touched in years suddenly boasted the most beautifully kept and most frequently visited burial site in all of Dublin.

Rather, the security was designed to protect Spiller and his crew from rival gangs whose territories Spiller had moved in on when he branched out into drug distribution.

It wasn't just his rivals' runners, who delivered the drugs to various dealers around the city, or their bagmen, who collected the weekly takings from the main dealers and handed over the proceeds, whom Spiller had recruited for his own business. He had been much more ballsy than that. Spiller had spent months tailing his rivals' couriers, following them overseas, tapping their mobile phones, bugging their cars and generally launching twenty-four-seven surveillance on them until he had the full picture on the finest points of their operations. Then he moved in on one of the biggest crews in the city, led by the fearsome Octopus Tierney from the south inner city, and decimated his business.

Now Spiller Cummins was a marked man and he took every precaution to ensure that he was never in a vulnerable position.

'What are you going to do to him, boss? Do I get to play with him for a while?' No Knickers Grimes asked, licking his lips with anticipation as he awaited the nod from his boss.

'Jesus, Grimes, you're bleedin' disgusting. Do ye know that? You're a fucking pervert, so you are. If you weren't so fuckin' frightening to the enemy, I'd have ye shot meself, ye bleedin' little wanker.'

Grimes sat back into his big leather chair, swivelling nervously. That was the problem with psychopaths like Cummins, you never knew if you were just being rattled, or whether they meant what they said. He crossed his legs and placed his hands, subconsciously, over his testicles.

Spiller, Knocker and Breaker Daly all burst out laughing in unison: 'Ah relax, ye stupid little bollocks. I already told ye, you're too valuable for me to waste you. But no way I'm letting you anywhere near Vaughan. I'm going to make him suffer in a way that will be much more painful than anything you could ever do to him. I'm going to hit him where it really hurts. Aren't I, Knocker?' Cummins said, a steely determination to his voice. 'How is our grand plan comin' along, me son, anyway?' he asked.

'Very well, boss, even if I do say so myself. I'll have the next one delivered any day now and if that doesn't get his heckles up, nothing will,' Knocker told Cummins.

'Where is she now?' Cummins asked.

'She's safely ensconced in her own place, with not a clue of what's about to happen to her, just like the rest of them, boss. Silly cow,' Knocker said. 'That's what amazes me about these professional types, they haven't got a friggin' clue about nothing. Bleedin' deadheads, the whole lot of them.'

Cummins sat forward in his huge leather padded chair, his eyes wide and his pupils dilated. 'Does Hunt know about this one?' he asked urgently.

'Not a hint of it, boss. I've kept this one all to meself, Mickser,' Knocker replied, knowing that this would indeed please his boss.

'Good man, Griffin. That's exactly the way I want this one kept. Play it close to your chest at all times around him. If he gets to hear about this last one, he might lose his bottle and then where would we be? Out at Balgriffin Cemetery, burying him six feet under, that's where.'

'But that's what's goin' to happen to him anyway, Mickser,' Breaker Daly intervened. 'If the filth get wind of his involvement in this, he'll be dead and buried before any of us!'

They all laughed. Hunt, more so than any of them, would certainly come off the worst if any of this got out. He was in it up to his eyeballs. Whereas, as far as the rest of the crew were concerned, there was no physical evidence linking any of them to this business.

Just as Spiller Cummins had planned it all along.

15

Kate walked into Timmy's office. She hadn't bothered knocking so he jumped when he saw her
standing there before him, a vision of freshness
in a pair of Levi's and a soft cream cashmere
v-necked sweater. Her black hair was loosely swept
back from her face and clipped in a chignon, with
strands falling casually here and there. She looked
like one of those carefree women American
perfume companies always seemed to use in their
adverts. Pure class, Timmy thought.

He self-consciously tucked his creased shirt into
his creased chinos. Timmy wasn't big on style.
Another reason why she probably isn't interested,
he thought ruefully to himself.

'It's been two days, Timmy. This is ridiculous.
How on earth can we keep working together on
this case? I just can't deal with this silent treatment, it's so unprofessional.'

She stood facing him, her arms resolutely

crossed as she waited for an answer. He knew that stance, knew that she meant business.

Timmy leaned back and did what he always did when he was troubled or trying to buy time: he ran his fingers through his mop of unruly black hair. Kate thought the gesture made him look sexy, a bit like the Irish actor Gabriel Byrne, with the dark hair and the high facial colouring. Albeit he was carrying a few more pounds in weight than the actor.

She had predicted he would go straight into defensive mode when she accused him of being less than professional. She had been right.

'Oh, so you screw this case up, Kate, then you decide that you are going to sail off into the sunset because you don't like what I have to say about it. That's rich, Kate. I would have expected more from you,' he stormed.

Kate spoke evenly: 'More what, Timmy? We are working together here. To work this case, I need to hear from you. If you expect more on a personal level, I'm afraid I can't give it to you. Not any more. That's the whole problem, Timmy. You expect more from me.'

He pushed himself back angrily on his battered chair, creating even more of a gap between them. 'No, Kate, you *won't* give me more. Not can't. Just won't.'

'Ability and desire are two totally disparate things, Timmy. I gave you a lot more once and look where it got us. I can't and I won't go down that route again.'

'Ah, don't talk down to me with your psycho-babble crap, Kate. We both speak the Queen's English. What is it? Am I too old for you all of a sudden? Or is it that a humble cop is just not good enough any more? Now you've moved on to better things, I suppose?'

Kate was furious. She was trying to do a job and deal with their past as best she could, but he just would not let it happen.

Her big brown eyes bore into him. 'You know what, Timmy? That's it. You're just not good enough for me any more. I've found a younger, better model. You've outlived your usefulness. Is that what you want to hear? There you go then, you have the full picture now.'

Timmy looked as if she'd driven a stake through his heart. She didn't try to appease him. Sometimes, you just had to be cruel to be kind.

He spoke slowly: 'So you're just going to up and leave this investigation now. Is that it? You've potentially exposed us massively by losing all of those files and now that the heat is up, you're just leaving it.'

'No, Timmy, I've given you the profile you were

after. I've given you my professional judgement on the type of person who is most likely behind this and now it's your turn to do your job. As for the files, I didn't *lose* them. They were stolen. I was being watched, if you recall.' She took a deep breath. 'But, if it does emerge that the files were stolen, I have no problem admitting to the fact that they were in my possession. There. Case closed. Mea culpa, Timmy.'

'You are indeed to blame, Kate. Why are you doing this to us?' His voice was raised in agitation now. She thought she could see tears too. 'Who is he, Kate? What's so special about him that he's got such a hold over you? He must be some operator to steal the heart of a woman as cold as you.'

Even before the final words were out, Timmy was regretting them. But it was too late. The damage was already done.

Kate turned to walk out. Before she opened the door, she looked back, her beautiful face full of sadness. 'You're right, Timmy. I am cold. I've been cold since our last night together, since the night your daughter died.'

She did not normally share the details of her police work with anybody, even her closest friends and family. But Kate had felt vulnerable after discovering that she was being watched and that her office had been burgled. She had telephoned Pete on the afternoon of the discovery and asked him to come and stay with her.

Her companion of the past five months had not even hesitated for a second. Over the past few weeks, her uneasy state of mind had been hard to miss. At one point, he had even been fearful that she was going to call a halt to their relationship, but it soon became clear to him that she was worrying over work-related issues and that his concerns were without foundation.

Never before had she breached confidentiality on an investigation. It was pro forma in her consultancies with the police, probation and prison services that none of the information divulged to her ever went any further. That was one of the reasons she was held in such high esteem by the authorities. She had a reputation for being the consummate professional.

Deep down, she knew that discussing the case with him was wrong, but she was feeling overwhelmed by Timmy's attitude and she needed somebody to turn to. Pete had been close to hand and she figured it was time to start trusting again.

Although they had only been together for a relatively short period of time, Kate felt at ease

around her new man. He was the first since she'd
ended her relationship with Timmy and she hadn't
really expected it to last as long as it had. The
only reason she had agreed to date him in the
first place was because her two best friends, Jill
and Ruth, had been plaguing her to get a new
life and not to let the tragedy with Timmy destroy
her prospects for the future.

They had been with her that night in Doheny
and Nesbitts pub on Dublin's Merrion Row. They
couldn't fail to notice the looks he attracted as
he made his way through the crowded front bar,
populated on any given night by the city's business, political and legal hotshots.

He had worn a crisply tailored black suit –
Armani, they had guessed – and it had made him
stand out from the crowd. The strong jaw line
and piercing blue eyes gave his lightly tanned face
a distinguished air and in a pub that often attracted
the most distinguished in the city, he definitely
had the edge.

After ordering himself a pint of Heineken, he
had moved towards the snug at the back end of the
bar and begun reading his *Irish Times*. Jill and Ruth
insisted that he was giving the eye to Kate, but she
refused to respond to it. Her friends knew that she
still wasn't over Timmy, but they also knew that the

only way she would ever move on was to get out into the world again. Sure, she could at least return a smile in his direction. What harm could it do? And before the pair had time to badger her any further, Pete had come over and asked Kate if they hadn't met somewhere in the line of business.

The previous day, Kate's picture had been in the *Irish Times* after she'd given evidence for the prosecution in the trial of a teenager charged with rape. Otherwise, she would have considered his chat-up line a bit clichéd. But her work had increased her public profile and she was often stopped by strangers these days.

Jill and Ruth proved themselves to be less-than-subtle matchmakers that night, informing Pete after half an hour in his company that it had been nice meeting him, but they had to go. 'Both of us have dates,' Ruth told him, with a coy smile on her face. The inference was clear: Kate didn't. She was a single girl.

Kate had wanted to strangle them, Ruth in particular, but instead had decided that it wouldn't harm to stay for the drink he had offered. He was, after all, very good company and extremely handsome to boot.

The girls were thrilled when they heard from her the next morning that she had accepted an invitation to dinner. Since then, work permitting, Kate had been seeing Pete on a regular basis.

After the break-in at her office, she hadn't exactly asked him to move in permanently, but it had been three days now and she hadn't exactly asked him to go home either. Now he was at home waiting for her most evenings.

'Hey, sweetheart, what's up? You look miserable, baby.'

'I am bloody miserable, Pete. I have just had the most dreadful argument with the lead detective on the case and I'm just fed up with the whole lot of it. In fact, I think I have just resigned from the investigation.'

Pete was involved in Human Resources consultancy and one of his fortes was his ability to read people, a bit like her own job really. She was ready for the attempt to talk her out of her decision.

He put his strong hands on her shoulders and began massaging them. It felt good. She put her head back.

'You know what, Kate? You're totally stressed out by this case. I think you need a break. How about we get away from it all?' he said, his voice full of concern.

Kate flared up. 'I can't just walk away, Pete. That's not my style. I'm not a quitter, for God's sake. I have never quit anything in my life.'

He turned her to face him, looking her solemnly in the eye. 'You know what the most important thing has been for me over the past five months, Kate? You know what has made me realize why God put women on this earth?'

He didn't want her to give an answer. 'You, Kate Waters. You have made me realize what it really means to love. And nobody upsets the woman I love. You're not a quitter. You have just quit the bad situation that is going on with Vaughan. That's totally different.'

She gave in to the tiniest of hesitant smiles. She was flattered. But she was shocked also. He had not told her before that he loved her and she certainly hadn't uttered the sentiment to him. The thought hadn't even occurred to her.

She thought about her feelings for him. He was a great guy, good-looking, extremely handsome in fact, with his tall, muscular build and mischievous blue eyes. At thirty-eight, he was greying prematurely, but it only served to give him the appearance of an extremely distinguished and dishy businessman. Her friends were mad about him. She had it all, they said;

a fabulous guy, with good looks, considerate, well-off and mad about her. What more did she want?

But Kate knew that there was infinitely more to a great relationship than these superficial attributes. Five months in, she still did not really know if there was any significant depth to the whole thing. Yes, she liked him, a lot in fact, but she was also a firm believer in the 'gut feeling', the instant chemistry, the immediate knowledge that this was 'the one'.

Sometimes she felt guilty, wondering if she was just using him until 'the one' came along. Or maybe he was the one for her and she was just avoiding acknowledging the fact.

And then there was a whole other troubling scenario: if the traumatic events of that last night with Timmy Vaughan, that night two years ago, had not turned out as they did, would she still be embroiled in a passionate relationship with the only man she had ever regarded as her kindred spirit?

She snapped out of her reverie. He was still looking deep into her thoughtful eyes. Her face reddened with guilt. She felt he had been able to read her mind. It was as if he had been reading her mind. It was one of the traits about him which disturbed her. He seemed to know what she was thinking, even what problems she had, a lot of the time.

'Come away with me, Kate. Let's take a short break together, two or three days. Just you and me. It might help you see things a bit clearer. No pressure, OK?'

If it had been any other investigation, she would automatically have dismissed the suggestion with a firm 'no'. Any other detective would rubbish her reputation to high heaven if she just disappeared in the middle of an inquiry, but despite the current impasse with Timmy, she knew that he would never bad-mouth her around town. That wasn't his scene with her.

Anyway, as far as Kate was concerned, this was not merely an impasse in good relations, this was possibly the end for her and Timmy – professionally speaking. It seemed obvious to Kate that they could not spend time together again. But to be certain, she needed to get away from him to get a clear perspective on things. She was in no doubt that if he needed her professional services, he would not be slow to pick up the phone.

She stretched back in acquiescence. 'OK, Pete, I'm all yours, for a few days at least. But don't expect me to be the best company in the world.'

As always, Pete was the embodiment of understanding. He kissed her tenderly on the neck, rousing her passion with his hot breath. 'Don't worry, sweetheart. We'll have the most relaxing time in the world. By the time we're finished, you will wonder why you ever let Vaughan get you so stressed out in the first place.'

He took her to bed and they stayed there for hours. Their sex was full of raw passion. After the first hour, Kate had pleaded that she would explode from tension; by their third time, she was only beginning to feel the release of all of that pent-up frustration in her body.

She fell asleep and when she woke it was nearly midnight. She rolled over and stroked his head and called him. 'Timmy, Timmy, hold me,' she said. Then she sat bolt upright, startled, remembering Pete was the one she was with now.

She cupped her head in her hands in distress. 'Oh my God, Pete. I'm so sorry. What must you think of me? It's just this case and he's on it and I can't stop thinking about it, that's all. I'm so sorry, Pete.'

'Don't worry about it, Kate. I know you have had other things going on in your life before me.

But it's OK. I am prepared to do battle against Timmy Vaughan. I want to take you away from him for ever.'

She lay back in the bed, half-relieved, half-shocked. It had been a strange thing for him to say. Still, maybe that was exactly what she needed – to be taken away from Timmy Vaughan for ever.

16

The woman sat in the back corner of a tiny little pub in the village of Greystones. Spiller Cummins was of the view that they should not be meeting in public at all, but she had made it one of the conditions of her continued cooperation that they meet for frequent updates. She did not trust telecommunications. She was well aware what technologies were at the disposal of the police and how easily any communications over the airwaves could be traced. Sure hadn't she done it herself, with some considerable success? It was the main reason she was where she was today.

The pub was a typical spit-on-the-floor kind of place, complete with tobacco-stained woodwork and sawdust-covered ancient flagstones. Were it a weekend evening, the place would be packed to the rafters with customers of the seaside town piling in to hear the session musicians beat out their traditional melodies, but of a Wednesday afternoon, the only thing to be heard apart from the two old men sitting at the bar was the sound of the waves crashing up against the harbour wall outside.

She loved meeting with Cummins. It gave her a huge thrill. She knew that what she was doing represented pure evil and her blood warmed every time she thought of the trouble she was causing. If only they knew.

As she waited, she nursed a gin and tonic. The drink was supposed to be the preferred tipple of depressives. It made you melancholy, they said. But as far as the woman was concerned, it was the opposite. It always filled her full of exciting thoughts about the endless possibilities life held. The difficult choices always seemed so much easier to make when she had gin warming her liver. With a few glasses inside her, she could achieve anything.

Spiller walked into the pub, self-consciously dropping his head as he strode the narrow pathway to where she was seated. She knew a bit about the psychology of hard men. They hated to be off their own turf. It took away the element of control. That's why she chose Dan's bar. Spiller's unfamiliarity with the place unnerved him and that gave her the upper hand.

'How's it goin'?' he said in his harsh north Dublin accent, his eyes not quite meeting hers as his right hand fumbled in his breast pocket for the packet of Rothmans. Then he uttered the words he always said at their meetings: 'Ah fuck. Here we go again. Can't even have a fuckin' fag in a pub now. Bleedin' smokin' ban. Bleedin' fascists, that's what the government is, a load of bleedin' fascists. Ye can do nothin' these days in this effin' country.'

'Mine's another gin and tonic, thanks very much,' she told him, with a mischievous glint in her eye.

He hated the woman's cockiness, but he knew where it came from. It came from the knowledge that he needed her and it came from arrogance, an arrogance derived from the certainty that she was protected from the likes of Spiller Cummins. As she had told him at the outset, if she was to help him, she would take steps to protect herself. Later, she had outlined exactly what measures she had taken.

She had even taken him to visit the safety deposit in her bank, and shown him the letter – to be opened upon her death or disappearance – detailing her dealings with him. It had been a very clever move, considering their first encounter.

That had been six months earlier, just two months into Cummins' reconnaissance mission for his latest scheme. His men had done their homework and Knocker had come up with the suggestion that she be the first woman to be taken. It had been a risky decision to go for her, given the grief it was likely to bring, but they had wanted to make an impact and get the cops in a spin and her disappearance would certainly have caused havoc.

They had worked for an age on the plan, tailing her, tailing her husband, meticulously noting her every move for weeks. Then they had pounced. Knocker and Cummins had walked right to her front door in full police uniform and asked for a word, 'in private' of course.

At the time, the woman had assumed they were there to deliver the news that her husband was dead, the news that every person not used to receiving uniformed police officers to the home, expects to hear – that some horrible accident has befallen a family member.

Instead of delivering that dreaded news, they had covered her mouth and tied her hands behind her back and shoved her violently onto a couch, telling her to 'shut the fuck up and listen'.

To this day, she could remember Cummins

mentally undressing her as he watched her lying sprawled on the couch, her summer slip dress riding high up her thighs. At the time, she'd thought they were going to rape her.

She had sat in her undignified sprawl in total silence for fifteen minutes and when they had terrorized her into believing that they would rape and then kill her if she made a commotion, they removed the gag to allow her to answer their questions.

But once the woman had begun talking, a whole new scenario unfolded and a deal was made shortly after. Cummins and Griffin had been shocked by her sensational revelations and were then incredulous when she offered to be a party to their scheme. After two hours, at the end of which they were left in no doubt that she would be more than glad to assist them, the bindings were removed and Cummins and Knocker Griffin had quickly exited the house feeling like they had just been handed the crown jewels. Indeed, she was the jewel in the crown of their elaborate plot to take revenge for the loss of the millions from their broken drugs route.

If any other woman had instructed Mickser Cummins to get her a drink he would have slapped her one good and hard, but at the moment he would do anything for her. She had given him what he wanted on a silver platter and for that, like any decent criminal worth his word, he was grateful.

'So, what kind of an effect is our antics havin' on the whole team?' he asked, his eyes glinting with anticipation.

She sat up straighter, happy to embrace the subject of the grief they were causing. 'Oh, they're not happy campers at all. Detective Vaughan is constantly chasing his tail and screaming and shouting at everybody and, in general, he is in such bad form that, to be honest, I would say this is the worst piece of investigating he has done in his whole life.'

Cummins was thrilled. He still found it hard to believe that he was working with such a malleable and pliable 'civilian' – that was the term which he and his cohorts afforded to people who did not qualify for the title of 'practising criminals'.

'What's his theory? Are they anywhere near to getting a lead on this thing?' he asked, praying that the answer would be a firm no.

'If it's affirmation of your brilliance you are looking for, then you've got it. He hasn't got a clue about you.'

Mickser was a bit confused about her first sentence. He wanted to tell her to 'speak bleedin' proper and not be usin' ridiculous long words', but to do that would have been to show weakness and that was one thing he never displayed. Anyway, she had used the word brilliance, so he was sure she had just paid him a compliment.

'I know you've got the first three, but when are you moving in on the fourth woman?' she asked, her eyes steely.

Mickser knew that she was motivated by a desire to hurt the fourth woman. Her face carried a positively venomous look whenever they talked of her.

'It's all in hand, mam. Don't you worry. She is already under our control,' he replied.

The woman licked her lips in delight, a slow caressing movement with her tongue which hinted of future pleasure to be attained.

'What are you going to do to her?' She was almost quivering with excitement as she contemplated what she supposed lay ahead for the fourth woman.

Cummins raised his eyebrows in mock innocence as he responded: 'Why I am going to treat her just as all women should be treated. I'm going to lavish her with my undivided attention and never let her go.'

The woman downed the rest of her gin and rose to leave the pub. As he watched her walk away, he contemplated that she was indeed one sick psycho. Another to add to his collection. Perfect.

17

A whole week had passed and still she had not made contact. But harsh words had been spoken and Timmy knew that he would have to allow time for the bitterness to heal before he made an approach. He knew that she wasn't gone from the case for good, although if he was truly honest with himself, he knew that she had given him what he had asked her for and that she was justified in staying away until he contacted her for more help.

If the team unearthed new information to suggest that the profile of the abductor was other than the one she had provided them with, then they would need her to re-examine things. On the one hand, it would be great if the profile did change dramatically, because then he would have a legitimate reason for contacting her; on the other hand, that would throw the whole thing into disarray – not that they were any nearer to coming up with an identity anyway.

But the meeting this morning could change all of that. He was sitting in the incident room at Blackrock police station, where they had relocated to and from where the entire investigation was now being run.

Some of the lads had drifted in but there was still five minutes to go before the official start of the ten o'clock meeting. He studied the cork board where they had details of each of the three women pinned up for their examination and chuckled quietly to himself as he did so. If only the public knew, he laughed inwardly.

The reason he was chuckling was because when reporters on TV told their viewers to call incident rooms with *any* information regarding the crimes they reported on, he knew that the image conjured up was of a high-tech nerve centre with phone-tracing equipment and teams of hardened detectives waiting round-the-clock for that big break. In reality, the rooms were merely used to collage fresh information relating to the big case of the day and the high-tech equipment was likely to consist of little more than a mid-range computer and a knackered fax machine which nobody knew how to operate.

Ever since his first big investigation, Vaughan had spent a lot of time in incident rooms. At first he started off answering the phones with his officious 'Incident Room' response into the handset after the very first ring. The instructions to the rookies, as he was back then, were always very clear: answer the phone immediately because you never know who is on the other end and you don't want to give them time to lose their bottle.

In those days, he would immediately pass the phone to a more experienced detective, until, eventually, he was allowed to deal with some of the calls himself. These were usually what were termed 'the psychos' – people who called in with information that involved long-winded crackpot theories on who was behind the crimes under investigation. Few of the calls were of substance. But unfortunately, because of the nature of the job, the calls could not be avoided.

In one instance, he had even dealt with a psychic who claimed to know who murdered a young child and said that she needed a piece of the child's clothing to locate the perpetrator. When she had arrived at the station with three crystal balls and incense sticks and demanded access to the forbidden environs of the incident room, he had been berated to high heaven by his superintendent.

And the more experienced he became, the more

easily he was able to spot 'the psychos'. As his career progressed, he was also able to identify the repeaters who telephoned incident rooms for a hobby.

The calls from the repeaters usually came after pub closing time or in the middle of the night. Lonely sods they were, and one night, after recognizing a voice that had telephoned on two other investigations, he had an inspiration. He said that the information they were providing was so important that they would have to phone another top-secret phone number. From that day on, every incident room contained a poster for the Samaritans, with the number in big bold writing within the eye-line of the rookies answering the phones.

Still, in this investigation, there was no likelihood of the team having to deal with 'psychos' or 'repeaters'. They had not alerted the media to this investigation and the tight-knit team was under the strictest orders from the top brass not to do so.

Ordinarily, that in itself would immediately lead to a leak, because there was nothing the ordinary cop liked doing more than embarrassing police management; but in this case, Vaughan had reinforced the instruction with such ferocity that his loyal colleagues had not broken the embargo. He didn't want the team under more pressure from the inevitable media scrutiny that would follow.

Additionally, if this was the work of some publicity-crazed freak, the last thing they wanted to do was give him the attention he sought. That had been Kate's advice and Vaughan happened to agree with it. Her theory was that if there was no publicity surrounding the case, the perpetrator would be *forced* to make contact, if it was attention he was after.

But so far, there had been no communication and whoever was behind these disappearances did not appear to be bothered by the lack of attention they were getting. That either meant that the perp did not want publicity, or that there was a more sinister motive behind the whole thing.

Vaughan was a believer in the gut instinct style of policing and, by and large, that had not failed him through his career. In this case, his gut was telling him that there was more to it than simple abduction. He couldn't say what, but his gut was his gut and he was ever-hopeful that a lead would emerge eventually.

Which is exactly what happened ten minutes later when the team sat down to run through the 'jobs' they had conducted on this case so far. The jobs represented each task – no matter how small or apparently insignificant – conducted by an officer. Each such job was given a number and the designated jobman then detailed the nature of the inquiry and its result, then recorded that job in the jobs' book. It sounded pretty old-fashioned, but it was the most effective way of keeping track of developments in investigations where hundreds, if not thousands, of people were sometimes inter-viewed.

Paddy Daly from the Number One inquiry team was the man who brought the good news to the table. The name made him sound like an old-timer, but Daly was actually only thirty-five and one of the brightest young detectives on the force. He was the acknowledged expert when it came to dealing with the telecommunications companies.

What Vaughan admired about Daly was that, unlike many of the other bright young guns who were fast-tracking their way up the ladder, Daly's career success did not come from politicking, but from sheer talent and hard work. Just like his well-respected father before him, who had been Vaughan's mentor, Daly was of the old school of hard knocks. As far as Vaughan was concerned, that was a plus.

'I think we've got a go, boss,' Daly said when everybody had settled down and Vaughan had asked for latest developments. He nodded his head for Daly to spill the beans.

'Well, as you all know, lads, none of the phones owned by each of the three women showed information regarding any unusual or suspicious calls.'

'Yeah, as you said . . . as we already know. Get to the point, Daly,' his colleague John Finnegan jibed.

'OK, Finners, hold your horses. Did nobody ever tell you that patience is a virtue?' Daly retorted.

They all knew he was savouring the build-up. Who could blame him? It was the first lead in the investigation. Any of them would have done the same.

'Anyway, at Cracker's suggestion, we ordered a complete search of all incoming calls and, hey presto . . . I think we have just secured our first decent lead on this case.'

Some of the lads sat back in their chairs in visible relief.

'Now the thing is—' Daly continued.

'Ah jaysus, Paddy, don't say that. When you start like that, we know there's going to be a *but*, and I for one am not interested in hearing any more buts in this bloody case.' It was Jack Farrelly from the Andrina Power team.

Daly ignored Farrelly's rant. He was known amongst the lads as Moaner and certainly lived up to his name. With him, the glass was always half empty. Literally, in Farrelly's case. He had the reputation of being one of the tightest detectives on the force and he would rush to the pub and order his pint before anyone else arrived, then nurse his pint for the night rather than get in a round system. A right old scrooge.

'The thing is,' Daly said, 'all three women received calls from unregistered mobile phones to their land lines in the week before they disappeared. That's three different phones, mind you, but the calls were pretty frequent and, in the case of each woman, they occurred in the week before the disappearance.'

Moaner Farrelly was on his case again: 'Big swinging you-know-what, Daly. Sure, where is that going to get us?'

'Would you shut the hell up, Farrelly, and let the lad continue,' Vaughan interjected.

Moaner crossed his arms defiantly and sat back in his chair. A scowl came to his face as he said, 'I was only being devil's advocate, Vaughan.'

'Yeah, well, less of the devil and more of the

advocate wouldn't be a bad thing for you, Farrelly. Just cut the crap and let's see where Daly can take us.'

'I'll tell you where I *hope* it is going to take us, Farrelly,' Paddy Daly said. 'I *hope* it is going to take us to a common link between those phone calls and our three missing women. If the same person called all three women, we are dealing with one smart cookie, lads. But every Tom, Dick and Harry criminal has at least one unregistered phone and the bigger fish have several. So we can no longer just run a trace on a number and find out the identity of the phone owner – because they haven't registered any personal details in the first place. It's a bloody nightmare, lads.'

'That's why the Commissioner is making constant representations to the Minister for Justice to introduce legislation to force the phone companies to change their practices. These unregistered phones are literally becoming one of the most effective tools of the trade for hardened crims,' Vaughan reminded them.

'So we have no way of tracking this fella down then,' Moaner Farrelly said. The man just couldn't help himself. He was like an institutionalized grumbler.

Daly was back on the case again: 'That's where

Farrelly here is wrong, lads,' he said, addressing everyone around the table except Farrelly. 'Thanks to advances in technology, the phone companies have just introduced some very high-tech gadgetry which allows them to pinpoint the areas from which these unregistered phones are making calls.'

'So have we got locations?' Vaughan asked.

'Not yet, boss. It's not as simple as the phone companies going through their computers and coming up with a quick answer. Once a call is made from a mobile, it's logged on the mobile's SIM card and that information is logged, in turn, on the central database of whichever phone company controls the number. That's the information that we already have and which was relatively easy to obtain. What requires a lot more time is pinpointing the locations the calls were made from. They do that by tracing the signals sent from the SIM cards. In a nutshell, when any of us makes a call on a mobile, a signal is transmitted from our SIM card and that signal bounces off an invisible waveband and that leads us to the geographical location of the nearest mast from which that call was transmitted. That's it, boys. Advanced communications made easy.'

'How long will it take?' Vaughan asked.

'At least another twenty-four hours, boss, and

even then, it's a long shot; it's not as if they are going to be able to point us to the house each call was made from. They can only point us to the mast and that could be in a catchment area of up to fifty thousand houses. Our saving grace, however, may be the fact that under the deal the phone company in question did with the police authorities, the majority of their masts in the Dublin area are located on police buildings and in Dublin most police stations are no more than three miles apart. So if the calls were made from the Dublin area, we will be able to significantly narrow the field of concentration.'

Daly's briefing had lasted half an hour and they spent another forty minutes going over details they already knew. Somebody suggested they get Ken Jones to make a spreadsheet to cross-reference the phone calls in the hope that his super computer might come up with some fantastic comparison they may have missed. Vaughan didn't relish the thoughts of dealing with the little nerd again, but he accepted that it was a logical necessity and instructed Daly to brief him when he returned from leave.

The meeting broke up and they each returned to the tasks they had been assigned. More legwork to take them to the endgame. Vaughan told them to be sure to keep their mobiles on in case of developments. He was certainly keeping his in close contact – just in case she called.

18

Barbados, December 2003

Sophie Andrews lay on a lounger on the stunning
white sand beach. They had swum from their villa
towards the west, where a string of the most
opulent hotels in the Caribbean occupied the best
beachfront money could buy.

Jonathon had thrown the beach boy at the
famous Coral Reef Club thirty dollars for the use
of two of the club's sun loungers and they were
now happily ensconced, just ten feet from the
fabulously warm and near-translucent waters of
the Caribbean.

It should have been perfect, but Sophie was
feeling tense. She did not know why a feeling of
unease had enveloped her just six days into their
holiday, but no matter how hard she tried to block
it out, it just wouldn't lift.

The man in the dreadlocks approached them,

his voice booming and his body oozing energy.

'Hey, sir, may I say that your lady is lookin' a little edgy here. Maybe she needs a little loosening up, man. She needs to relax, sir. A beautiful woman like this, she needs to let go,' the dread-locked man said as he addressed Jonathon.

Jonathon Hunt was not a man to sit idly by and let others tell him how to relax his women, but he had to admit that the beach bum was right. Sophie was definitely very tense.

'What exactly have you got in mind for her?' he asked in a playful voice.

'Hey, man, call me Doctor Cool, 'cos that's what I am, man. I am one cool dude.' He cast his eyes over the full length of Sophie's lean and now very tanned body. It was clear that he approved of what he saw.

Doctor Cool removed a sharp knife from the pocket of his three-quarter-length trousers. Sophie sat bolt upright, almost paralyzed with fear. Jonathon held up a calming hand. 'It's okay, sweetheart.'

Sophie wasn't reassured.

Doctor Cool removed a slender green plant from his other pocket and expertly slashed it in half with his knife. She visibly relaxed, a wide smile on her face.

Doctor Cool knew that he had the all-clear and

he began his spin about the healing properties of the aloe plant: 'This will make you feel cool and relaxed, beautiful lady. This plant is not just for sunburn. This plant has properties that go onto your skin and into your bloodstream, lady, and it cleanses the body of the impurities that make you go all tense. This plant is the real thing now.'

Sophie lay back and enjoyed the sensation of Doctor Cool running the soothing plant up and down her legs, from the tops of her thighs to her toes. She didn't normally go in for the sales pitch of beach bums out to make a quick buck, but she had to hand it to him, she felt utterly relaxed as he massaged her body.

Ten minutes later, Doctor Cool had thirty American dollars in his hand and was thanking Jonathon for his generosity: 'You is one generous man, sir, but you got to give to your lady too, man. I ain't talking about cash, man. Doctor Cool is talking about RE-LAX-ATION. You got to get your lady to relax more often. Maybe she need more lovin', man.'

Jonathon was affronted, but he didn't let it show. He laughed off the remark as Doctor Cool and his dreadlocks bounced away in search of his next target.

As Sophie thanked him for the treat, he searched her eyes for signs of trouble. Perhaps the man was right? Perhaps it was time to put the girl out of her misery? He knew what she was thinking: why hasn't he touched me yet? Why the big tease? How much more does he think I can take?

He answered her unspoken questions with just three sentences. 'Later. I will deal with you later, Sophie. Didn't anybody ever tell you that patience is a virtue which carries extreme rewards?'

And yet again, he had managed to drive her into a state of pure frenzy, a state of absolute desire, a state of such desperation that she would do anything he told her to. Which was exactly what Jonathon Hunt expected of his women.

Jonathon had misjudged his first victim. He had expected her to remain under his spell for considerably longer than the first six days of their holiday. But back at their villa that evening, Sophie Andrews had come right out with her feelings of insecurity.

'I'm not happy staying here and not being in contact with home, Jonathon. I think it's time I was in touch with them. People will be worried about me. I've got to let them know where I am.'

They were sitting on the floodlit wooden deck watching the fish swarm in with the incoming tide below them. Jonathon had been preparing to put her out of her misery, to take her like she had never been taken before. Now his plans were in tatters. There was no way he could keep her under his spell when she was questioning him and issuing demands. He was indignant.

'Let's go inside, sweetheart. We'll talk about it in there,' he said, already rising from the over-sized deck chair he was occupying.

'There's nothing to talk about, Jonathan. I just want to make contact with home, that's all,' Sophie said.

There was an adamant tone to her voice which he did not like.

'Whatever happened to spontaneity, Sophie? I thought that this was what this whole thing was about. Where is your sense of romance?' he asked, trying, with a considerable degree of difficulty, to keep his temper under control.

Sophie, on the other hand, had no problem letting her temper fly: 'This is not about romance, Jonathan. This is about me wondering why you are so insistent that nobody knows where we are. I've got to contact people and let them know that I am safe. My family will be worried sick. I will lose my job, for God's sake.'

He could see that she was beyond pacification. 'OK, sweetheart. Have it your own way, if you must. There is a phone in the upstairs bedroom, it's in the safe. I'll get it out for you.'

They both went inside and Jonathon locked the double doors behind them.

Relieved at his change of heart, a half-smile broke over Sophie's face. She was beginning to relax again. But as far as Jonathon was concerned, she was too late.

He touched her face with his right hand. Sophie took the opportunity to gently lick his index finger as it brushed by her lips. It was the wrong move. Immediately, a stern look came to his face. He drew his hand back and slapped her face with ferocious force.

'There *is* no point in telephoning anybody, my dear.'

She stepped back, astonished by the metamorphosis in his personality. It was like listening to a totally different person.

He took her jaw firmly in his right hand. She tried to back away, but his grip was too strong.

'What are you talking about?' she asked, bewildered.

'I'm afraid that you have ruined everything, Sophie. You have questioned my authority and therefore you must suffer. You must learn a lesson from your disobedience. And your first lesson, now that we are on more formal terms, is that you will never *ever* address me as Jonathon again. In the future, you will address me as sir.'

Sophie was frozen. He took her towards the antique writing desk at the other side of the room. Jonathon sat in the chair behind the desk and ordered her to come and stand before him.

'Did you hear what I just told you?' he demanded, his eyes blazing with fury.

'Yes, I heard you, but I don't know what this is all about. If this is some sick joke, it has gone way out of control.' She was shouting now. The tears were streaming down her face.

He stood up and placed his hands on her shoulders, pressing his full weight on her body until he had brought her to a kneeling position before him. Then he sat down again.

'I do not like to have to repeat myself, Sophie. I will ask you again. Did you hear what I just told you? Did you understand my instruction?'

Her voice quivered as she responded meekly: 'Yes.'

'Yes what?' he bellowed.

'Yes, sir,' she quivered.

'I'm afraid that is not clear enough. Could you please repeat your response?'

'I said yes, sir,' she said, even less audibly this time, her voice muffled with tears.

He opened his trousers and roughly pulled her head towards him. 'Get to work and do a good job, you bitch. Do not stop until you have pleased me.'

Four minutes later, he zipped his trousers. 'Next time, be quicker,' he said, then dragged her to the corner and made her face the wall. He had placed a mirror where she was to stand, 'so that I can be sure you are maintaining your composure'.

He placed a handcuff on each wrist and attached them to hooks on the walls. She did not dare move. He then repeated the exercise with her ankles and pushed her bikini wrap high around her waist. In the mirror, she saw him walk away to the desk and then return with a long leather riding crop.

He laughed as he whipped her, all the while repeating the words: 'He that has lost his credit is dead to the world . . . He that has lost his credit is dead to the world . . .'

When he was finished, he instructed her to thank him for the lesson. When she omitted to use the word 'sir', he slapped her hard with the palm of his hand.

'Don't worry,' he said, his face full of menace as his eyes penetrated hers through the mirror, 'there is plenty of time for you to learn. After all, you are effectively dead to the world.'

19

Los Angeles, March 2004

'The really great thing about the United States of America is that one can keep to oneself for as long as one chooses.'

He strode up and down the room with the over-sized crop in his hand, every now and then lashing it against the floor to imprint on her what he was saying. The sound of it against the marble floor terrified the living daylights out of Andrina Power. She knew that if she said the wrong thing, she would be on the receiving end of the ferocious pain she now knew he was capable of meting out.

'You see, you turn up in a place like this and nobody takes a blind bit of notice. Everybody comes to Los Angeles for their fifteen minutes of fame, but in a city where everybody is trying to get noticed, nobody does. That's the beauty of this place, you know. That's why I chose here.'

Jonathon Hunt let a long and sinister laugh escape from the bottom of his stomach. He was enjoying this. It was a power trip, she now knew. He was a complete psychopath and she was caught in a catch-22; if she didn't do exactly as he said, he punished her; on the other hand, if she did precisely as he told her to, he became frustrated because he had no excuse to punish her.

Earlier, he had made her clean the floor on all fours – naked. She had spilled a glass of orange juice and had promptly been given a scrubbing brush and told to clean the entire floor of the large living room as a punishment.

'Now, for the last time, tell me what you have learned today. I will not ask you again, young lady.'

'I have learned not to make mistakes. I have learned to have respect for those around me, sir.'

His eyes blazed with fury as he pulled her long hair away from her face and jerked her head back towards him. She thought her neck would snap.

'But you have not learned, have you?' he shouted. 'Look at the mess you made. This floor is still filthy. You have not followed my instructions properly, you stupid bitch. Lick it. Lick it clean. Then I will deal with you.'

Two hours later, he ordered her to stand before him, as he did at the end of every session.

She stood shivering for twenty minutes before he bothered to address her. 'Now, it's a good job I hired this house. Isn't it? Had we stayed in that stuffy hotel there would have been no special room to send you to at times like this. Then where would we be?'

He let out an exasperated breath as he told her: 'Finally, you are learning to have respect. But you have a long way to go, my girl. Do you know, it took me a good sixteen years before I learned respect and it is only recently, I might add, that I am reaping the rewards of my lessons. These things take time and patience. You are still too impatient. It's back to the basement for you, I am afraid.'

Obediently, she knelt before him, as she had been ordered to do on earlier occasions. He jerked her head towards him and placed the metal collar around her neck. Then she walked the forty feet to the basement and took her position in the centre of the room, not daring to move. If she did, he would feel the tension on the long chain and she would suffer for it.

She prayed that he would leave her there in the windowless room, just as he had on two previous occasions since he had moved her here. She presumed that he was not planning on killing her – he seemed to be having too much fun.

Much later, in the middle of the night, he came down to check that she was still standing. When he saw that she was, he broke into a lascivious grin. 'Ah, you are learning at last. Enjoy your stay alone here. Next time I come, it will be my final visit. And remember, do not try to cross me. After all, as far as everybody else is concerned, you are dead to the world anyway.'

20

Manhattan, one day later

'I am very tired, you know. I hope you realize the trouble I have taken to get to you here. And look at the state of you. You are a disgrace. How am I supposed to have pride in myself publicly when you behave in such a disgraceful way? Didn't I tell you to always be prepared for my return? Didn't I?' he bellowed.

They were in a brownstone house just west of Central Park. It was a traditional two-storey house over a basement and he had moved her there after her initial induction period at the Pierre. The method he had used had been the same as he had used in Los Angeles for Andrina: the date-rape drug, Rohypnol. He had checked out of the hotel with a woman who appeared to be very much in love with him on his arm.

They may have been in a city of eight million

people, but Nikki Kane had remained in total isolation since the move. The place had been completely soundproofed and all of the windows blacked out. Neighbours did not interfere in New York City but, had anyone become curious, it appeared that the house had merely been adapted to the feng shui principle of decorating. Total uniformity and all clean lines.

Nikki was in the kitchen, in the basement at the back of the house. He had left her there after the move from the hotel six weeks ago. He had removed anything she might have used as an instrument of escape and all that remained was a fridge stocked with enough food to keep her going until his return. And a bucket which she had used as a toilet. The smell in the room was rancid now.

She was chained to the kitchen sink by her left ankle and then her left wrist. There was a tiny amount of give which allowed her walk three feet to the right to the fridge and then three feet back into the centre of the room.

On his return, however, he was angered by the fact that she had clearly tried to escape by attempting to pull the chain away from the tap to which it was attached. But all she had managed to do was spring a leak which, after eight days, had left her soaking and the kitchen flooded.

When he saw what had happened, he removed her clothing, leaving her naked. 'Don't want you catching pneumonia now, do we? You stupid cow. It was welded on.'

Nikki stood shivering before him. She had been severely ill over the past four days. The kitchen was now covered in vomit.

'Get down on your knees and eat it up,' he told her.

But Nikki Kane was the most stubborn of his three victims. Plus, she plainly did not care any longer. 'Go screw yourself, Jonathon. You're probably going to kill me anyway, so what's the point? I'm not following your orders any more.'

His menacing laugh echoed around the bare room. 'Oooh, it's sooo good to have a challenge at last. I was beginning to think that all of you were weak, but at least one of you has a bit of fight in you.'

'What the hell are you talking about, you bastard?'

'Go ahead, shout as loud as you like,' he said, 'nobody will ever hear you. In fact, I am your only audience. Just as well too, the way you are conducting yourself. So, do as I said and eat it up.'

She was huddled beside the fridge now, her

knees close to her chest and her arms wrapped protectively around her. Still she refused to move.

He placed his travel bag on the counter and removed a jar from it. 'I brought you a present, you know. Imagine the fun these little guys would have with your naked body pinned to the floor. New York is crawling with these things. Cockroaches love the damp. Perhaps I should leave you here with some company after all.'

Nikki bent down and began eating her own vomit.

'No stockpiling in your mouth. Make sure you swallow.' She did as he said, but threw up again and again.

Only when she had finished did he replace the roach he'd been dangling just millimetres from her body. Then he took a blowtorch from his bag and welded the neck of the tap back into place. It was still red-hot when he pointed it close to her face. 'I don't need to tell you not to try this again, do I?'

Nikki quivered as he awaited her response. As he raised his hand to slap her face, she answered: 'No, sir.'

'That's more like it,' he said. 'Now, it's time that I got going. I have other business to attend to.'

Nikki wondered what he meant.

'I am a very busy man and it makes me angry to have to waste time disciplining you. But what choice do I have? There is so little respect for others in the world these days. That is why I chose you. I could tell straight away that had you not thought I had friends and money, you would not have respected me. That's what this is about, my dear. Teaching people like you not to look down on people like me.'

Nikki knew he was mad. She was absolutely terrified now. Clutching at straws, she told him: 'But I do have respect for you. It's not because of your money, Jonathon. I do respect you.'

'Oh *per-lease*,' he said, a scornful look on his face. 'DO NOT TREAT ME LIKE A FOOL. Your type never have any respect for the likes of me. The only reason you have respect for me now is because I HAVE TAUGHT YOU TO.'

As he turned to leave, he looked back over his shoulder. 'It's just as well that you have me for a friend. As far as everybody else is concerned, you are dead to the world.'

21

Dublin, two days later

The big house in south Dublin was cold. He had been away for over a week and had not set the heating to come on with a timer. A chill ran through his bones, especially having come from the balmy climes of Los Angeles, and New York in late spring. Still, there was no point in being extravagant with money, even if it was not his own money that was being used for this house.

In any case, the woman should not be given the benefit of any comforts. She had lessons to learn. She was there to learn about respect and if that meant depriving her of her creature comforts, then so be it.

She had to have respect before she received any rewards. That was the way he had been brought up and it hadn't done him an ounce of harm. Look at the powerful position he was in today as a result of all the hard lessons he had learned. You had to be cruel to be kind, that was for sure.

Anyway, she was also the one who had caused him most trouble; daring to question him so early on during the operation in Barbados. She had almost ruined the whole thing. There they had been, having a lovely time together, just like any other normal devoted couple, and she had begun asking questions. The insolence of it still infuriated him.

And what had she forced him to do? He had had to reveal his true colours far too early in the game for his liking and he had been compelled to return home with her. She had almost ruined everything.

Just as well he had the use of the private jet then. Had he not come up with the brainwave of chartering it, he would have had no way of getting her back into the country without the authorities being notified. Thankfully, he had been able to stroll back into Ireland with her on his arm and nobody was the wiser. Rohypnol was a great help too. He loved it for the subservience it created in his women.

Finally, he went down into the basement of the house – a snip at ten thousand a month, and small change to the people who were paying the bill anyway – to survey the scene. He was disappointed. Everything was in order. Although he had to concede that Sophie was looking quite dishevelled. He was glad to see that his chastisements had reduced her to a quivering mess. Do the girl good to be brought down a peg or two. That would teach her to go after men just because they had money. And power and authority.

Not so long ago, he would have questioned that some people could be so shallow and that there seemed to be automatic respect for those in positions of power and wealth. Now those questions had been well and truly answered. His father had been right all along. Of course.

The fun had almost gone out of it for him with this one. They did not know that he had her back here. To tell them would be to compromise the security of his scheme. But he knew that he would have to hand her over soon. He was quite forlorn about the prospect really, because he knew that this woman had a lot more to learn about respect.

Sophie's eyes widened in surprise as he went to leave the basement, without having uttered a word to her.

'Where are you going, Jonathon? What's going to happen to me?' she asked, her voice desperate for some scintilla of hope.

'I'm glad to see that you missed me, my dear,' he said, a menacing look in his eyes. 'But don't worry, I think I'm finished with you now. I think it's time for you to move on.'

She recoiled in terror.

He laughed. 'No, I'm not putting you out of your misery, if that's what you are thinking. Just moving you on. And if you think I'm bad, wait until you see what's in store for you at your next port of call.'

With that, he closed the door firmly and went to organize the handover. One down. Two to go.

22

County Limerick, March 2004

Kate's heart skipped a beat when she saw his number flash up on the screen of her mobile. Sure, she had told him she wanted out, but in her heart of hearts she knew that was not the case. If she was completely honest with herself, she had to admit that she still wanted a part of things with Timmy – at least on a professional level.

She was with Pete in a cute little hotel in the village of Adare in County Limerick. It had been consistently voted the prettiest village in Ireland and it was not hard to see why. With its smattering of antique shops and gourmet restaurants and a five-star castle, Adare Manor, which had played host to some of the most famous people in the world, it was pure postcard perfect.

Kate adored the manor. It was a stunning location, particularly when it was snow-covered at

Christmas time and the crackling log fires acted as a magnet to all who entered its environs. It was very difficult to leave. But her personal favourite in the village was what actually looked like a long cottage, complete with traditional thatched roof, across the road from the imposing manor.

The Dunraven Arms hotel was the epitome of subdued elegance. The food was Michelin-starred, but, unlike many other establishments which received the accolade, the Maigue restaurant, named after the river which flowed through the village, was anything but stuffy. The cosy bar, with its blazing fire and resident piano player, was the perfect place to while away a late afternoon after a walk in the woods, and the suites, complete with four-poster beds, were the ultimate in pure indulgence.

After the initial excitement at seeing Timmy's number, she felt a pang of guilt. He was the one who should have been lying beside her. The guilt was not about Timmy's absence, but about the very fact that she was having these thoughts, minutes after making love to another man.

Pete looking up adoringly at her. She blushed.

'Work?' he asked.

'I'm sorry, Pete. I thought you were still

sleeping. It was only on vibrate. I'm sorry if it woke you.'

Pete, as always, was the essence of discretion. 'It's OK, Kate. I know that you are probably ready to get back to the job. Three days is a long time when there's only one thing on your mind around the clock. If this break has helped put things into perspective for you, then I am glad.'

Kate was confused. He had certainly spoilt her over the past few days as if she was the only woman in the world. He had told her that he adored her, that he was falling for her big-time. Heavy words indeed. But was he telling her now that she should go back to Timmy?

'You think I should go back then?'

Before he had time to answer, she added: 'I want to give us a chance, Pete. I just don't know if I can.'

She knew that she was pushing the boundaries of relationship politics here. Most other guys would already have told her to take a running jump. But not Pete. That was why she wanted to be totally honest with him and why she did not want to lose him altogether at the same time. There was certainly something special about him.

'I think you should go back, Kate, and at least

sign off on this case. I think you need to get closure on this thing before you come to any final conclusions, sweetheart.'

It was all Kate needed to hear.

23

Dublin, March 2004

The mobile-phone operator had come up with the goods for Paddy Daly. They had managed to pinpoint where each of the calls to the missing women's land lines was made from.

'But now we have a bigger problem, boss,' the young cop told Timmy Vaughan.

'Jesus, Daly, give us the good news before you shower me with foreboding, would you? There's little enough joy in this investigation as it stands,' Vaughan said.

'OK, what we've got so far is the locations.'

'Which are?' Vaughan asked impatiently.

'Blackrock and the north side, on each occasion. Sophie Andrews received her first call from the north side, somewhere between Sutton and Howth to be precise. And then she received five subsequent calls from the Blackrock area. Now, here's the thing. The pattern for both Andrina Power and Nikki Kane was *exactly* the same. Each of the women received her first call from the north side and then *all subsequent calls were made from the Blackrock area.*'

'Christ, Daly. That's some coincidence, isn't it? Either each of the phones was bought on the north side and the initial calls were made immediately, or whoever made the calls possibly lives on the north side and made the first calls from there, or they work or live in Blackrock and made the rest of the calls from there. Either way, it's a good lead.'

Daly hated to dampen his boss's spirits with his next piece of information.

'As the man says, Timmy: Houston, we have a problem.'

Timmy sat back and folded his arms. 'OK, let me have it.'

'Well, because we weren't tapping the lines at the time, we have no idea what the content of those calls was. And whoever made the calls is not likely to do so again. Not unless they are planning on taking a fourth woman and even then, by the current pattern, they would most likely get a fourth phone to go along with the new woman.'

Timmy stood up abruptly. 'I thought you said

that the preliminary information was that texts were sent from those phones, Daly.'

'Yeah, but we have no way of knowing what was written in them. I'm sorry, boss, but it's as simple as that.'

Timmy wasn't giving up, though. 'These signals bouncing off masts and logging our calls? What about all of that stuff you told us about, Daly? There must be something on those computers somewhere.'

'Twelve million text messages a day are sent in Ireland alone. I'm not surprised that they can't keep the details of each of those texts. What kind of a super computer could do that?'

Timmy stood against the wall in his office, his hands dug deep in the pockets of his chinos. 'So how is it that they were able to tell us that texts were sent and they can't give us the contents? I don't understand that.'

Paddy Daly explained patiently for his pupil: 'When anybody makes a call, or texts, from a mobile, it's logged by the operator on what is known as a CDR system. That's the Call Detail Record. When the computer recognizes the call as having been a text or an actual call, it logs the appropriate information for billing purposes and then dumps the details. In the case of texts, because of the sheer volume being sent, we are talking a matter of an hour or two before the details are dumped.'

'OK, so we can keep track of each of the phones and see if any further communications come from them. But I won't be holding my breath on that one. I'll get Donny Nolan to set up the paper-work on the numbers for you and I want to know *the minute* we have an iota of information regarding any of the phones. Meanwhile, I want you to go back to your friends in the phone company one more time.'

Paddy Daly raised his eyebrows quizzically. What could Vaughan possibly have thought of that he might have overlooked?

The question was answered almost immediately. 'When these unregistered phones are purchased, obviously the retailer who sells them has to activate them as working phones. Am I right?'

The younger cop could have kicked himself for not thinking of it. 'I'll get on it immediately, boss. You're right, the agent who sells the phone has to notify the service provider of the sale. Otherwise the phone won't be activated. It's all about letting them know about the volume of people using the network.'

Vaughan smiled. 'And my guess is that these phones were probably bought in the same shop and, if we are really lucky, the sequence of the numbers will show us that they were all bought at the same time.'

Daly looked at the print-out he had given Vaughan. Shite! He had missed this too.

All of the numbers ran in sequence; the number of the phone which telephoned Sophie Andrews finished with the digits 306; the number which telephoned Andrina Power finished 307 and the number which telephoned Nikki Kane finished 309. It was almost a dead cert that all three phones were bought together and that significantly increased the chances of the sales person remembering something about the identity of the purchaser.

'Praise for your lateral thinking,' Daly said, as he smiled and shook Vaughan's hand. He made his way back to his own office and said to himself, not for the first time, that it was no wonder they called Vaughan 'the survivor' behind his back. Just when you thought it was safe to lie down, he always came back at you with one more punch. His latest observation was about to deal a major body blow to whoever was behind this plot.

24

Kate was not given to capricious behaviour. In fact, in all the time he had known her, he could not recall an incident where she had changed her mind or gone back on her word. Even with the chicken wings in the Elephant and Castle, if she said she wasn't having them, she just wouldn't – no matter how great the temptation. And while he conceded that she had effectively walked off the job, he knew that he had effectively forced it on her. He had allowed their professional relationship to become complicated by their personal history.

Yet when he arrived at the Sorrento pub in Dalkey – named after the road it was located on, which led down to sweeping views of Dublin bay, but known to locals as Finnegan's, after the family who owned it – there she was, sitting waiting to meet with him.

It was half-past eight on Wednesday night and

the place was fairly quiet. It usually picked up about an hour later, when the mid-week malaise began to lift and the customers, including famous musicians, writers and sportsmen who lived in the village, started to come out again.

Dan Finnegan, the pub's ruddy-faced proprietor, was sitting talking to her. It wasn't often that Dan sat down with the customers. He was usually busy behind the bar, but Timmy regarded Finnegan as one of the soundest publicans he had ever met.

Dan seemed to sense Timmy's presence at the door and immediately beckoned him over. In the past, Timmy and Kate had been a regular item in the pub and Dan was clearly happy to have him back again.

Dan handed Timmy his usual, a pint of Guinness, then promptly disappeared to the other end of the bar.

They sat in silence for a few seconds. It wasn't uncomfortable, but more like a mutual acknowledgement that everything was fine now that they were together again.

'Thanks for coming,' Kate said, breaking the ice and smiling at him in the process. 'I didn't know if you would, to be honest.'

He could tell that she was nervous. This was not the Kate Waters he was used to.

'To be honest with you, Kate, I didn't know whether I would myself. But I guess your call means that you're back on the job?'

Kate was taken aback by his demeanour. All business. This was so unlike the Timmy she knew. And loved. Had she been analysing a subject, she would have said that he was playing a game of reverse psychology, but this was personal stuff and professional detachment did not enter the equation.

'Timmy, I just want to say that I'm sorry. I'm sorry if I hurt you. It's just that I'm confused. It's difficult for me to think of you, of us, and not think of what happened that night . . . of what happened because of us,' she said.

Timmy had had a long think about how he was going to approach things and he had resolved to stick to his guns, professionally speaking.

He took a long gulp of his pint before speaking. 'Look, Kate, there's no point in going over what is now water under the bridge. I'll say one thing to you about that night and one thing alone. *What happened was not our fault. We did not kill her. Somebody else did. You know that.*'

Kate tried to interrupt, but Timmy continued. He was determined to get his point across. 'The fact of the matter is you can't cope with the idea of us. You have been unambiguous about that and I just choose to ignore the fact. But I have thought a lot about what you said and I accept your position on things, Kate, so let's just put the past behind us and get on with the job. For both our sakes and for the sake of those missing women.'

Kate was shocked. She knew that her face must have turned white, but she couldn't think of anything else to say on the subject. He had obviously decided he was better off without the grief.

'So what's been happening with the case?' she asked. It was an effort to cover the devastating blow he had just dealt. Over these past few weeks, this was what she had thought she'd wanted from him all along, but their past had resurfaced and he had gotten under her skin again.

He told her about the development with the mobile phones and about his planned trip to the north side of the city tomorrow with Paddy Daly to interrogate the shop owner who sold the phones. Kate was genuinely thrilled with the news.

Then he told her about their plans to profile a list of all known sexual deviants who lived or worked between Howth and Sutton, or in or near the Blackrock area, and he invited her to the case conference later in the week to assess the list of suspects.

When he finished his pint, Timmy signalled Dan for another. Kate refused a second, giving a lame excuse about being exhausted, and left. Timmy was not surprised. He knew that he had really startled her with his declaration about forgetting the past and just getting on with the job. Just as he also knew that, in some cases, you had to be cruel to survive.

On the short drive up Sorrento Road and along the stunning Vico Road, which led down to her coach house in Killiney, Kate was a nervous wreck. She felt empty, broken and frustrated. She pulled in at the side of the road and stared out at the stunning panorama before her, then finally dissolved into tears. She hated herself for feeling this way, because she knew that she had been dealt a good hand in life and that her relationship with Timmy was the only thing which caused her to bow her head in shame.

Her conscience was clear regarding their affair. His assertion about his marriage to Laura being dead had not been a convenient tale concocted just to get her into bed. He had been upfront from the outset. She knew that she was not the temptress who caused him to realize that there was nothing left. When Kate arrived on the scene, all that remained was the paperwork and his child.

But she carried a Herculean burden regarding the fact that Laura had been en route to confront them on the night their daughter died, on the night she had been drinking heavily before putting the child in the car. It was this fact which prevailed each time she had entertained going back to him. And yet here she was, devastated that he had put the final nail in the proverbial coffin of their personal relationship.

When she'd accepted the offer to work on this case, she had hoped his attitude would be one of the acceptance of closure and now that she finally had it, she was devastated. She felt such a fraud and a weakling. Her friends would be thrilled to learn that Timmy no longer pined for her, but Kate was gutted and she was disgusted with herself for feeling this way.

An hour later, she dried her swollen eyes and began the journey down the hill to her home, where she knew Pete would probably be waiting for her. But she was kicking herself for having invited him to stay. Everything felt uncertain now.

Perhaps she wasn't such a good judge of men after all.

25

They ambled into the shop as if they were two bored husbands just killing time while the wives shopped in the up-market boutique next door. That's the way Timmy and Paddy Daly had planned it and that was exactly how it looked to the fifty-year-old proprietor of the Home Office Centre, where the sign declared you could buy 'everything you need for the ultimate home office'.

'Wives out spendin' your hard-earned money, lads?' Martin Tierney asked jovially.

'Not quite,' came the response from Paddy, the designated 'bad cop' for the operation. 'We're on a bit of a shopping trip ourselves actually and we are looking for your cooperation in a very important matter,' he added, flashing his police badge.

Martin Tierney recoiled instantaneously. It was just as they had discussed. He probably knew who his customers were all right.

Timmy was playing the 'good cop' and, contrary

to the often hammish portrayal of this scenario on the television, the routine usually worked. With his affable manner, he was often thought of as a gentle giant by those on the receiving end of his charms.

'Steady on, Daly. Don't send the poor man to an early grave. We're just looking for a bit of assistance, sir. You're the proprietor of this establishment I take it?' he asked.

'I am, to be sure,' came the response. 'The name is Martin Tierney, but I can't for the life of me see how I can be of any assistance to you fellas in your line of work.' It was said as a joke, but all three of them knew he was lying. It was written all over his face.

Paddy Daly was back in like a light. 'We'll be the judges of that,' he said as he walked over to the door to turn the 'closed' sign to face the street.

Martin Tierney didn't want any trouble. He opened his palms in a gesture of transparency. 'What can I do for you then, lads?'

Daly went to speak, but Timmy dramatically silenced him with the sweep of his hands. 'Young fellas these days. You just can't keep them back, Mr Tierney. Some of them would do anything to get on in the job,' he said, whilst never taking his eyes away from the proprietor of the little business.

Martin Tierney was no fool. The threat from Timmy was implicit. Either Tierney cooperated or the young buck Daly would make trouble for him. He knew that the cops had links to the tax man now and one phone call could bring huge pressure to bear on his one-man show. Tierney knew immediately that it was the gentle giant who controlled this duo.

'The thing is, Mr Tierney, we are conducting an investigation into serious organized crime and a number of items purchased in your shop have come into the equation. We would like you to clarify some things for us,' Timmy said.

'And what items would they be, do you mind my asking? And sure before you answer that, detective, I don't need to tell you that I'm not responsible for what my customers do with the products they buy from me.'

'Oh of course not, Mr Tierney, and there is absolutely no suggestion from me – the name is Timmy Vaughan, by the way – or from my young buck of a colleague here, Paddy Daly, that you are in any way involved in any of these crimes that have been committed. We are merely seeking a bit of assistance from you in this matter. Now what we were wondering is if you keep a list of regular customers, or perhaps some of your regulars keep accounts with you and maybe you could help us this way.'

The shopkeeper remained silent, but his eyebrows lifted, indicating that Vaughan should continue.

'Would you have any regulars who buy a lot of telecommunications equipment from you, by any chance?'

The question hung in the air. Both detectives knew what Tierney was thinking: did they want to know about anti-bugging devices or scanners or walkie-talkies or listening devices? The list was endless. He had countless customers on his books who required such things.

'I'm afraid you will have to be more specific, gentlemen. I sell a lot of different things to a lot of different people.'

'Mobile phones. Three of them. All bought on the same day.' Paddy Daly was back in again. He didn't take his eyes off Tierney for a second.

'There are a lot of small businesses around here. A lot of them buy mobile phones from me,' Tierney said, his voice faltering along the way.

'I'm sure you offer special discounts to your regular clients then. Perhaps you can check your records for us. Or we could always get a warrant and check ourselves. Of course we'd have to hand the details of your books over to the Revenue Commissioners, as a matter of professional courtesy, you understand.'

Martin Tierney understood Paddy Daly only too well. He also understood that if he revealed the identity of his most regular purchaser of mobile phones, and if it ever got back to that person, he would probably be found dead in a ditch with a gunshot wound to the back of the head.

As Tierney contemplated his options, Timmy Vaughan came back with the good-cop routine. 'Perhaps we could help you along. These were three pay-as-you-go phones. No billing needed. They were all bought together. Let's see, just over four months ago. And, of course, all information you give us will be treated in the strictest confidence.'

'Yeah. And I'm the Angel Gabriel.'

Tierney was sweating now. He rubbed his clammy palms together and then wiped them on the sides of his trousers: 'What guarantees do I have that my customer won't accuse me of a breach of confidentiality?'

'Well, I suppose if we were to come in here with a warrant and search the place, that might alert them,' Daly said. He was getting impatient and, quite frankly, he had no time for people who catered to criminals' needs and he had absolutely no doubt, from the look of terror on Tierney's face, that his customer was indeed a crim.

Vaughan, on the other hand, felt a bit sorry for the shopkeeper. He knew how intimidating serious faces could be and it was not for the likes of Tierney to take them on and come the moral high ground with them.

'I'll let you into a little secret, Mr Tierney. This is an undercover operation and as far as we are concerned, nobody will ever know that we were here. I expect for your own sake that you will want to respect that confidence also.'

Martin Tierney tore a piece of paper from the top of a bundle of Post-its. His hand trembled as he wrote down the name.

Timmy Vaughan looked at it and was wide-eyed with shock. He understood now why the shopkeeper was so reluctant to provide them with assistance. God knows what was going on here.

Vaughan was afraid. Very afraid . . . for the fate of the three missing women.

26

'This is going to be a big one, lads. Make no mistake about it. This case is going to go down as one of the all-time GUBU cases. Grotesque. Unbelievable. Bizarre. Unprecedented. That's what we are dealing with here. An absolute case of GUBU.'

Vaughan had the undivided attention of the entire investigation team. He had called each of them back for an emergency case conference as soon as he and Daly were back from interviewing Tierney.

Things were too serious now for him to have contemplated breaking the news via the phone lines.

Kate, too, was sitting anxiously waiting for the promised bombshell to drop.

The tension in the room was palpable as Vaughan stood up and his broad six-foot frame towered over the top of the conference table in the incident room.

'There has been an earth-shattering development of enormous proportions, lads, and before

I deliver the news to you all, I want to be sure of one thing.' Vaughan paused. 'I need to be certain that we have checked the double-life scenario for each of the victims in this case. Are we absolutely airtight on each of our three victims? I need every one of you to be absolutely certain that we are before we go any further in this investigation.'

Vaughan's choice of the word victim was not lost on the team. The women were no longer merely considered missing. They were victims of serious crime. The case had clearly moved on to a new level.

They all knew where Vaughan was coming from when he asked them about the double-life scenario. In police investigations of missing persons, investigating detectives always presumed that the missing person had a double life. Even when the parents, or partner or spouse insisted all was well, the officers privately operated on that basis.

The families were never informed of this because it only added to the trauma. But the flip side of the double-life approach was that it complicated investigations. Very often, leads were missed because the police didn't inform families that they were looking at other angles.

'There wasn't a trace of anything untoward in

any of their lives. The scenario for each of them is the same. They were pretty much creatures of habit and every piece of information we have been given about them has checked out according to the way their families and friends described them,' Moaner Farrelly said.

Farrelly had been given the job of 'collator' of all of the information gathered to date and it was his responsibility to ensure that each task assigned by Vaughan was completed and the results logged in the collators' book.

It was an important job: the collator was essentially the keeper of the investigation secrets. In Farrelly's case, it was also a useful way to ensure he could not infect the investigation with his negative attitude. At the same time, he was such a moaner that he persisted in nagging his colleagues until each of them returned with a result – just to get him off their backs.

Vaughan looked around the table, a worried, troubled look on his face.

'OK, lads, then we have a major plot going on here,' he said. 'This morning, myself and Daly paid a visit to the shop where our three mobile phones were purchased and we learned the identity of the person behind the purchase of the phones. It's very disturbing news, I'm afraid.'

There was total silence in the room. There was no way a seasoned cop like Vaughan would look so worried if it wasn't merited.

'It would appear that the man behind the disappearance of each of the three missing women is none other than my old friend, Spiller Cummins, king of the drug barons himself.'

He took in the incredulous look on the faces of his men. Even Kate appeared to know who Cummins was. She had heard about him from her journalist friend, Jenny, and knew that he was bad news. But she couldn't, for the life of her, understand why he would be behind something like this.

John Finnegan from the Sophie Andrews team was first to speak. He was one of the older cops on the team and thought he had seen it all. But this one confounded him.

'Christ, Vaughan, are we sure it's the same Cummins? I mean, Spiller Cummins . . . he has no rep for anything like this. Why would this sort of thing interest him? What could possibly be in it for him? It makes no sense at all.'

Tommy Curran from the Nikki Kane camp was equally perplexed: 'This isn't Spiller Cummins' scene at all, lads. Drug-running, gun-running and hard-core violence, sure. But this . . . There has to be some mistake. I mean, the profile that Miss Waters here gave us – that doesn't fit Cummins at all.'

As all eyes turned to Kate, Curran felt sorry for her. He had not meant to stab her in the back, but that was the way it had come across. She had profiled the potential abductor and the mental picture she had supplied them with came nowhere near the likes of Spiller Cummins.

Kate, herself, was in shock. She had never been so far off base in all her career. It just didn't add up for her.

Vaughan immediately came to her rescue: 'How can we blame Cracker here, lads? Now is not the time for that. We were all off base. None of us could have predicted that the likes of Mickser Cummins was behind this.'

'That's what happens when you bring civilians on board police investigations. They don't understand policing. Look where it gets us.' Moaner Farrelly looked around the table for the support of his fellow officers. He didn't get it. Each of them, despite resenting Kate's involvement in the investigation, happened to agree with Vaughan. They could never have predicted this.

They also knew their boss was in love with her. A blind man could see it.

'I stand over everything.'

Everybody, including Vaughan, stared at Kate. Most of them were glad of the excuse. Her beauty was compelling.

'Go on,' Vaughan said, as another of the men went to question her judgement.

Privately, Vaughan was flabbergasted by the statement she had just made, but it was so like Kate to put her reputation on the line when she believed in something. It gave him confidence in her.

Kate stood to address the men. Her demeanour showed total confidence. She was on her own turf now.

'How do you think a man like Cummins can pull the likes of these girls, gentlemen? If the so-called double-life scenario has been ruled out, then he has to have persuaded them in some way to become involved with him. These are educated, young, refined and relatively affluent women. There is no way that any of them would become involved with a villain like Cummins.'

Now it was Kate's turn to look accusingly around the table. A few heads bowed indignantly as she did so.

'The person who managed to persuade these women to go with him is urbane, not unprepossessing and certainly educated. I don't think we can apply any of those characteristics to Mr Cummins. As I said before, I stand by what I said earlier.'

Paddy Daly was intrigued. He figured that Waters was only about his own age, and here she was, telling a team of pretty hardened detectives that she knew more about the job than they did. She had guts. That was obviously why Vaughan was so smitten.

'How do you explain Cummins' involvement in this, then? We may not know what the links are yet, Miss Waters, but we know *for certain* that he has links to these women. Where is the rationale behind that?'

'It's very simple, gentlemen. I think this is a set-up. Cummins may well be the person behind this thing, but he has used somebody else to get to these women. When you find him, that somebody else will have all the characteristics I outlined to you at the beginning of this inquiry. I stake my reputation on that. There is already one major fact supporting my theory, by the way. You already have a significant indicator that somebody else is involved.'

'All of the calls, bar the first one to each of the women, being made from the Blackrock area.' It was Vaughan who spoke.

'Precisely.' Kate smiled. 'Whoever he is using as bait for these women lives somewhere in the Blackrock vicinity. And I would put money on it that previous surveillance operations on Cummins have not shown any contact with conduits in that area. These people generally stick to their own turf, don't they?'

'Absolutely,' said Tommy Curran, who was buying into her theory now. 'Better the devil you know than the devil you don't,' he said. 'The likes of Cummins would never do business with a distributor who lived so far away from his own turf. That's not the way these gangland guys operate.'

'So whoever this person is, he is not part of his normal coterie,' Paddy Daly said. 'Are you saying it is a totally different type of crime from his normal MO? Is that what you are suggesting?' he added.

'That is precisely what I am saying. Cummins may well be the architect of whatever plot is underway here, but in order to get to him, you need to find the person he is using as his conduit. When you find that person, you will get your link to Cummins,' she said and then sat down, leaving the business of plotting policing issues to the big boys.

'There's just one thing about this whole scenario I don't understand,' Paddy Daly said.

'Shoot,' said Vaughan.

'Motive. Why would the likes of Cummins bother to become involved in such a messy business? It has absolutely no relevance to his normal criminal activities . . . and another thing, it's not like there is any money in it for him. That's what normally motivates him, is it not?'

'You're absolutely right on that one, Daly,' said Vaughan. 'And that, my boy, is the ten million dollar question . . . What in the hell lies behind this crime?'

27

They sat in a tiny wine bar in Greystones in County Wicklow, where Kate had grown up. Even though the village was a fair bit out of the city, Kate loved to come back. Had it not been for the traffic, she probably would have stayed living there, but her office in Trinity and her work with the police meant that she had needed to move further up the coast.

Upstairs in the building, the Hungry Monk restaurant – named for the Gregorian decor and chants of the monks which echoed from the speakers in the hallways and bathrooms – was busy catering to its patrons. Some were locals, others had made long trips to get a seat in the famous restaurant.

Downstairs, where Kate and Pete were seated, the owner of the establishment, a gregarious man named Pat, and Nic, his very French maître d', welcomed their regulars, Kate among them, into the cosy environs of the dimly lit wine bar.

Pete was impressed. He had never been to Greystones before and had imagined it as a sleepy seaside town with little in the way of sophistication to its credit. But he could see now that his preconceptions were wrong.

'This place has great cachet, Kate. It's quite a find. You'd be hard-pressed to discover anywhere like this elsewhere in Dublin,' he said, as he took in her beauty across the candlelit table.

Count Basie was playing softly in the background and they were drinking a bottle of lovely heady red wine. It seemed to Pete like he was on the set of a Woody Allen movie. There was a real off-beat feel to the place. It certainly wasn't what he expected in a small West Wicklow town.

Kate had taken him there because it was one of her 'special' places and she had decided that it was time to work on their relationship. The friction with Timmy had made her realize that she had to try and make a new start in life, that she had to give somebody else a chance.

'It's a pretty cool place all right,' she said. 'I love it for the understated atmosphere and the simple food. It's one of the best-kept secrets of Dublin dining – although, strictly speaking, it's not in Dublin – and it always seems to come more alive just as you try to leave! There's something unique about the ambience here.'

Pete agreed. The Hungry Monk was clearly a great spot, and he noticed there was definitely something unique about the mood between the two of them tonight. It felt to him as if Kate had finally turned a corner. He breathed a sigh of relief that he was getting to her at last, that she was finally letting him in. There was so much more he hoped to learn about the lovely Kate Waters.

Kate sensed what he was thinking and broached the subject right out. 'I have had other things going on in my head. I think you might have guessed that already,' she said, her wavering smile lighting up her beautiful brown eyes through the candlelight.

She told him about her relationship with Timmy, but not why, or how, it finished and not about how she found it difficult to commit to a new relationship because she did not want to experience the pain again.

'You know, Kate, you are not the only person in the world with emotional skeletons in the closet. We've all had that one experience, even me, which we think we will never recover from. But, you know what? We do. You have just got to give yourself, and others, a chance. That's all.'

Kate was taken aback by his patience and honesty. 'God, you're something else, Pete. Most other guys would walk away. You're special.'

Pete took her hand across the table. For the first time, she felt that perhaps there might be a future for this relationship.

'You're the special one, Kate. That's why I'm here. There's so much that I don't yet know about you.'

It was time to start trusting Pete Connors. She had already let him into her private life, and a little of her professional one too. Tonight, she wanted to tell him more. It was as if by doing that, by sharing her secrets, she would be validating her trust in him. Her job was, after all, very exciting at times. Her friends discussed their professional lives with their partners and she knew that, once upon a time, Timmy had discussed details of sensitive investigations with Laura, and with her. It was what relationships were about after all. Trust.

She told him pretty much everything; about how Ken Jones discovered the pattern of the disappearances in the first place; about her initial assessment of the perpetrator; the discovery of the purchase of the mobile phones and the shopowner's confirmation that the phones had been purchased by one of the biggest criminal outfits in the city. The conversation was cathartic for her. She felt good to have somebody else to share things with, especially somebody so far removed from her line of work. It was definitely less intense than dealing with Timmy.

Twenty minutes later, Pete sat staring at her. 'Are you telling me that one of the biggest criminals in the Dublin underworld scene is behind these disappearances? Oh my God, that is absolutely sensational. Maybe your guys got it wrong? That really is an amazing turn of events, Kate.'

'I know, Pete. I'm still trying to absorb the information myself. It seems incredible, doesn't it?'

Pete was genuinely fascinated by her line of work. 'My God, this certainly puts HR consultancy in the shade, I can tell you that. Who is this guy? What's the theory behind his involvement then?' he asked, full of curiosity.

She had let her guard down with him, but she could not possibly identify the individual concerned. Pete said he understood and warned her to be careful: 'You're so young and so beautiful, Kate. I'd hate to think of these guys knowing that you are involved in this investigation. For all we know, they could come after you.'

Kate was flattered, but reassured him that the likes of the individual concerned would have no way of knowing of her involvement with the police.

'How can you be so sure? Please be careful. If he knows that they are on to him now, you might become a target,' he said. He was just getting to know her and he didn't want to lose her, not to Vaughan and certainly not to criminals, he added.

She laughed off his suggestion. 'Don't be ridiculous, Pete. These guys never get to hear about the likes of me. And anyway, there is no way he could possibly know that we are on to him. The only way that we know he's behind the whole thing is because we've traced the shop where he bought the mobile phones that he used to contact the women.'

'All the same,' Pete said. 'Take every precaution to protect yourself. Just in case this guy does find out about your involvement.'

'I intend to,' Kate said as she smiled knowingly at him. 'I want you to watch over me every minute that I have free.'

He leaned across the table, looked into her dark eyes and kissed her on the lips. 'Let's go home,' he said. 'I think I should begin watching you right now.'

28

Timmy and Kate sat in Ken Jones's office at head-quarters. They had been waiting all of twenty-five minutes for Jones to appear for their eleven-thirty appointment and Timmy was already becoming very agitated.

'Little fucking shit. This guy is a control freak. What does he think he is doing keeping us waiting?' Timmy grumbled.

'Just play along, Timmy. It's his MO. The guy is basically extremely insecure and this is his way of exerting a bit of control. He thinks it will get him more respect,' Kate said in response.

'Yeah, Kate, well screw that. We're here to do a job and we need his help NOW. That's the thing. Every second counts . . . if those women are not already dead.'

Timmy looked like he was about to explode from frustration.

Bright Spark Jones hurried into the office, but made no apology for his lateness. 'I understand that there have been some developments in the case on which you require my expertise. Let me have it, folks,' he said, donning his spectacles and pressing a few buttons on his computer screen.

Supercillious little prick, Timmy thought as he ran through developments so far and told Jones that they needed him to start cross-referencing all of the data relating to the mobile phone calls to each of the women. 'We're reckoning that this guy is going to surface using one of these phones again and when he does, we want to see if we can establish a pattern. It's our only hope of finding him at the moment.'

From the look on Jones's face, it was clear he did not approve of the approach being taken. 'Quite frankly, detective, I see this as a complete waste of my time. What can you possibly hope to achieve from establishing a database of a few phone calls? It's not as if there is any specific program designed to do any in-depth analysis or comparisons which might point you in his direction.'

Timmy's face blazed. Kate knew that he was about to blow up any minute and that she had to intervene. There were ways of handling egotistical guys like Jones and antagonizing them was most definitely not one of the best approaches to take.

'Perhaps you could enlighten us, Ken, on what approach you think might best assist us. It is a matter of life and death, you know. Your assistance would be invaluable.'

Jones peered earnestly at Kate through his spectacles. He knew that she was manipulating him, but he also knew that she was the only person on the entire investigation team who respected his skills. He was prepared to deal with her, but not with the likes of the jumped-up, ignorant Vaughan.

'I guess what I could do is set up two databases. The first could log all the calls from the unregistered phones and the second could log all of the calls to Cummins' personal mobile and land line. I'm figuring that between the two, we should be able to find a link somewhere. I'm assuming one of your touts can get you the number of Cummins' current mobile phone?'

This last question was, with a thick measure of derision, directed at Vaughan. The implication was clear: Jones was hinting that Vaughan and company might be too incompetent to get the number.

'Of course we have his current mobile number. We're a bloody investigation team. What the hell do you think we are, Jones? Morons?' Timmy replied.

'That, detective, is an opinion I will keep to myself,' came the sarcastic response. 'Anyway, this will only work if Mr Cummins has *absolutely no idea* that you are on to him. Otherwise, this exercise will be a complete waste of my time and yours. Can you fully trust every member of your team?'

Kate thought it was a strange question to ask. But still, Jones had a point.

'Detective Vaughan has absolute confidence in the entire team,' Kate said hurriedly.

Vaughan called the meeting to a halt, roughly pushing his chair back and slamming it on the tiled floor. 'Let us know as soon as you discover anything,' he said as he stalked to the door.

When they got to the car park outside, Kate patted his shoulder in mock consolation. 'There there, Timmy. Why do you let the guy get to you so much?'

'The guy makes my blood boil. I don't want to set eyes on him ever again once this case is finished.'

Kate had a feeling that Timmy would get his way. It certainly did not do to mess with one of the most respected detectives in the force.

29

'Hello again, Mr Tierney.'

Martin Tierney recoiled in horror.

'Jesus Christ, lads, I had no choice,' he said, his eyes ablaze with panic and his voice quivering with fear.

Martin Tierney was under no illusions about the capabilities of the men standing before him. Their violent reputations preceded them the length and breadth of the city.

Breathlessly he told them what happened: 'They came in here threatening all sorts about warrants and the tax man unless I gave them the name they were looking for. For God's sake, I have a family and children. Please don't harm me.'

Knocker Griffin just smiled. Breaker Daly's face displayed pent-up hatred and anger. He also had the appearance of a man who was anticipating more rewarding things to come. This was his favourite part of working for Mickser Cummins:

the violence. The money, the perks and the respect he got from other crims because he was part of Cummins' crew were all great, but for Breaker, the real perk of the job was the adrenalin buzz of knowing he had the power to beat the shit out of whoever he liked – so long as he had Cummins' say-so of course.

'Shut the fuck up, ye scumbag and take your fucking dues. You're going to get what's coming to ye. Ye bleeding poncey prick. Do ye realize the fucking trouble you've caused our crew?' Breaker said.

Martin Tierney began to cry, the first time he had done so as a grown man. 'For crying out loud, pal, I have a wife and family. I'm only trying to get by in life. I had no choice.'

Knocker had already locked the door to the tiny office-supply shop. 'Don't you realize the importance of customer confidentiality? Why in the hell did you have to go and bite the hand that feeds you? You fucking prick. You've caused no end of trouble for us.'

Gone was Knocker's elocution-perfected south Dublin accent and in its place were the thuggish tones he used to intimidate those who needed intimidating.

A Pajero jeep was parked on the double-yellow

lines directly outside the shop. 'We're going for a ride, mister, and before you think about screaming blue murder, I suggest you think of your lovely daughter and her three-year-old girl. Have you ever heard of a fella called No Knickers Grimes?' Knocker asked.

Martin Tierney had not, but the name was enough to terrify the living daylights out of him. He could only imagine what a man named No Knickers would do to his adorable blonde granddaughter.

Knocker continued: 'No Knickers is a friend of ours. He's keeping an eye on little Stephanie as we speak. Don't worry, though. He loves little girls. Very fond of them he is.'

Martin Tierney vomited all over the counter. Then he quietly accompanied the men outside to their jeep.

They drove for twenty minutes and then stopped on deserted wasteland at the back of Dublin Airport. Dusk was falling and as he looked up at the darkening sky, Tierney knew that he would never again see the light of day.

Breaker Daly roughly pushed him to a kneeling position and then tied his hands behind his back. Then he removed a Stanley knife from the inside pocket of his leather bomber jacket and held it up to Tierney's right cheekbone.

'I was going to use a claw hammer and nails and pin you down to a plank of wood and leave you to wriggle away in agony,' he sniggered, 'but the boss wants a more speedy conclusion to your demise than that. Anyway, I used that trick on me last big job. It doesn't do to go repeating yourself, now does it?' Daly said, clearly enjoying the terror he was instilling in his victim.

'Oh Jesus, no. Please, no,' Tierney begged him, for he had indeed read the extensive newspaper coverage of the crucifixion of another gangland figure not three months earlier. The police had described the man's death as the most savage and brutal they had ever witnessed and now Breaker Daly had just admitted that he was the man responsible.

'Come on, Breaker. Enough of your antics now. You know the boss wants this dealt with quick-sharp. There's no time to waste on this one,' Knocker said as he watched Breaker carve a delicate incision right across their victim's face.

'Just a few more minutes,' Breaker said, as he made another incision from the forehead, down over Tierney's nose and finally to his chin. 'There you go now, my man,' he smiled gleefully. 'I didn't get to crucify you, but I least I got to make the sign of the cross. Think of it as the last rites.' Daly fell to his knees, convulsed with laughter.

Impatiently, Knocker Griffin pushed his colleague to one side and looked Tierney straight on in his blood-spattered face.

Just as a 747 made its noisy take-off nearby, the shots were fired.

Tierney jerked backwards with the impact of the first. The second was unnecessary, but it sent him crumbling to the soil in a sorry mess.

Martin Tierney was a dead man.

Knocker Griffin and Breaker Daly headed back to Howth to celebrate their invincibility.

30

Timmy stood looking in the mirror in the hallway of his Monkstown home. He wasn't prone to vanity and he didn't make much of an attempt at grooming. In fact he couldn't care less what he looked like, so long as he was clean and had on relatively decent-looking chinos. No matter that they were always a mass of creases.

He examined his tired eyes and ran his fingers through his thick head of hair. He tried to compose his face into a more neutral expression that belied the frustration he was feeling over this investigation, the slow pace it was moving at and the disturbing turn of events involving Cummins.

Ever since the incident with his daughter – he still found it difficult to describe it as the death of his daughter – he had developed this habit of checking himself in the mirror before he went inside to Laura. It was as if he felt he had a duty to his wife not to bring home the troubles of his day. He had caused her enough grief already.

Timmy knew that he and Laura should have gone their separate ways a long time ago. Childhood sweethearts they had been, and once she had finished her nursing training and he had finished training in the police college in Templemore, they had done what was expected of them and gotten hitched.

Their relationship had never been all flames of passion and candlelit dinners, but they got on extremely well together and he had loved her in those early years. They were like many other couples at a time when there was no divorce in Ireland and marriage was for life. You found some- body you wanted to be with and you didn't push your luck and expect a never-ending passionate affair. That was the stuff of Hollywood.

But ten years in the job had taken its toll on their relationship. There were no actual discernible problems to speak of, but once Kyra, the beau- tiful raven-haired baby, was born, Laura had chucked in the job, chucked in socializing and pretty much chucked in life.

'I don't like going out with bunches of policemen and their wives and chatting policing all night. It's just not for me, Tim,' she would tell him time and time again.

Timmy had pleaded with her to have a bit of a life. He loved little Kyra with every ounce of his heart and totally appreciated the way Laura had sacrificed her career, as she constantly reminded him, to see to it that their daughter had a secure upbringing.

After five years of pleading, Timmy eventually gave up. Kyra had been at school for a year already and still Laura insisted on living her stay-at-home life. She had no women friends and adamantly refused to socialize unless it was for a birthday or an anniversary. She totally lost interest in her appearance; why should she bother with make-up or up-to-the-minute fashions?

On more than one occasion, Timmy had reminded her that she was still in her late twenties and sure they were only young and why couldn't they live a little? But the answers were always the same; she did not like socializing with members of the force and Timmy and Kyra were enough for her.

As Timmy entered his early thirties, he had begun to realize that his wife was a bit of a control freak. Although he also suspected that she was oblivious of the fact. He had come to the conclusion that the reason she did not want him socializing with his colleagues was so that he would devote himself to her and Kyra. When he finally decided that he needed a bit more to his life, Laura did not take it well.

'Wake up, woman. What do you think is going to happen to us if we keep living in this malaise? One of us is going to go stir-crazy,' he had told her. Privately, he had feared that he would go offside because he needed some stimulation in his life.

'But why can't you be happy with just us?' Laura had screamed at him. 'Why do you need all of those other people around?'

And when she had refused to go for counselling, Timmy had decided that he had to save himself. He applied for the post of detective, totally threw himself into the job, and met Kate Waters during the course of an investigation into an internet child-pornography ring.

It was one of Kate's earliest assignments from the police and he had been completely blown away by her performance. She had had to cope with an array of utterly disgusting images of children paired with grown men, and including animals in one scene. Yet she had remained calm and collected all through the six-week inquiry and had given them an almost perfect profile of the lead perpetrator in the ring, from a selection of seventeen possible suspects.

What had impressed Timmy most, however, was the way she had dealt with the unbelievable resentment levelled at her from the other detectives. It was the first time an outsider had been brought in to advise that particular group of detectives – aside from the legal eagles or professionals appointed to assess suspects – and they had not been kind to her.

But instead of trying to ingratiate herself with them, Kate had taken an altogether more practical approach: she got on with the job and ignored their jibes and snide remarks. Within weeks they were singing her praises, albeit behind her back.

Initially, they were just friends, although it was obvious to all and sundry that Kate and Timmy had a serious bond going on. The air was just filled with chemistry when they were in the same room.

Kate, in fairness, had known that he was married and it was only when a deep bond had formed that he admitted his feelings for her were more than friendship.

Kate had been angry, very angry, when he told her at first, but she had believed him when he explained that he had done all he could to make his marriage work. She had backed away, but they just kept coming back together again. They were drawn together by some powerful magnetic force that, no matter how hard they tried, neither of them could resist.

They enjoyed almost two years of absolute passion. Neither of them ever mentioned Laura, although she was always in the back of their minds. Both knew, that were it not for beautiful Kyra, Timmy would have done the brave thing and ended the marriage a long time ago – with or without Kate Waters. But Timmy could never have left his pumpkin and Kate could never have lived with the thought of separating a little girl from her father.

In the end, it was Laura who separated Timmy from Kyra and although he resented her every single day for causing the little girl's death, he was burdened by huge guilt because he also accepted that it was his behaviour which was the biggest contributory factor to Laura's actions on the night of Kyra's death.

'You're home early. It's only nine o'clock, Tim. This is not like you at all,' Laura said, as she came out into the hallway.

Timmy couldn't understand it. Lately, it was as if Laura had started to come alive again. She was paying a lot more attention to her appearance. She was talking to him a lot more and she was even out some of the nights when he arrived home.

He wondered if she had found out about him

working with Kate again and if that was the reason for the metamorphosis.

'Tough case?' she asked, placing her hand affectionately on his arm.

Timmy was gobsmacked. The last time he'd had any physical contact with his wife was on the day of Kyra's funeral.

Timmy nodded.

'Why don't you tell me about it?' she said cheerfully.

They walked into the small sitting room where a blazing fire had been lit for the first time in three years and she poured him a brandy and moved his old favourite chair closer to the fire.

Of all the bizarre turns of events Timmy had experienced in his thirty-eight years of life, this night was certainly the strangest. He had barely had a conversation with Laura since Kyra's death and suddenly she was being all sweetness and light.

He warmed the balloon glass with his large hands and stared at her, a perplexed look on his face.

'Don't look so stunned, Tim. I've been doing a lot of thinking lately. You were right all along. I let myself go. I didn't pay attention to us. I know now that I fell into the common trap – I took us for granted, Timmy. I thought I had it all and I thought I didn't need to make an effort. I know now that relationships are all about work.'

Timmy was stunned. Not in a million years had he expected this. Laura was talking about relationships. They hadn't had a relationship in a very long time.

She read his thoughts: 'Am I too late with this, Tim? Have I already ruined it for us?' she asked.

He had had enough of bombshells for one day.

'I still care about you an awful lot, Laura, but a relationship needs more than that. It needs love. Do we still have that capacity?' He paused a moment, before adding, 'I honestly do not know.'

Her pretty blue eyes focused on him earnestly. 'All I am saying is that we could perhaps give it another try. I know that I was unfair. I know that I destroyed us. I never gave us a chance. If it's not too late, I would like another try. The question is, are you prepared to try too?'

Well, what could he say to that? He had to at least consider it, didn't he? He owed her that. He knocked back his brandy in one gulp and told her that he needed time to think.

Laura said she understood. What Timmy Vaughan understood was that his adult life appeared to be turning into one long guilt trip.

31

All hell broke loose the next morning.

Monica Smith, a housewife living in a laneway close to the airport in north Dublin, had been out walking the family basset hounds when one of the two dogs broke free from his leash and ran onto a piece of wasteland. Monica had followed and came upon Martin Tierney's disfigured corpse.

Now she was under sedation at home and the scene where her basset, Henry, had made the gruesome discovery was cordoned off by a host of police and forensic specialists.

The problem was, Timmy and his team hadn't even been notified about this development because, as far as the local boys were concerned, it was a crime on their turf and had nothing to do with Timmy's team. In fact the officers handling the discovery of the body could not possibly have known to contact Timmy because the ongoing missing-women investigation was still top-secret.

Timmy heard the news from Laura who, much to his astonishment, was waiting for him in the kitchen with a full Irish breakfast when he got up at half-past seven.

'Did you have the radio on upstairs?' she asked cheerfully when he walked into the room.

'No,' he answered. 'Should I have?'

'Well, your lot are going to be getting it from the media today,' she said. 'There's been another gangland shooting.'

'Mad bastards,' Timmy grunted. 'All the fuckers can kill each other for all I care. It's less of the scumbags for us to deal with in the long run.'

That was the view of most seasoned police officers. The gangland world was so tight-knit that it was extremely difficult to solve the frequent murders which occurred within that community, and the more experienced members of the force believed that if justice couldn't be served through the courts, then the fuckers might as well save the system the effort and do the job for them.

'Well, actually, Tim, I should correct myself. It appears it was a gangland-style killing, but the news says the victim has no associations with the gangland scene,' she volunteered.

'Thanks for the breakfast,' Timmy said as he

dipped his crispy toast into the yolk of a perfectly cooked free-range egg.

'Where was the killing anyway?' he asked, not that it concerned him one iota. He had bigger fish to fry at the moment and dealing with the scumbags involved in a gangland murder would be a piece of cake by comparison to the mystery he was trying to solve.

'Out somewhere on the north side. Apparently the victim was in his fifties, a local small businessman,' Laura replied.

A chill ran along Timmy's spine. Call it second sight, or good old-fashioned cop's intuition, but Timmy knew instantly who this latest victim was. He pushed his breakfast away from him, sending the cutlery and a milk jug crashing to the floor.

An hour later – thanks to Dublin's gridlock problems – he was at the scene and he was fuming. John Flood, the superintendent in charge, was standing in the centre of a circle of detectives and Timmy did not want to be noticed. Had Flood, or any of the detectives known the reason for his presence, the horde of reporters gathered at the scene would get the news within fifteen minutes and then the secret of Timmy's investigation would be blown wide open.

Paddy Daly was with him. 'Jesus, Timmy, we've

got to tell them. It's going to get out eventually and when it does, our heads will be on the chopping block. There will be a huge internal investigation and we will be accused of withholding information. We've no choice in the matter, man.'

Timmy pulled his sheepskin jacket around him. It was twenty to nine in the morning and there was no heat yet in the day. But even if it had been thirty degrees, Timmy would still have been freezing. His blood was running cold, even though things were clearly hotting up.

He stood silently behind a news jeep owned by one of the television stations. All the reporters were so busy staring at Flood and waiting for him to come and make some kind of statement about the slaying, that none of them noticed Vaughan. If they had, the more seasoned ones would have been over to him like a light, knowing that if he was there, there would definitely be another story behind the scenes.

What was he to do? Nobody, except for Kate and his team knew about poor Martin Tierney's links to Mickser Cummins. The poor sod had only been doing a bit of business and now he was dead, because of Timmy's investigation.

Timmy was trying to think things through. Why hadn't he protected Martin Tierney after extracting the information about Cummins? That was the question the media would ask if they got hold of this. Why was a little-known sole trader, who was forced to provide information to the police about one of the biggest gangland figures in the land, not offered protection?

Then there was the whole issue about the missing-women investigation. If the news leaked that Martin Tierney's murder was linked to Mickser Cummins and a secret police investigation into missing women – an investigation which was being kept secret – there would be hell to pay. Opposition politicians would be screaming blue murder about incompetence at the Department of Justice and the media would be screaming about cover-up and transparency.

The fact that all three women were from solid middle-class backgrounds would increase the pressure tenfold. It was always the same. If somebody from a working-class area went missing or was murdered, there were the usual few days of coverage and then the whole thing was forgotten. It was almost as if it was expected that the poverty-stricken and working classes would suffer in such a way.

But if somebody from a middle-class area became the victim of a serious crime, the media went ballistic. The families mounted huge publicity campaigns and big rewards were often offered. Then the media went on a tirade about how crime was spiralling out of control and how even those on the more privileged side of the fence were being affected. It was as if crime should be confined within particular socio-economic boundaries. That made Timmy sick.

There was also the question of the blame game. Each police division fought hard to get more resources for overtime and more credits for crime-solving. If Johnny Flood's division learned the real reason for Martin Tierney's death, they would run to the media with it. Allegations would follow about a cock-up and Flood's team would sit back and enjoy watching Vaughan and his team take the flack for causing the death of an ordinary civilian.

'If we tell them, this whole thing will be exposed and we will never get to solve it. We've got to leave them to work this case in isolation.' He was thinking out loud now.

'Jesus, Timmy, we can't do this. We can't be party to covering up a crime. It will look like we were point-scoring when it gets out,' Paddy Daly said.

Timmy turned and walked towards his Volkswagen Passat. 'We've got to, Daly,' he said. 'We've got a much bigger problem on our hands than the death of poor Martin Tierney. We've got to think of the bigger picture.'

Daly put a hand on Timmy's shoulder, stopping him in his tracks.

'What the hell are you talking about, Timmy? What could possibly be worse than this?' he asked.

'Isn't it obvious?' Timmy asked him.

Daly just shook his head. He was totally in the dark.

Timmy leaned in close to him. 'Do you think that Martin Tierney called around to Mickser Cummins last night and told him that he'd assisted the police in their inquiries? Is that why he's dead now?'

Daly turned white as he answered: 'Oh Christ, Timmy. We've got a mole on our hands.'

'Not just a mole, son,' Timmy said gravely. 'Somebody on our team is on Cummins' payroll. We've got a bad cop on our hands.'

32

'That will teach the fuckin' bastards. That will fuckin' learn them that they can't bleedin' well put one over on me. Fuckin' dickheads the whole bleedin' lot of them. Well, now they've got their first body on their hands. And you know what the beauty of it is?'

Mickser Cummins was in his den, surrounded by his cronies. He paused to let his words sink in. His crew were hard men but, aside from Knocker Griffin, they were a bit short on brain matter. No Knickers Grimes and Breaker Daly had to have everything explained to them in great detail. Cummins wasn't waiting for an answer from these two. He would be there for ever if he had to wait for a modicum of intelligence to emanate from either of their gobs.

'The beauty is, me boys, that they still haven't got within a mile of their missing women. Fucking ponces, the whole lot of them.'

Everybody laughed. It was what was expected of them.

There had been no need to murder Martin Tierney. It wasn't even the principle involved in Tierney giving Cummins' name to the police that motivated Cummins to order his death. In general, Cummins tended to reserve such punishments for fellow gangland associates or other crims who crossed him.

Tierney's death was all to do with sending a message to the filth. The rough translation was: 'Fuck with me and I'll fuck you right back. Only ten times worse.' It gave Cummins great pleasure to know that while one investigation team would be tearing their hair out trying to find a motive for this slaying, Timmy Vaughan and his sidekick Daly would know exactly what it was all about. What was more, they wouldn't be able to pin so much as an ounce of guilt on him.

It was all about arrogance really. Ever since Cummins had conceived this plot, he expected Vaughan to discover who was behind it eventually. But discovering the perpetrator and actually fingering that person were two totally different scenarios.

Cummins was aware, from personal experience as well as his own knowledge of numerous vicious gangland crimes which went unsolved, that in nine out of ten cases, the dogs in the street – and that included the police – knew who was behind the crimes. But it was a rare occasion when anybody was brought to justice for them.

There was a huge irony surrounding the whole gangland crime scene. Few people realized that gangland crimes were *much* easier to solve than ordinary civilian-type crimes because word was always on the street within hours about the motivation behind gangland slayings. In the case of 'ordinary' murders, the cops often spent months trying to identify the culprits because the motives of private individuals were much more difficult to pin down.

Cummins had exploded with fury when he had learned that Vaughan had tracked the three mobile phones to him. It had been a major oversight on his part to purchase the phones locally, but he had never in his wildest dreams expected that the network operators would be able to trace them to the point of purchase. It was a new lesson and one that would, no doubt, serve him well in the future.

In the meantime, his arrogance forbade him from accepting that he was about to be rumbled by Vaughan. Hence the murder of Tierney. Cummins believed that he was untouchable.

But the brilliance in the plan was that, even though Vaughan was now on to Cummins, he still would not be able to finger Cummins for the disappearance of the three women. The fact remained that the only word Vaughan had was the word of a dead man. More importantly, Cummins had never made a single call from any of the phones, nor had any of his crew. So Vaughan would never be able to prove any connection with the missing women.

To add insult to injury, Cummins was about to throw Vaughan's world into even more disarray. He was going to take away something which he knew was even more important to Vaughan than solving the case of the missing women.

He smiled as he contemplated the prospect. Instinctively, Knocker Griffin knew what his boss was thinking.

'Is it time, boss? Do you want me to put the next phase into motion then?'

Cummins spun himself around in his swivel chair. When he arrived back at the point where he was facing his men again, he smiled a crazy, demented smile. It was the signature smile he was famed for. It was a smile that signalled that Mickser Cummins meant business.

'Get out there and wreak havoc, Griffin. Let's

really put the cat among the pigeons now,' he said.

No Knickers and Breaker looked at each other quizzically. They hadn't got a clue what Cummins was on about and they knew better than to ask. But they felt certain that there was a fair amount of violence involved. Anything less just wouldn't have been Cummins' style.

33

'He's tapping all of your phones.'

'I know,' Knocker said.

'They've got taps set up on all land lines and on all mobiles.'

'What's the next likely step then?' Knocker asked.

'They will be waiting for your lot to make a mistake.'

'Well, they will be waiting a long fucking time. What do they think we are? Fucking morons? Probably.' Knocker paused. 'Especially after the death of Tierney and all. You'd think they might have copped that *we are on to them*.'

'Of course they are aware of that. But they appear to have touts working for them. They have the extra numbers too.'

'How could they have gotten hold of our extra numbers?' Knocker asked.

'They seem to have accessed them through the families of Breaker and No Knickers.'

Knocker was shocked. 'Surely their families wouldn't double-cross them?'

'I don't think it was a question of double-crossing. Through their touts, they got hold of the lads' brothers' numbers and they monitored their mobiles until calls were made to your boys.'

'But it's only twenty-four hours since Tierney was killed. How could they have gotten hold of the numbers that fast?'

'Easy. Once they got hold of the numbers for Breaker and No Knickers, they got the phone company to access its Call Detail Record system and they examined the numbers until they came up with those bouncing off the masts nearest Cummins' home. It's a piece of cake for the cops to do something like that these days.'

'Did they get anything useful from the calls over the last twenty-four hours then? Those two pricks have been warned not to talk on those phones. Tell me they didn't.'

'No, Knocker, they got nothing. But all the same, you'd better watch out, and the other pair had better be warned. You don't call them dumb and dumber for nothing, remember.'

'Fair enough. I'll see that you're taken care of, mate. Thanks for the tip.'

'No problem,' said the source. 'It's entirely my

pleasure. I'm having the time of my life, thanks to you and your three missing women.'

Knocker bade farewell to the source. He couldn't stand being in his company. The sooner this came to an end the better as far as he was concerned. Then he could have his own bit of pleasure and finish off the source once and for all. Obnoxious little prick.

34

The source was indeed having the time of his life. He was back at his house now, where Sophie Andrews was safely ensconced in the basement. He didn't even have to bother going down to check on her – a CCTV monitor, connected to a camera buried deep in the wall of the room she was imprisoned in, gave him a clear picture of what she was up to.

'Insolent bitch!' he shouted out loud as he observed her on the screen. He had told her to stay standing at all times, but there she was, huddled in a ball in the foetal position on the floor. He could see her torso shivering from the cold. Or was it the fear, he wondered. He chuckled to himself. He hoped it was!

He had wired the basement to connect to an audio system attached to the CCTV control unit, so that he could project any sound he wished into the room. He pressed a button on the audio machine now, and smiled. He had had the basement soundproofed, so he couldn't actually hear her screams, but he could certainly *see* her screaming on the screen.

Jonathon had purchased the rattlesnake CD in a special-effects store in LA. Where else could one buy such a thing, he asked himself as he saw the reaction it brought forth in Sophie.

Right now, he sniggered with pleasure as he watched Sophie – chained to the wall and semi-naked in complete darkness – struggle to get away from the rattlesnakes she thought had been put into her cell. It was beautiful. The sight of her wriggling like a deranged person, clearly utterly terrified, brought the old memories flooding back. For he knew from experience that until she learned about respect, the torture would never stop. Not while he was on the scene, at least.

Pleasurable and all as watching Sophie's obvious discomfort was, it was time to check up on his other charges. The satellite link-up he had installed in the properties in New York and LA proved just as effective. However, this was the first time he had had an opportunity to link into them, as he had been busy in his 'other' life; managing people and projects took up a lot of his time, but he was usually able to juggle things to fit everything into his busy schedule, as he frequently reminded Griffin.

It had been so easy, it was child's play, even though he had never wired so much as a plug before in his life. He had merely installed cameras in the ceilings of each of the rooms the girls were held in, then run the wires out into adjoining rooms which housed computers, which in turn were linked to a computer he had installed in the house he was now in. And, hey presto . . . he could watch them live via the internet!

'Poor old Andrina,' he said out loud as he watched her via the link to LA. She was still standing naked in the centre of the room, the metal collar still attached to her lovely neck.

Clearly the sound effects he had left running in the house had fooled her – she obviously believed that he was there!

And in New York, Nikki Kane was under the same illusion. She was still chained to the kitchen sink. He wanted to play the same trick on Nikki that he had just played on Sophie, but he couldn't. It was still bright in New York and enough light was seeping through the sealed-up basement window to allow her to see what was going on. It was a pity, he thought, because he dearly wanted to frighten her with the snakes, having gotten so much pleasure out of her reaction to the cock-roaches on his last visit to her!

Still, soon enough he would have all three of them together and he would play great games with them before handing them over. That was the wonderful thing about being in a position of authority, he reminded himself; he could do what he wanted and had nobody else to answer to because everybody automatically gave him the respect he so richly deserved!

35

'Why do you think he's doing this, Kate? That's what I don't get. This is not Spiller Cummins' style at all. I need a motive here to help me on this. It just doesn't add up for me, I'm afraid.'

Timmy had called into the coach house in Killiney to see Kate. It was the evening of the day after the discovery of Tierney's body and Timmy and the team had been up to their proverbial eyeballs trying to get a lead. They were all over the place. Not one of them could figure out why the likes of Cummins would be involved in this business.

She poured him a glass of red wine and Timmy could not help noticing that the bottle was already open and that two used glasses already stood on the coffee table before the fire. Instinctively, he resented the cosy set-up.

For her part, Kate had been relieved when Pete had said he had to go out to a last-minute meeting.

She did not want the two of them to meet. The whole situation would have been far too awkward, for her, and for Timmy.

Kate had been thinking long and hard since she learned of Tierney's murder and the more she thought about it, the more she arrived at the conclusion that Tierney had been finished off because of his dealings with Timmy. It just seemed too coincidental to be anything other than a message for Timmy.

'You know, I can't help feeling that Cummins' motive for this has something to do with you.'

Timmy had a look of absolute revulsion on his face. The last thing Kate wanted to do was put the burden for this whole business on Timmy's shoulders, but that was her gut instinct and she trusted her instincts.

'Why me? Why would he go to such drastic lengths to get at me, Kate? Where are you coming from with this? I don't understand,' he said.

'I don't understand yet, Timmy, but I think what I am saying is correct. I really feel that he is doing this to get at you. It's only a gut feeling. But look at the evidence: you are the lead detective and everything that has happened to date appears to have been designed to cause maximum embarrassment to the investigating team.'

Timmy sat there in silence. The gravity of what she was saying to him was just too much for him to bear. Why would a hardened crim like Mickser Cummins go to so much trouble, and risk, just to get at Timmy Vaughan?

'How so? How does it point to me?' he asked, an accusatory tone to his voice.

She ticked off possible reasons on her fingers.

'Look, you were the one who busted his drug distribution network last year. Then a series of crimes are committed that don't come to light until very late in the day, potentially exposing the investigating team – and most specifically you, as the most senior investigator on that team – to extremely embarrassing and bad publicity. Then, after three weeks, you make your first major advance in the case and within hours – literally hours, Timmy – you get a big message, in the form of Martin Tierney's body. It's almost as if he was just waiting for the opportunity to give you the proverbial two fingers, to let you know that he is there and ahead of you in whatever sick game he is playing.'

Kate waited while he absorbed her reasoning. He wondered if she was paranoid, or if he was not paranoid enough.

'Then it becomes apparent that you can't

release the information that you have about Martin Tierney's murder to your colleagues on the north side because if you do it looks like your team screwed up and the whole thing will turn into a PR fiasco. Cummins knew that, in order to cover your back, you would have to keep quiet. It seems to me, Timmy, that this whole thing is a set-up. A set-up designed to damage you.'

He looked devastated. Since discovering that Cummins was the architect of this grand scheme, Timmy had been perplexed, for sure. But Kate's theory was just so much more disturbing.

As always, Kate followed her theory with further analysis. In this case, it was designed to soften the blow to Timmy.

'If I am correct, Timmy, I think we can take comfort from the fact,' she said.

'No way Kate'. He paused, an incredulous look on his face. 'Well, I've heard it all now.'

Kate smiled at him. This was *so* Timmy. A fantastic investigator for sure, but not much of a lateral thinker.

'Bear with me here, Timmy. There *is* a method to the madness of my reckoning.'

'Yeah, well, I'm just *dying* to hear what it is, Kate, because as it stands, Hercules with his labours never had a patch on the way I feel now.'

'Well, if this is some bizarre plot to get at you, Timmy, then it's good news for our three women. It means that they are not with some sex fiend whose intentions would probably be very different from those of Mr Cummins. If that's the case, they are probably still alive. Why would a guy like Cummins expose himself to such risk by harming them, if I am right?'

Timmy thought about her scenario for a few minutes. She had a point, he had to concede that. It was at least one point of consolation he could take from her lateral reasoning.

'I hope you're right with this scenario, because if you are, and Cummins is just doing this to get at me, then at least it gives these women a fighting chance,' he said.

Timmy didn't want to get overexcited about the merits of what she was saying. She could see it in his face and she knew why.

'I know what you're thinking, Timmy. You're thinking, quite rightly I might add, that he's not in this alone.'

'Absolutely,' he conceded.

'I think he's got the help of whoever it is tipped him off about Martin Tierney. That's what's really bothering me at the moment.'

As always, Kate Waters was way ahead of the game.

Or so Timmy thought.

But after he'd left her he realized that there was one fundamental flaw in her reasoning. If this thing was just a big scam to expose Timmy as a useless investigator responsible for cocking-up a serial-abduction case, then that meant that Cummins had taken extreme measures to cover his tracks, so there would not be a shred of evidence to link Cummins to the disappearances.

Additionally, if Cummins was using outside help to stage this scam – and surely he must be – then he was left with two options: to kill the facilitator or to kill the women.

It didn't bear thinking about. He wondered if Cummins had another motive altogether. If he did, Timmy, for the life of him, could not figure out what it was.

36

One thing really bothered Kate. Mickser Cummins was intent on goading Timmy. That much was clear. Not only had he sent him the two fingers regarding Martin Tierney, he was almost advertising the fact that he had inside help. Otherwise, he would have left Timmy thinking that Cummins had no idea that Timmy was on to him.

But he had not done that. Instead, Cummins had committed a bare-faced murder. He may not have pulled the trigger himself. Indeed, knowing the likes of Cummins, it was almost a dead certainty that he had not. But he may as well have.

Kate believed wholeheartedly that she was correct in her theory that this was a vendetta against Timmy. But she was also of the firm opinion that it was about something very personal, that Cummins was intent on really *hurting* Timmy. Why she felt this way, she was not quite sure, but again her gut was telling her that there was definitely more to this case than was on the face of it.

She had not discussed all of her thoughts on the case with Timmy, but she also suspected that Cummins was using somebody else to do most of his dirty work and that the finger would ultimately point elsewhere, and not specifically to Cummins.

She continued her reasoning with Pete, who had returned to the coach house about an hour after Timmy's departure. 'Think of it, he has got to be using somebody else to play this thing out the way it is going.'

'Why, sweetheart? I don't necessarily see it that way, not that I'm used to your way of thinking or anything. Why would a hardened criminal like Cummins use somebody else to do his dirty work? Aren't guys like him well able to take care of themselves?'

'Well, that's the whole point,' Kate said. 'He is using somebody else because he can and, more importantly, I think that this somebody else – whoever the hell it is – is going to be Cummins' fall guy, though they most likely have no idea that they are being set up too.'

Pete didn't understand her thinking at all. 'How

can you rationalize it that way, Kate? Surely if he has been using somebody to abduct these women, then that person is fully aware of what he is doing? You can't be party to the abduction of three women and not know that you are committing a *very* serious crime. It doesn't stack up for me.'

But Kate already had the answer to that conundrum. 'Three mobile phones are purchased on the north side of the city and on each occasion, the first call from each phone is made from Cummins' neighbourhood. The records from the phone companies prove that. Then every subsequent call from each of the phones is made from Blackrock in south Dublin. It's as if Cummins has deliberately distanced himself from everything to do with the crimes.'

Pete said he didn't really see her point. 'So where does that take you to then, Kate?'

'Well, this is the point I'm getting to. Cummins obviously feels totally secure in what he is doing. I think that if we solve this crime – actually, *when* – we solve this crime, we won't find Cummins' fingerprints on it at all. It will be the fingerprints of whoever it is he is using as his pawn.'

Pete was intrigued. Ever since he first met Kate, he had been totally blown away by the depth of her intelligence. Her insight was so acute that she almost frightened him at times. He often wondered what she really saw when she analysed him.

'So who do you think it is then?'

Kate put her arms around Pete's broad shoulders. 'If I knew that, I wouldn't be sitting here with you now. But one thing is for sure: Timmy Vaughan should not be concentrating solely on Mickser Cummins. The clues to solving this crime lie much closer to home.'

Pete kissed her deeply and led her up the stairs to bed. He wanted to hold her tight, to make her feel protected. He feared that she was getting perilously close to the truth in what was clearly turning out to be a very dangerous game.

After they made love, Kate found that she wasn't falling into her usual exhausted state of mind. In fact she was buzzing. There were too many unanswered questions about this case and she needed somebody else to put a few theories to. She knew it was late, but she thought that the woman she was going to call wouldn't mind being interrupted.

She crept out of the bed so as not to wake Pete and hurried down to her little study at the back of the house. She knew that what she was about to do wasn't exactly ethical, but this thing had more twists than San Francisco's Lombard Street and she figured they needed all the help, inspiration or whatever they could get at this stage in the game.

She took out her Rolodex and searched for the number of the only journalist in Dublin she had ever been willing to deal with – Jenny Smith.

Jenny was an investigative journalist whom Kate had first met two years earlier at a conference on the socio-economics and demographics of crime in Dublin. The journalist was a few years younger than Kate, but what Kate really liked about her was the fact that Jenny, unlike so many of her counterparts who were only interested if there was a sensationalist angle to a story, was actually interested in what made the criminals she dealt with tick. Around town, among the police and criminal lawyers, she was well regarded, particularly for the pieces she wrote which didn't focus so much on the crimes as on the psyche of the criminals who committed them. In the business, she was famed for writing so-called 'colour' pieces, which gave great background information on the more controversial criminals of the day.

If anybody involved with the case knew what Kate was doing, they would go ballistic, particularly Vaughan. But Kate appeased her guilty conscience with the fact that she was not about to tell Jenny any of the details of the case: she just wanted to put out a few feelers about Cummins and his crew. If it was known within the criminal fraternity exactly what Cummins was up to, Jenny Smith, with her vast array of criminal contacts, was the journalist who would find out. As Jenny had put it once to Kate, even the shrewdest of crims could hardly resist boasting of their exploits when they managed to defy the law. It was human nature, even in a game with high stakes.

Four rings later, Jenny answered her mobile. She was on the ball as usual and Kate was relieved to note that Jenny, whom she had not seen or talked to in about four months, still obviously had her mobile number stored in her phone.

'Hi, Kate Waters. To what do I owe the pleasure of a midnight call from you? It must be pretty big if you're calling at this ungodly hour,' the journalist teased.

Kate let out an inward sigh. Jenny was no fool. Still, Kate had to play it cool.

'Ah nothing huge, Jen. I'm just doing a bit of background on an ongoing case and I was wondering if you could put a few feelers out for me?' she asked.

'Sure,' Jenny responded in mock agreement. 'The premier criminal profiler in the land is burning the midnight oil, rings me and tries to tell me that it's nothing important. Sure, Kate, what can I do for you? Anything I can assist you with, you know that I will. And we know it goes without saying that you will return the favour some day.'

'I'm wondering if you have heard anything from any of your sources lately about Mickser Cummins?' Kate said bluntly.

'Wow!' Jenny exclaimed, the glee positively dripping from her voice. 'It must be something really big if he's involved. Do tell me more.'

'I don't know any more, Jen, that's why I'm calling. I just need to know if you can find out what he's up to at the moment. You know, if there are any rumours going around town, that's all.'

'Come on, Kate, you will have to give me a bit more to go on than that. I can't start delving until I know what to look for. What do you think I am, psychic?' she said.

'In this case, I wish you were,' Kate responded forlornly and then could have kicked herself for doing so, for surely Jenny would know for definite now that she was on to something big.

'I can't give you anything else at the moment, Jenny. I just need the favour and I need you to be absolutely discreet about this request.'

'OK,' Jenny replied. 'But I have one question I need you to answer for me.'

'Fire,' Kate told her.

'Does this involve a particular detective with whom you have worked closely in the past? No names, Kate. Just a yes or a no will be fine.'

It was the time for the coded language often spoken between journalists and unforthcoming sources.

'Look, Jenny, I've already said, I'm bound by serious confidentiality on this one. I can't answer that,' Kate responded, an exasperated tone to her voice.

'But you haven't said no,' Jenny ventured.

'That's right, Jen, I haven't.'

'I'll get back to you in a day or so,' Jenny replied, before hanging up abruptly to dash to her computer to examine her ongoing file on Mickser Cummins.

As she waited for her Dell notebook to boot up, Jenny rubbed her hands in eager anticipation. Kate had just confirmed that she was working with the one and only Timmy Vaughan. Everybody knew that Vaughan had rumbled Cummins' distribution network last year and set the criminal back by millions. It was common knowledge within the criminal fraternity that Cummins was completely pissed off with Vaughan, because even though Vaughan had not been able to pin any criminal charges on Cummins, he had still cost him a fortune.

If Kate Waters and Vaughan were involved in something with Cummins, it had to be something spectacular, particularly since Kate had taken it upon herself to call a journalist to find out what was going on.

Jenny could hardly wait for tomorrow to come to start making calls. It was six weeks since her last big scoop and she was really looking forward to sinking her teeth into this one. It had trouble, with a capital T, written all over it.

37

Dublin, 1986

'You will never amount to anything in this life.
You are nothing. Look at you. Nobody, but nobody
respects you. You are dead to the world. You are
dead to me.'

The eighteen-year-old boy stood before his
father. The man was seventy-three now, but he
was still as cruel and heartless towards his son as
he had been through his younger years. Age had
not softened him in any way.

The boy had nursed him for the past three
months – the summer holidays before he began
university given over to the care of a man who
had taunted and abused him all his life.

Was it through fear or love that the boy had minis-
tered to the dying man? The boy did not know. All
he knew was that he felt compelled to look after the
cancer-ridden monster who had ruined his life.

His mother had died five months earlier. At the funeral – which was attended, of course, by hundreds of his father's friends (though the boy noticed that few of them came back to the solemn house for the reception) – the boy had shed a few tears. But they had not been tears lamenting the loss of a good mother. The boy hated the woman with a vengeance.

He had often told her so through his miserable childhood. He hated her for allowing him to endure the suffering at the hands of the man he privately called 'the Monster'. How could a mother permit such a thing to happen to her child?

So no, the tears at her funeral had not been tears of love, but tears of regret and resentment. The boy resented the fact that she had not paved the way for him to have a normal life. He resented the fact that she had stood by all those years and watched his father ridicule him, beat him and reduce him to a quivering wreck who had never known a day's love.

As he stood before his dying father, he acknowledged for the first time the reason for his mother's silence. She was weak. And it was from her that he had formed the basis of his overriding impression of *all* women. They were there to be dominated. They deserved nothing but contempt. They were *spineless* creatures who would *put up with anything*, so long as they had the façade of a happy marriage and the comforts of a good home. That was all women wanted and for that they did not deserve a modicum of respect.

'You have ruined my life. You have left me to die a shamed man. I have nothing, nothing whatsoever to be proud of in you. You will never amount to anything.'

The old man's words drove a stake through the boy's heart. It was then that the boy realized why he had cared for the man these past months. He had been hoping, against all the odds, but nonetheless hoping, for a scintilla of compassion and love from his father.

He had not known it until this very minute, but he now recognized his loyalty towards his father for what it was – a last chance for love, a last chance for respect. Despite everything that had happened, the boy craved the man's respect.

Clearly, from what the man had just said, he was never going to get it.

The boy took the syringe from the bedside table and held it up clearly for his father to see. The man's eyes widened with surprise. 'What are you doing, you stupid fool? It's not time yet. The nurse has just left. Wait for another four hours,' he barked.

But the boy did not wait. His father had chosen to die at home. This way, he was just dying a little sooner than expected.

The man was heavily drugged already, but he was still alert, still able to taunt the boy. That's what drove the boy to do it: the knowledge that until his father was gone, the torture would never stop.

He took a firm grip of the man's left wrist. His father was right-handed, so they would assume that he had injected himself in the left wrist using his right hand.

'Don't be a fool, boy. Do not disobey me. Do as I say. Take the needle away now.'

His voice was as stern as ever and his face was as indignant as it always had been whenever he was challenged.

Very slowly, the boy pressed on the plunger of the syringe. He felt sick, not because he was killing his father, but because he was forced to touch him. He had not willingly touched his father since the commencement of his teenage years, when the unrelenting taunting had begun.

He waited until the syringe was emptied and then held his face close to his father's. The man's eyes had begun to blink rapidly, but the boy knew that he was fighting the morphine, that the man could still hear him.

'You have just lost your credit here, Father. It is you who is dead to the world.'

38

Dublin, March 2004

Sophie Andrews held her breath when she heard the key turning in the door. Was this it, she wondered, remembering Jonathon Hunt's final words to her the last time he'd left the house. What was it he had said? That she was going somewhere much worse than where she already was . . .

'Mother of God,' she said out loud when he opened the door to the basement.

She stood there, wide-eyed, open-mouthed. She wasn't the only one in his clutches.

He smiled at her, that vicious, lascivious smile that spoke of sinister thoughts and lewd acts. The smile of smugness and all-consuming power. He had it perfected to a fine art.

Jonathon could see the reaction on her filthy, drawn face. He liked it. It spoke of fear and uncertainty, but also of relief.

'Glad to see you're not the only one who has been suffering, then? How selfish of you. Bitch!' He slapped her hard across the face as he uttered the last word.

But it was true, Sophie was relieved to see the two other women with him. It gave her hope, a feeling of solidarity. Perhaps they could work together to escape from his clutches? What was it they said? There was strength in numbers.

The other two women clearly had not been subjected to the same type of confinement and degradation as she had, she thought to herself as she took in the groomed appearance of each. They were well dressed and looked as if they had been well fed too. Not like Sophie, whose rations had run out four days ago and who had since been living on water.

Again, it was as if he could read her thoughts. 'Don't worry, they have each had as rough a time as you, my dear. They have been learning about respect too and I can assure you that I have been every bit as severe with them as I have with you.'

He was smiling confidently, clearly proud of his *achievements* with these women. Sophie had the feeling that he was waiting for her to congratulate him.

'And if you are wondering why they look so –

how should I say it? – well. Well, that's because they have just come back from overseas. You see, Andrina and Nikki here, they did not question my authority so early on – as you did – so they have had a longer holiday. But look beneath the surface and you will certainly see the marks of the punishments I have doled out. Their outward appearances are just that, my dear – for appearances! We are just back, you see. From Los Angeles and New York. I have been flying all weekend. They are drugged, of course, that is why they appear so meek and mild-mannered. It's the same stuff I used on you.'

He clapped his hands loudly then, causing Sophie to jump with fright.

'Now it is time to get back down to business. We have just one night left together before I hand you all over. I think we should all enjoy it. It will be like a revision course, to see what you have all learned. If you pass, I will tell the people you are going to, to treat you well. If you don't, then I am afraid I will have to tell them to be very harsh with you.'

He began stripping Andrina and Nikki of their clothing. 'Don't want you to feel left out now, do we?' he laughed, looking at Sophie's bruised and scarred body. 'Best that you see for yourself the evidence of their suffering, Sophie.'

Sophie retched when she saw the evidence of his brutality. Both women were badly and freshly marked. He had obviously beaten and abused them before transporting them back home. At least she assumed they were at home, in Ireland. That's what had kept her going all these weeks, the hope that if they were in Ireland, somebody would eventually find them. But she didn't know for sure because she could not remember actually getting to the house, or even getting off the jet in Dublin. But it certainly seemed cold enough for Ireland. Sophie felt like she was suffering from hypothermia.

'What do you mean that you are handing us over? What are you talking about, Jonathon? What are you doing with us?' Sophie knew that he would probably beat her for asking the questions, but she didn't care. If they were going elsewhere, perhaps an opportunity would arise for escape.

'Do I have to keep repeating myself?' he said with a sigh, sounding like a weary parent who was fed up of asking a child to perform a task over and over again.

He had chained Andrina and Nikki to the wall in separate corners of the room by now. He walked to the centre, where Sophie was standing and pushed her face down on the ground. 'Did I not forbid you from speaking unless you were spoken to?' he shouted into her ear, as he crouched over her body.

Sophie didn't answer him. She was too terrified to speak. He went to a shelf on the wall and removed the whip he had used on her before.

'Say it,' he shouted, as he lashed her sprawled body. 'Say it now. You know the words. Saaaaay iiiiiit,' he bellowed like a crazed madman.

But Sophie remained silent. She wanted him to shout. She half-suspected it was in vain, but perhaps somebody would hear him.

Abruptly, he stopped and stood over her, kicking her chin upwards with his foot so that she was looking up towards his face. 'I know what you are at, you bitch. But it won't work. *Nobody* will ever hear you here. Trust me, I am the last person they will suspect.'

And with that, Jonathon Hunt made to leave the room. Just before he went out of the door, he turned and added, 'By the way, for your insolence, I am going to rape you later. All of you. All three of you. Here's a bell. I'll hear it through my sound system. Ring it when the others wake up.'

39

The woman sat with Mickser Cummins, or Spiller, as she knew he was nicknamed, again. This time, they were in the village of Dalkey. They were in the very same pub, in fact, where Kate and Timmy had sat less than two weeks earlier.

Spiller Cummins had been dead set against meeting in Finnegan's bar, but the woman had insisted. It was a high-risk game and she was already beginning to reap the rewards; the risk factor just added to the thrill for her. She had him over the proverbial barrel and she was fully intent on exercising that control.

As usual, she was half-sauced by the time he got there. She had a gleeful look in her eyes as they talked about the case. Spiller Cummins acknowledged that the woman had given him assistance and inspiration, but he despised her for it. In his world, it was one thing for men to enjoy committing crimes against women – if the crimes served a purpose. But for a woman to take such pleasure out of crimes against other women . . . well, it was downright unnatural, bleeding disgusting. As he had said to Knocker Griffin on many an occasion, put a woman in a position of power and she was capable of being ten times more evil than any man ever was.

Mind you, Spiller was not actually certain that the three missing women had undergone any physical pain. All he knew for sure was that Hunt had conned each of them into going away with him; beyond that, he was totally unaware of Hunt's modus operandi.

But Cummins couldn't stand Hunt and he suspected that the man was an out and out pervert who was probably having a whale of a time with the women. He could only imagine what kind of acts all that new-found power had driven Hunt to. As far as Cummins was concerned, the guy was a seedy little cunt, probably worse than No Knickers Grimes too. It was fine to be one thing so long as you admitted to it, but to prance around masquerading as a respected member of society and then behave as Hunt did, well that was a different matter. That was two-faced and Cummins himself was a straight-up kind of man, even if he was a crook. Criminals had their standards as well. It bugged him that not a lot of people acknowledged that.

'I thought there was going to be some action soon,' the woman stated accusingly.

Cummins clenched his jaws. He was getting really pissed off with her constant demands and interference. In fact, if it wasn't for the information on their deal stored in her bank's safety deposit box, he would finish her off for sure. She was turning out to be an evil bitch and a royal pain in the ass, if ever there was one. Albeit a useful evil bitch.

'It's all in hand. My lads are going to move soon,' he said.

'That's what you said *the last time* we met. When am I going to get some proof?'

He really wanted to punch her one now. This was the last time he would do business with a woman, for sure. He was almost regretting not finishing her off when he had the chance earlier on in the game.

'*I said things are in motion. I can't be more specific than that. These things take time.*'

He was speaking through gritted teeth and she could see why he had such a violent reputation. Until now, she had not regarded him as posing any real threat to her.

'I'm only asking because I need to know. I need to know how to read the situation. I have a game plan too,' she said.

Spiller Cummins hadn't got a clue what she was talking about, but it was the first time that he realized that she was actually *using* him. He had not looked at it like that before, but that was exactly what she was doing. He didn't like it one bit. He should have stuck to plan A.

'We're moving on it this week. Now, is that good enough for you?' He didn't care about this woman any more. In fact, as far as he was concerned, she had more to lose than he did if this whole thing went belly-up. *He* could finger *her* quite easily. But what did she have on *him*? *Nada*. That was what she had on him. Abso-fucking-lutely nothing, except an alleged letter in some bank box and he knew that she wouldn't really drop him in it.

The more he thought about it, the more tempted he was to drop her in it too. After all, Hunt was going to fall. Vaughan was going to fall. And that snooty bitch Kate Waters was going to fall too. She was such a gullible bitch and the more he heard about her, the more he considered her to be a dangerous cow. He wanted her to suffer for sticking her nose in where it wasn't bleedin' wanted, as he'd told Griffin.

It was all part of his grand plan, to screw the lot of them, the so-called fucking establishment.

This was all down to Timmy Vaughan. If Vaughan hadn't fucked up his drugs business in the first place, there would have been no need to take revenge. But the wanker had crossed onto his turf and the whole bleeding gangland world in Dublin knew that Spiller Cummins had been screwed by Vaughan. There was no way that Cummins was going to rest until he proved to everybody that nobody messed with him and got away with it. Waters and Hunt just happened to be peripheral players, but they would suffer too. An example had to be made and that was the long and the short of it.

The one thing he was good at was distancing himself from physical evidence and Cummins was certain that there was no physical evidence to link him to any of it. If this bitch he was sitting with now wasn't careful, he would land her in it too.

He downed the last of his pint and enjoyed the look of astonishment on the bitch's face as she saw him rise to leave. She was so taken aback that she couldn't even utter the objections he knew she wanted to raise.

'Save your voice, love,' he said mockingly. 'I believe I've got business to attend to. And that business is the one and only Kate Waters.'

40

It was the first time Hunt had allowed Knocker Griffin to call on him in the rented house and he knew that some might say he was getting careless. But Hunt was beyond the stage of caution now. All of the women were totally under his control and, what was more, he was about to hand them over and he knew that the finger would never be pointed at him. That was the beauty of this whole scheme. Somebody else would finish them off.

He had just informed Griffin that the women were, in fact, in the house at that very moment. He could hardly contain the arrogance he felt at having gotten them back into the country without Griffin and Cummins' knowledge. To him, that had been proof – if any were needed – that he was just as capable of skulduggery as these thugs were.

'You must be bleeding joking, mate. We can't

take them away now. Not when this heat is on,'
Knocker told him.

Hunt was indignant. 'I told you I wouldn't keep
them all here together. It's just too much to expect
of me –' he paused – 'given my own professional
circumstances.'

'Listen here, man. You're playing with the big
boys now and you will damn well do as you are
bleedin' well told. This is not open to negotia-
tion,' Knocker said, enjoying the look of shock on
Hunt's face as he absorbed what he was being
told.

Hunt tried to object, but Knocker intervened.
'You see the thing here is, I'm not asking you.
I'm *telling* you that this is the way it's going to
be. You don't have a say in the matter.'

Hunt was apoplectic with rage and indignation. Never before, well not in recent years at
least, had he been spoken to like this. This kind
of behaviour was totally at odds with the way
they had treated him hitherto. For the last few
months, he had been travelling the world in a
private jet, staying in the best hotels and being
treated with the utmost respect – by Knocker
and Cummins as well as the women – and now
this. It was preposterous.

He told Griffin so.

The kick in his groin sent him flying on his back and left him sprawled on the floor. Griffin stood over him. 'Perhaps you didn't hear me, mate? I said this is the way it has to be. Do you understand now?' he asked, his angry eyes bulging from their sockets and betraying for the very first time exactly what Griffin thought of Hunt.

Hunt struggled to regain his composure, but Griffin planted the sole of his shoe very firmly on Hunt's chest and asked him again: 'Do you understand me?'

'Perfectly,' came the meek reply. Hunt realized that he was exactly back where he had begun: without a modicum of respect.

Griffin stretched out his hand and offered it to Hunt and when he was halfway off the floor, his left hand clutching his swelling testicles, Griffin laughed, then took his hand away, causing Hunt to tumble unceremoniously on his back again.

'You big bleedin' prick.' Griffin was speaking, in an accent Hunt had never heard him use before. It was Griffin's accent before he attended the elocution lessons, rough and menacing and it frightened the living daylights out of Hunt.

'Did you really think that you were one of us? You stupid bastard. Who the fuck would have you on their team? You're a fucking spineless waste of space. Now do as you're told and you might survive this thing. Do ye hear me?'

Hunt heard him perfectly well. This time he got up from the floor of his own volition and slumped in a chair facing Griffin. He was shaking all over.

'Well, when are you going to take the women from me? I need to offload them if I am to keep my cover,' Hunt asked gingerly.

'We've another job for you to do first. It won't be anywhere near as difficult as the other three,' Griffin said, a broad smile appearing as he took in the look of horror on Hunt's face.

Hunt went to speak, but Griffin pointed a finger at him. 'Don't be a bold boy now. Just do what you're told and we won't feed you to the piranhas.'

Griffin laughed uproariously when he saw the fear in Hunt's face. 'Jaysus, frightening the likes of you is much more fun that dealin' with me own fuckin' lot. Ye see my lot are trained not to show fear. It's how we all grew up. But you,' he said with derision, 'you're just a bleedin' howl. You're afraid of your own fuckin' shadow, Hunt! Now listen up, boy. There's no travel involved in this one and the woman will come to you quite easily. There will be no problems with her at all and the beauty of it is, this is the one that will really hurt Detective Vaughan. He'll never get over what's going to happen to this one, cos ye see, mate, I want ye to go the whole way with this one . . . no holds barred, if ye know what I mean!' Griffin said.

Hunt's face whitened. 'Oh my God. Not Vaughan's wife? Jesus Christ, man, don't tell me it's her. The wife of a copper, for God's sake. They'll move heaven and earth to find her. She's been through enough already. Don't you guys know that? Besides, if you're saying what I think you're saying, I'm afraid you've got the wrong man. I think you'd better get your friend No Knickers to do this one. This is not what I agreed to.'

But Hunt had wasted his breath. Griffin ignored him, gave him the details and then left.

Hunt sat slumped in the chair. He was so shocked by the revelation that he didn't even move when he heard Sophie ringing the bell to signal that the two other women were awake.

He realized he would have to follow the orders. Otherwise, they would never relieve him of the women and the whole thing would point straight to him.

41

'I do not bloody well believe this,' Timmy said.
'How can it be? How can one of our own men
double-cross us like this? The turncoat. The
bastard must be on the take. I always said he was
a supercilious wanker.'

Timmy and Paddy were sitting in a dingy pub
in Dun Laoghaire, just a five-minute drive from
the station in Blackrock. Daly had requested the
venue and Timmy had not asked any questions.
He knew the drill; if a colleague asked to meet
off-site during an important investigation, it was
usually because they did not trust those in their
midst.

There was always the possibility of conversations being monitored – even within police stations
– and both men knew that their superiors were
just as capable of monitoring those conversations
as the criminals were.

Under the current circumstances, they could

not afford to let *anybody* know what they were discussing. If management got hold of the link between the missing women and Martin Tierney's death, there would be hell to pay. It was one thing not having placed the man under protection when he had dobbed-in the likes of Cummins, but then to withhold information from the investigating team about the real reason for Tierney's death . . . that was professional suicide, for all of them.

Paddy Daly gulped down a huge swallow of his pint before elaborating on the devastating news he had just delivered to Timmy. He was having difficulty digesting it himself.

'To be fair to Ken Jones, I have to say that the guy has come up trumps for us here. Even I didn't cop it – if you'll pardon the pun – when I was downloading the information on the calls from the mobile-phone company.'

'I still think Jones is a wanker, Paddy. But if he's gotten this break for us, I suppose I should credit him with that. Mind you, it's just like Jones to work extra hard to show up one of our lot. He has always made it quite clear that he assumes we're a shower of arseholes anyway. But how did he come up with the link?'

'He was cross-referencing all of the numbers that the phone company passed on to me when he noticed an 8282 number calling Cummins' phone on the evening of the day Martin Tierney's body was discovered.'

Timmy knew that all 8282 numbers were for members of the Irish police force. The mobile phone company retained that sequence of digits exclusively for the force. It made the identification of police numbers much easier and was handy for police administration purposes.

'What in the hell was Moaner Farrelly doing phoning Cummins' number? Jesus Christ, I knew he was a bit of a gobshite when it came to interpersonal relationships, but I thought we could trust him. This is astonishing,' Timmy said.

'Beats me, boss, but *nobody* on our team had sanction to go phoning Cummins' number. Remember, nobody but yourself, myself, Jones and Kate Waters was aware that Jones was monitoring Cummins' numbers. Farrelly is our man all right. There's no doubt about that.'

'I just hope to God that we haven't made it easier for Farrelly to help Cummins any more than he already has between the end of last week and today. And why are we only getting this information today anyway? We should have had it by last week,' Timmy moaned.

'For God's sake, boss, give the guy a break. He

was on a half day on Friday when I gave him the information. As soon as he analysed it and discovered that the 8282 number belonged to Farrelly, he was straight on the blower.'

'More importantly, what are we going to do about Farrelly?'

'We can't exactly report him to Chief Nolan or that will surely blow the game regarding Tierney's copping it, and then we'll all be up the creek without the proverbial paddle.'

Timmy drained the last of his pint while he thought about this. 'We are just going to have to let Farrelly think that he is still in the loop. In fact maybe we can *use* the nasty little shit to feed inaccurate information to Cummins. That's what we'll do. Let's turn the tables and use Farrelly to get at Cummins.'

Paddy Daly had an issue with that approach: 'Aren't we placing Farrelly's life in danger by doing that, boss?' he asked.

Timmy raised his eyebrows into a cynical 'don't give me that crap' expression. 'Let Farrelly suffer the consequence of his actions, why don't we? The man will have to learn that you can't run with the hares and hunt with the hounds . . . at least not if you want to stay out of the trap.'

42

When Paddy Daly had shown Timmy the call list the telephone company had provided them with, detailing calls to all of the numbers they had for Cummins and his gang, Timmy had noticed that another number, all too familiar to him, had called one of the gang's mobile phones.

He had been shocked when the identity of the number-holder registered with him, but had not let it show. Even Daly, his most trusted lieutenant on this investigation, could not be alerted to what he had noticed, at least not until he had checked the details for himself. Jesus, he thought, this case was getting weirder by the minute. What in the hell was this thing all about? And why was Kate Waters telephoning one of the gang members? He couldn't believe his eyes when he had recognized her number.

Later that afternoon, he had gone directly to Chief Nolan and told him that he needed a top-secret search on the number, and although he had not gone into the details he had left his boss in no doubt that they could not, under any circumstances, have a paper trail involving this search.

The chief, good policeman that he was, knew better than to ask questions about the request. He had been long enough in policing to know that if Vaughan was seriously concerned about something regarding the discovery of this number, the less he knew, the better.

It was all about covering one's back and distancing oneself from certain developments. The senior members of the police force were experts in that field and Nolan had not gotten to where he was today by getting his hands dirty. So he had simply put the call in personally to the liaison officer at the mobile-phone company requesting a search on the number which Vaughan had given him.

Now it was seven thirty at night and the team were out on calls, or had gone home for the day. Timmy was sitting in the incident room staring at the cork board which held a chronological list of developments in the case to date. The list left out the murder of Martin Tierney, of course, but now he had information much more disturbing than the murder of Tierney.

He was so shocked, in fact, that he could not, for the life of him, put any rational explanation on this latest discovery. The number he had recognized from Daly's print-out had telephoned a member of the Cummins' gang on fifteen occasions over the past month alone. The phone company would provide details going back further tomorrow and Timmy had a sick feeling that when he got his hands on the full list, it would show earlier contacts too.

Why would Kate Waters have any dealings with Cummins' crew? And which member of the crew was it that she was in contact with?

This case was turning out to be one hell of a nightmare, from the murder of Tierney, to the discovery of Moaner Farrelly's involvement with the gang, not to mention the theft of the files from Kate Waters' office at the beginning of the inquiry. The more he thought about it, the more he realized that she had clearly tipped off the gang about developments in the investigation as they occurred.

First, there was the issue of the so-called stolen files. What was it she had said? That the files were stolen from her office and she had thought she was being followed, that was it. The story had obviously been a ruse to make him think that *she* was in danger, therefore removing any suspicion from her.

Secondly, he realized that she was one of a tight team of people who knew about the purchase of the three mobile phones from Martin Tierney. And within twenty-four hours of him informing Kate of Tierney's confirmation that Cummins' crew had bought the phones, Tierney was dead.

'Jesus, Mary and holy Saint Joseph!' Timmy exclaimed as he examined the list once more. He couldn't believe what he was seeing. He took out his black notebook to look at the date of Tierney's death again. Then he went back to the call print-out. He wasn't seeing things; Kate had telephoned the gang within hours of the case conference when he had told the team about the Cummins link. Tierney was dead because of her.

Little details came flooding back; there was her awkward suggestion to Timmy that *he* was the one to blame for these abductions. She had appeared to feel bad when she was planting that theory in his mind, a theory which had taken his concentration away from the investigation and focused it on Cummins' possible reasons for exacting revenge by abducting the women.

Then, of course, there was the whole question of her analysis of the perp at the beginning of the case. She had thrown them way off base with that too.

Timmy sat slumped at his desk contemplating this latest bizarre discovery. He conceded inwardly that he had obviously been double-crossed. Worse still, he couldn't see a way of keeping this whole mess quiet for very much longer and when the details of this screw-up of an investigation broke, there would be an internal inquiry and his head would be for the chopping block.

He rolled a piece of paper into a ball and flung it across the room at the cork board. Then he left the office, slamming the door behind him, and made his way to the car park. Just as he made to drive off, his mobile phone rang. Kate's number flashed up, but he decided not to answer it. He was too shocked, too incredulous at this latest development to even contemplate talking to her.

No, he needed to work out how to deal with the double-crossing Kate Waters before he had any contact with her again, because the last thing he wanted to do was give her further ammunition to take back to her gangland pals.

43

Kate pressed the intercom on the gates of the house in Blackrock and Ken Jones answered it immediately. Unlike the last occasion when she had met with him, he did not keep her waiting, but was standing at the front door when her car entered the driveway.

She stepped out of the car and was immediately struck by his nervousness. He was all edgy and shifty, as if he could not get her inside fast enough. Truth be told, she'd been taken aback when she got the call; never before had he contacted her outside office hours and she was surprised to be invited to his home.

During the fifteen-minute drive down the coast from Killiney to Blackrock, she had supposed that there must have been some major development in events to warrant him telephoning her, and on her home phone too. Normally, he would have called her on her mobile, but perhaps he had new information that calls were being monitored? Or was he using this meeting at his home as a chance to hit on her? She had certainly got the feeling earlier on in the investigation that he was the type who might use work as an excuse; his social skills were so lacking that she suspected he didn't have a life outside work.

In the end, she told herself that she was probably being a bit conceited and that the call was most likely to do with the case.

She was surprised to see that he had set the drawing room up as a type of incident room. There were several cork boards nailed to the walls, and on each of the cork boards he had the precise details of developments so far.

Full technicolour images of all three women were mounted on the walls. Sophie, Andrina and Nikki. The details available to the investigating team were contained in bullet points beneath a huge photograph of each woman.

He smiled as he saw her obviously surprised reaction. 'Got to keep my finger on the pulse, you know. Got to keep up to speed with what's happening in the investigation. In cases like this, the more you concentrate on the job, the less likely you are to let important developments pass you by,' he told her with a look of pride on his face.

She admired his professional approach, but she had not expected him to have the details on full view.

'What if somebody got into this house? What would happen then?' she asked him. 'This whole case would be blown wide open. That's what.'

'Oh relax, why don't you? I know what I'm doing. Besides, no uninvited guests ever get into this house,' he said.

Kate believed him when he said this. In fact she suspected that very few people would ever accept an invitation from him in the first place.

He offered her a drink and she didn't want to take it, but knew that she should. The last thing she wanted to do was offend his ego, to make him feel that she did not want to be alone in his company. After all, they were in this thing together and she needed his assistance to ensure that they got the results they wanted in the end.

Anyway, the wine he had opened was one of her favourites, a Shiraz bin 555. It was one thing not taking a drink with him during a working lunch, but to decline in his own home would be rude. She accepted a glass.

'Things are not quite going according to plan, Kate, are they?' he asked, a critical tone to his voice.

She took a sip of her wine and looked at him, shocked by the innuendo. It was as if he was accusing *her* of having messed things up.

He saw the look of indignation register on her face. He had hurt her. He was glad. As far as he was concerned, the woman had been given far too much involvement in this whole thing in the first place.

But she was savvy enough to let him think that he was in control of the situation. 'You're quite right there,' she said, taking another sip of her wine to buy time to ensure that she said the right thing. 'Things are moving far too slowly.'

He was smiling positively now. Kate was relieved. Clearly, she had said the right thing.

'I think we need to move things up a gear. We have got to take action regarding these women. This whole thing is in limbo at present and that does not bode well, for any of us,' he said.

Kate wanted to say that she could not agree more, but she found herself in a strange position, slumped in her chair and feeling confused and exhausted. She had only consumed a few mouthfuls of wine, but she desperately needed to sleep.

Ken Jones removed the glass from her hands, just as Kate Waters fell into a very deep sleep.

44

Mickser Cummins was truly enjoying the game he was playing with the Irish police force. It involved taunting them by letting them know that he knew he was being followed and then taking them on a wild goose chase, just for the laugh of it.

The game had been perfected by another gangland figure in the early nineties, but that man, nicknamed the General, had since met a grisly end. He had been assassinated – by other crims – whilst sitting in his car at a set of traffic lights. Mickser had no intention of being the subject of a hit, but he was getting a great laugh out of wasting police time and money.

Timmy Vaughan and Paddy Daly had been hot on Cummins' tail for the past seven hours and they had garnered nothing more than the two fingers, quite literally, for their troubles.

It was an age-old police trick, one that had in

fact been used frequently on the General, whereby the police would make their surveillance of a suspect very obvious in order to irritate that suspect. The cops knew that all it did was annoy the crims and the crims knew that all it did was signal that the cops were at a dead end.

Mickser Cummins, for his part, had spent most of the day driving around in his Grand Cherokee jeep because, at the moment, it was one of the few places which he knew for certain could not have been bugged by the filth. It had been locked in his garage at his mansion in Howth and Knocker had swept it with an anti-bugging device before they uttered a word.

'He's brought the women back, boss,' Knocker Griffin said as they meandered aimlessly through the lunchtime traffic along Fairview strand.

Cummins ordered Griffin to halt the jeep in the middle of a long line of moving traffic and, in doing so, forced Vaughan and Daly, a few cars back in the other lane, to drive right past them. As they did so, Cummins rolled down the passenger window and gave them the two fingers, grinning triumphantly as he did so. Both criminals then burst into howls of laughter as they lip-read a stream of expletives through the window of Timmy's unmarked car.

Knocker had expected Cummins to be apoplectic with fury at this latest development about Hunt and the women, but Cummins just laughed.

'Just as I thought he would!' Cummins said. 'The stupid little prick. What did you do then?' he quizzed his most trusted lieutenant.

'I did what I knew you would want, Mickser. I told him that he would have to keep them there, for the time being at least.'

'And how did the little wanker react to that news?'

'Suffice to say, boss, I had to belt him a few. But he's in no doubt now as to where he stands, or lies as the case was when I last saw him actually!' Both men burst out laughing again at this quip.

'What about the woman, then? Did you give him the message regarding her?'

'I did for sure, Mickser. I can tell you he was none too bleedin' pleased when I told him. He nearly had a fuckin' hernia when I delivered that bombshell. Anyways, it should be done by now. I gave him a deadline of last night.'

Cummins was delighted. Things were turning out just as he had anticipated all along.

'And how about your own meeting then,

Mickser? How did things fare out there?' Knocker asked his boss.

'I put her in her place well and good, son, so I did. I told her what's what and to have bleedin' patience. That's how I fared out. She's lucky I didn't belt her one, 'cos she's a bleedin' upstart, that's what she is.'

'Isn't that a bit risky, treating her like that? She could blow the whole thing on us if she wanted to, Mickser.'

'No, son, why should she? Look at this logically. As far as you and me are concerned, they haven't got an iota in terms of actual evidence. But as far as that woman is concerned, there's enough evidence to get her banged up on conspiracy to kidnap for at least ten years. Ye see, I have the whole thing taped. So if I go down, so does she.'

Knocker thought about this for a few seconds and realized that his gaffer was most likely right. After all, everybody knew that the woman was a piss artist and that she had cracked up at one point. She was hardly what you would call a credible witness.

They drove along in silence for a while, then Knocker asked: 'So what are you going to do about Mrs Vaughan, Mickser? Are you going to make a move on her as well?'

The answer that came back was cryptic: 'All will be revealed in good time, my son. All in good time.'

Timmy told Paddy to head back to the station. Daly exhaled a sigh of relief. He knew that this exercise in tailing Cummins was absolutely futile. More importantly, he knew that his boss had something much more worrying on his mind and that it wouldn't do to question him at the moment.

It was time for more drastic action.

'We're going public,' Timmy declared.

Paddy Daly nearly crashed the car. 'Jesus, Timmy, what are you trying to do? Crucify us all? There's more than your career at stake here.'

'We've *got* to go public, Daly. We don't have a choice. We've got to turn the heat up. We're getting nowhere at the moment. At least this way, we can apply a bit of pressure and hope that a few mistakes are made.'

Daly protested: 'But once the media get hold of this, they'll never be off our backs. Management will be looking for answers too. I think you're wrong, Timmy. This will destroy all of us.'

'You could be right,' Timmy said, 'but I have a different feeling on this one. My gut is telling me that when the pressure comes on, whoever is behind this thing will start turning the tables on Cummins. I think that a bit of pressure will help expose whoever it is, besides Moaner Farrelly, that is assisting Cummins. I'd lay my job on it, Daly.'

'I think you're going to have to lay your job on it, Timmy, because when this gets out you'll be lucky –' he paused, then corrected himself – 'we'll all be lucky, to have a job at the end of it.'

They drove back to the station in tense silence. Paddy Daly was furious at Timmy. Vaughan might be a fantastic investigator, but he could be a stubborn, intractable, pig-headed cop as well when he wanted to be and if he had one major shortcoming, it was that when he decided to go hell for leather at something, he didn't contemplate the consequences for his colleagues around him. Belligerent, that was how Paddy would describe Timmy.

For his part, Timmy was praying that his latest ploy would work. He was going public for one reason and one reason only. Kate Waters wasn't even bothering to answer her phone now. She was quite simply ignoring him.

If it was the last thing he did, Timmy would drag that woman out of the woodwork kicking and screaming and find out what this whole set-up was all about and why she had become involved with this group of seedy scumbags.

45

Kate rubbed her eyes with the back of her hands and tried to focus. It was difficult. She felt seriously groggy, disoriented, completely out of kilter.

She had slept deeply, for twelve hours in fact, although she had no idea it had been that long. She had not slept so much since Timmy's daughter had died and only then after she had taken some sleeping tablets in order to get some relief from the pain of the guilt she was suffering.

Her head was throbbing. Where had she been last night? Had she been drinking? She felt as though she had. She felt totally out of it.

She made to turn over in the bed and as she did so, she noticed that the ground beneath her was freezing cold. She wasn't in bed at all.

She turned fast, startled, ready to jump up and explore her surroundings. But something tugged against her arms and legs and she also realized that she was semi-naked. The only clothing she wore were her briefs and a black lace bra. Instinctively, she made to cover herself with her arms, but she could not get them to cross over her body. She realized then the reason for her restricted movement. The chains. She was chained to a wall.

Slowly, things came back to her. She had been with *him* last night. Yes, she had gone to his house. He had telephoned her and told her that they needed to have an urgent discussion. Straight away, that's what he'd said.

Kate had not thought twice about it. She had met with him alone on a couple of occasions before and had never felt threatened. And now this. Was she still with him, she wondered. Or had something happened after she left his house?

Vague memories of Ken Jones's drawing room seeped back. Pictures, he had pictures of the missing women all over the room and the investigation details, he had all of these also. He had let her see everything, almost boasted about the fact.

Then he had given her a glass of wine. She remembered now. They had been talking. He had told her that things were moving too slowly, and the last thing she remembered was taking another sip of her wine. That must have been it.

She did not remember that he had carried her

downstairs and undressed her, slapping her in the face a few times when her limp body had fallen away from him. Nor did she remember how he had laughed uproariously as he undressed her, how ludicrous the whole scene had been.

The room came into focus. She was lying flat on her stomach and the chains caused her arms and back to ache desperately as she tried to turn around to take in her surroundings.

'Oh my God,' she said out loud, not realizing she had an audience. 'I'm seeing double, no treble.'

She thought that she must still be drunk, or drugged more likely. For not only was she seeing an image of herself across the room, she was seeing three.

The images were all the same: long black hair, brown eyes, long naked limbs. 'Mother of God, what has he given me? Why am I hallucinating?'

'Be quiet. There's no talking allowed in this room,' a voice hissed.

Kate jerked around with fright. This time she knew that somebody had spoken, but it was not his voice. It was the voice of another woman.

The sound echoed and the room was damp and cold. There was a window in the room, but it had been blacked-out with some form of insulating foam. It was taped to the windows, but the tiniest bit of daylight was seeping through. Had she not been chained to the wall, she would have been able to reach it. A light was also on in the room.

She managed to pull herself up to a sitting position and turned to face the other images of herself. She had heard the voice. She knew that she had not been hallucinating. There were other women in the room.

She could see them now. There were three other women. Kate didn't need to ask. She knew who they were. They were the three missing women whose disappearances she had helped investigate.

They looked like hell, emaciated, terrified and beaten to a pulp. All had red welts on their bodies. They had clearly been beaten brutally and regularly. She wondered had he raped them. She wanted to ask, to know what was in store for her, but she didn't have the nerve. They all looked too shattered, like broken china dolls.

'It's OK,' she said. 'I know who you are. Try not to be afraid. Help is on the way for us.'

She wanted to reassure the women but, privately, she wondered if they would ever be found. This was the last place they would think of searching. Nobody in their right mind would ever suspect the nerdy Ken Jones of ever being tied up in this business. Kate was afraid, very afraid.

46

Timmy sat behind a long narrow table perched on a platform in a media briefing room at police headquarters in Phoenix Park. He was flanked by representatives from each of the investigating teams: Paddy Daly was there representing the Sophie Andrews team, Tommy Curran was there representing the Nikki Kane team and Moaner Farrelly was there representing the Andrina Power team. Even though Farrelly was the official collator on this investigation and was not specific to any of the individual investigation teams, Timmy had wanted him there to put some inadvertent pressure on him and, at the same time, to make him feel as if he was beyond suspicion.

Also present was Ken Jones. Timmy had not *wanted* him there, but he felt that he needed him to boost the image of the investigating team, to convey the impression that his team was firing on all cylinders. He wasn't identified to the media though, another not-so-subtle put-down.

The police press officer, Superintendent Colm Burke, had been warned not to let any of the media know what this was about. He was furious about this embargo because it went against the unwritten rule of police/media relations that correspondents would be kept in the loop – in so far as was possible – before information was released to the general media.

Most members of the public didn't realize it, but there was a symbiotic relationship between the police and security and crime correspondents. The way it worked was that these specialist journalists were always kept briefed of fresh developments by the police, so as to ensure that the journalists looked good to their editors – as if they had the information first. In return, police management were then able to apply pressure on those same journalists when they needed assistance in particular investigations, or when they needed to 'plant' leaks in the media in order to expedite investigations. Neither side would admit it but, in general, that was the way the game was played.

Colm Burke was also seated at the podium before a room packed full of journalists. The front row was reserved for the specialist crime reporters and there wasn't a face among them who had a decent word to say about Burke this morning. The national radio hacks were furious that they hadn't even been fed a line before the rest of the media and the television journalists working for the evening news were furious that they were not receiving any exclusive interviews. Meanwhile, the print journalists were up in arms because they didn't even have a line to feed their editors prior to the lunchtime conferences which set the agenda for the next morning's newspapers.

The whole thing was a mess and Burke had a feeling that the anger would spill over into negative criticism of this investigation. He had warned Timmy that these journalists would take no hostages, but Timmy, belligerently true to his reputation, had insisted they play it his way.

Burke went to the central podium and tapped the mike to ensure it was working. He then went on to outline the sensational details of the investigation that had begun several weeks earlier, revealing the identities of Sophie, Andrina and Nikki to the assembled media.

He informed the gathered posse, already stunned into absolute silence, of the reasons behind the delay in the formal establishment of an inquiry – the fact that no clues were left to indicate abduction or anything unusual in the women's lives – and outlined the extensive steps taken so far to trace each of the missing women.

None of the journalists did their usual 'snatch and grab' act, whereby they grabbed the first line and ran outside to telephone their news-desks with details of the sensational press conference. They were all too stunned that the details had been kept from them for so long, especially the crime specialists. Burke knew that they would blame this on him, but was damned if he would admit to any of them that he'd been kept out of the loop on this biggie until the eleventh hour. Instead, he would have to pretend that he had concealed it from them for what the police liked to term 'operational reasons'.

They were glued to their seats as he briefed them of the establishment of the database to try and cross-reference these cases with earlier cases of missing women, and of efforts to trace the women through Interpol.

'All of the efforts of the investigating team have been painstaking, thorough and tireless. This team has left no stone unturned and yet they have been unable to come up with any clues as to the identity of the perpetrator. We are now formally requesting the public's assistance in this investigation, and I hand you over to a man whom many of you will already know from his work on several other high-profile cases, Detective Timmy Vaughan.'

It was protocol at these press conferences that the media did not interrupt until the senior press officer finished his briefing. But then it was a free-for-all.

The room went mad. Cameras clicked furiously, television cameramen buzzed around the room ensuring they got the whole team from every angle, print journalists broke etiquette and took out their mobiles and dialled the numbers of their news-desks so that their editors could hear things first-hand. The radio journalists ran up to the podium to ensure that their microphones were displayed prominently for the television cameras to get them in their shots.

Have you any idea who is behind this, Detective Vaughan? Is this a serial killer we have at large? Why did you wait so long before releasing the details to the media? Do you think they are still alive? What about the forty-eight-hour rule? Isn't it most likely that they are dead by now? What do their families think? Have you engaged any criminal profilers? Have you got any help from psychics? Has there been any contact with the culprit? Do you have a photo-fit?

The question and answer session went on for twenty-five minutes – they had initially agreed only fifteen minutes, but it was Burke's job to call a halt to proceedings and he had decided to let Vaughan sweat a little. After all, Vaughan had well and truly dropped him in it with the media, so there was nothing wrong with a little payback.

When they left to drive back to Blackrock police station, Paddy Daly noticed that Timmy's hands were shaking. He offered to do the driving and commented that the session had not gone badly at all – 'considering, boss, that you never actually told any lies, but never admitted either that in fact we *know* who is behind these disappearances'.

Timmy nodded his head in agreement. He was too worn out to talk about it. Too busy praying that news did not leak out that they had had a criminal profiler working on the case, although he had just managed to avoid answering that question.

Paddy Daly was thinking along the same lines as Timmy: where was Kate Waters these days? The team had not seen or heard from her in days.

47

For the rest of the day, the phones of every member of the investigation team rang like crazy. Blackrock police station was inundated with phone calls from the general media, with journalists phoning every few minutes looking for updates on the situation.

Meanwhile, the crime specialists hounded Daly and Vaughan and the rest of the team on their mobiles. The only person who did not receive a call was Moaner Farrelly, because any journalist worth his or her salt knew that he was a cynical old sod who would cross the street sooner than look at a journalist.

Timmy had left the entire team in no doubt that no matter what allegiances they had to particular journalists, there was to be absolutely no leaking on this one.

'I don't need to tell *any* of you, that no matter how close you are to these hacks, there is to be no information released. We are all in at the deep end here and the last thing I want is for word to get out about Mickser Cummins' involvement. Any references to him will invariably lead to Martin Tierney and then we will all be in very hot water, lads.'

In fairness to the team, they all seemed to be taking his instructions seriously, although it probably had helped that he had reminded them about the new legislation that the Minister for Justice was bringing in regarding the prosecution of officers who had any unauthorized contacts with the media. Timmy did not agree with the new proposals, believing them to be draconian and indicative of a right-wing policing policy and he had said this to his union representatives in no uncertain terms. He happened to believe, in fact, that without the media acting as a watchdog, there would be far too many cover-ups within the force. But in this instance, he had used the threat to quite good effect. Desperate times called for desperate measures.

After a few hours, most of the journalists gave up, their shifts ended. The non-crime specialists had no real vested interest in the story anyway and the crime specialists who relied on the police for many of their stories knew that if they plagued certain officers too much, they would be blacklisted in the future. All in all, the policy of 'no comment' was proving pretty effective.

Except in the case of one persistent journalist who, two hours before the conference was called, had been on her way to meet an enemy of Cummins to try and discover what he was up to.

Now Jenny Smith, the senior crime writer with the best-selling Sunday newspaper in the country, the *Irish Sunday*, had a lead on everybody else in this case – thanks to Kate Waters. Had it not been for Kate's call two days previously, Jenny would never have linked the likes of Cummins to a case like this. Kidnapping women just wasn't his form. But Cummins obviously was behind this thing and she had a jump on everybody else in knowing this fact.

As the press conference had broken up, Jenny reflected on Kate's call. The woman must clearly have been desperate to have telephoned Jenny looking for help. And Jenny now realized that Kate had probably been worried for Vaughan. Why else would she have risked professional disgrace, except for the man everybody knew Kate had once been in love with?

When it came down to the chase for a good story, Jenny had a reputation for being like a dog with a bone. She was also savvy enough to know that because of the pretty successful embargo to date on this story, it was unlikely any of her usual contacts, and among them were several members of Timmy's team, would give her a dig out. Anyway, the last thing she wanted to do was expose Kate.

After the press conference, when all of the other journalists had chased after the detectives for 'a line' on the story, she had stood quietly at the back of the room and observed some of the other individuals involved in the investigation.

Jenny was thirty-one, but her maturity belied her years. Over the course of her career, she had developed certain methods of dealing with potential sources which she used to some considerable success. These methods had helped her to secure high-profile 'scoops' which had won her several awards for outstanding journalism.

Jenny's approach was simple. She would identify the outsider in a group of people and would observe that person until she got a 'read' on them and then she would move in. The approach didn't always work, indeed she had been told in no uncertain terms many times to take a hike. But on several occasions, it had been successful.

Now she was about to try her luck with a man whom she had noticed during the press conference as being quite isolated from the rest of the team. When they had chatted amongst themselves at the top table before the press officer formally launched the conference, he had been left out of the loop. And although Timmy had referred to the fact that a computer specialist had been on board for the duration of the inquiry, he had not referred to him by name. When the press conference was finished, the rest of the team had huddled together in a circle, but he had not been included. It was at this point that Jenny decided that this was her man.

What had further reinforced her belief that he was her best shot was watching the computer specialist while Vaughan spoke during the press conference of the functions of the database. Jenny could not help but notice that he appeared to be scoffing Vaughan's analysis. She concluded that he would have killed to have an opportunity to take centre stage and demonstrate the depth of his knowledge and intelligence. The man had an ego and, as far as Jenny was concerned, that often led to quality information.

Now she was sitting in her car outside the main gates to police headquarters. The press conference had finished five hours ago and she had sat there patiently, waiting for her man to emerge.

Liz Allen

She was just praying that he drove, because if he was walking, or taking the bus or using a motorbike, it would be almost impossible for her to shadow him.

At half-past six, he pulled up to the main gate and Jenny thanked her lucky stars for the barrier that guarded the entrance, because it gave her time to observe the occupants of each car to ensure that she had the right man.

The traffic down the quays, which led to the centre of the city, was murder, but for once she was glad because it ensured that her target could not get very far away from her. His car crawled the full length of the quays and across the toll bridge to take them to the south side of the city. And then another painstaking forty-five minutes were spent at the infamous chock-a-block junction at the Merrion Gates, before he passed through and made his way to the south-city suburbs.

It took eighty minutes in rush hour to complete what should have been a twenty-minute drive and then the man pulled up to his house, or at least she assumed it was his house.

Then another wait for the fastidious reporter. Her plan was not to approach him straight away, but to sit it out outside his house and then, hopefully, he would go somewhere nearby for a pint and she could 'accidentally' bump into him in the pub.

But at eleven o'clock, Jenny gave up. There hadn't seemed to be much action at the house. He hadn't come out at all. When the lights went out, she figured she would have to come up with another plan, or possibly even approach him cold, although she only did this as a last resort as she found that the element of surprise tended to intimidate a lot of people.

Just as she was about to drive off her mobile phone rang. She expected it to be her editor, calling to know how things went. When she heard the voice on the other end of the phone, her heart leapt with anticipation . . . What on earth could this man want from her on a day like this?

48

Kate sat huddled in a corner. She was freezing cold, still wearing her scant under-garments and nothing else. They had been in the empty basement for about twenty-four hours now. And Jones certainly wasn't making any efforts to keep their energies up with food or drinks, or even warmth. Privately, Kate wondered if they were all going to die, for she knew now that Jones was a complete psycho and nobody doubted Cummins' capacity to maim and murder.

'How long does he normally stay away?' she asked the women, not quite sure exactly which one she was looking at because it was dark now. They all looked the same anyway, dishevelled, battered and terrified.

'It was weeks for me,' Sophie replied. 'We were in Barbados and when I said I wanted to contact home, he went ballistic. He brought me straight back here and began beating me and telling me

345

he had to teach me about respect. He has a big thing about earning respect. He's obsessed.'

That figured for Kate. She remembered seeing his screen saver once. She had thought it odd at the time. It came back to her now: He that has lost his credit is dead to the world.

Kate shivered as she thought what must be going on in the mind of someone so disturbed.

'But he has been in almost every day since he brought us back; Andrina was in Los Angeles and I was in New York. Since we came back, he has been here a lot,' Nikki volunteered.

That figured for Kate also. He had appearances to maintain. He had done a pretty good job fooling her. She never would have guessed he was capable of this, not in a million years.

'At least we can take consolation from that,' Kate said. 'The more he is around, the more likely it is that Timmy Vaughan, the chief investigator on this case, will find him. He will know that whoever is behind this is around because I am missing too and just before I came here, I called Timmy.'

'Then why hasn't your friend Timmy come for us?' Nikki asked.

Kate just could not understand why he had not come for her yet. A whole day had passed and

Timmy must have known that she was in trouble. She had left a message on his message-minder telling him that she was going to meet Jones at his house and saying she would let him know the outcome. She knew he would never let her down.

Then a horrible thought occurred to her. Perhaps Timmy had checked with Jones and been fed some plausible story. After all, she had been fooled by appearances. It wasn't inconceivable that Timmy might be taken in too.

She shivered at the prospect of Timmy not realizing she was in trouble. If that was the case, they would all die. She was sure of that. After all, the three missing women could identify him by sight. More importantly, Kate Waters knew who he really was. If for no other reason, that was the reason they would all die.

'Oh my God, it's all my fault,' she said out loud.

'You're quite right indeed,' came the response.

He was in the room with them again. None of them had heard him creep in.

All four women pressed themselves even closer to the wall in fear, as if trying to distance themselves from their captor. But there was no point. They all remained securely chained to the wall.

He strode over to where Kate was huddled on

the floor and kicked her in the pit of her stomach. Then he squatted down so that his eyes were boring into hers. 'You and your profile. You think you are so clever, so smart. You stuck to your guns, trying to point them towards me the whole time.'

He spat in her face. Kate looked him square in the eyes. She was terrified, but she knew that she could not let him know this. She had to stand up to him. That's what was needed in this situation, not to let him thrive on the fear he loved to instil.

'Bullshit. It was never you I was pointing them towards,' she spat back. 'Who would ever have thought it was *you*? Somebody like you, perhaps, but never you.'

She had just insulted him, letting him know that she never would have credited him with having the bottle to do a job like this. It was a risk, she knew, but one she had to take to let him know that not everybody was intimidated by him.

He straddled her then. He was kneeling right across her mid torso. She could feel his member pressing into her pelvic bone. It was throbbing. She knew that his adrenalin was pumping now. It was the power.

She was trying to exorcize the terrible fear from

her mind, trying to remind herself how a psycho-pathic control freak like him should be dealt with. She cursed herself for all the advice she had given the police before; it was *very* different when you were dealing with the person, very different indeed.

'Go on, do it. Use me, even though I have no respect for you. Use me, even though it will never make me respect you. If anything, you will be held in even lower esteem than before. These women,' she swept her chained arm as wide as it would go, 'these women have no respect for you. They find you repulsive, *Mr Hunt.*'

She uttered his name with a derisory snort, letting him know that the women had told her everything. He used the opportunity to deflect attention away from her criticism of him and jumped to his feet, shouting at the girls: 'Who spoke? Which one of you told her my name? Whoever it was will be punished.'

'What difference does it make who told me your alias, Ken? What difference does it make now? They may know you as Jonathon Hunt, but I know who you really are. You're exposed well and good now. Is your friend Mr Cummins going to come to your rescue now? I should think not. You've been used!' she taunted.

He paced the room like a demon, eyeing each of the other women, wanting to know who told Kate his alias. Now they could track everything back to him: the private flights, the hotel and house bookings. Everything. He was wild with fury.

None of the girls would answer him. They were strengthened now, it seemed. They were taking some solace from Kate's treatment of him and standing up to their torturer.

He looked at them with utter contempt. 'On your knees, all three of you. Now!' he roared.

None of the women moved and so he walked calmly over to where Sophie was lying and kicked her in the face. When the blood gushed from her mouth, she coughed so violently that Kate thought she was going to choke. Unperturbed by the scene, their captor bent down and punched Sophie violently in the stomach. 'You're worthless,' he screamed. 'You worthless bitch! How dare you question me? How dare you disobey me?'

Slowly, Nikki and Andrina got to their knees, but Jones did not move until Sophie, teeth dangling from their nerves, struggled into position too. He seemed to reserve a special hatred for Sophie. Kate supposed that it was because she had objected to staying in Barbados with him.

Then Jones removed the long whip from the

wall and lashed her with it, ordering her to thank him for the punishment.

Kate observed the scene in complete astonishment. Clearly, this had happened before. The three women – although it was difficult to understand a word from Sophie's blood-spattered mouth – began chanting in unison: 'He that has lost his credit is dead to the world. He that has lost his credit is dead to the world . . .'

Kate did not know how long it went on for. But she knew that they had just won part of their first battle against the man who called himself Jonathon Hunt. They had stood up to him, albeit momentarily, but it was a start. A tiny inroad in Kate's campaign to shatter his confidence. It was their only hope now.

49

The woman was on the phone to Cummins the minute the story on the nine o'clock television news was finished.

'Where are ye ringin' me from?' Cummins asked, his voice tight with anger and his face pinched with fury.

He had specifically *told* her that she was not to call him, except from a pre-arranged number and at a pre-arranged time.

'I'm calling you from home actually,' she said, apparently oblivious of his fury.

'Are you out of your bleedin' mind, woman? You'll get us both done,' he shouted.

The woman didn't seem to take in what he was saying. He could hear the slur in her voice. She was obviously hitting the gin bottle again.

'I thought you said you were going to take the fourth woman. That was the deal we made, Mr Cummins, that you would take the fourth woman.

She's my only interest in this whole thing. Why have you double-crossed me? I want an answer, now!'

Spiller Cummins had had enough. Once again, he was cursing the day he ever got involved with her, but he was going to show her what's what now. The woman had to be put in her place.

It was late and, given the day that it had been, he was no more bothered with going out, but she had to be sorted and that was that. He knew that he was taking a risk, but if he scaled over the back perimeter of his property, he could cross the big field and be in the little car park at the edge of the village in fifteen minutes, a quarter of the time it would take her to get to Howth. He would use the rest of the time to check out the lie of the land and ensure he had not been tailed by the filth.

When she pulled into the car park, he was surprised that she had actually made it that far. She was absolutely pissed; three sheets to the wind. The woman was a walking time-bomb.

She staggered over to him, the index finger of her right hand pointing at him every step of the way. 'You sh-sh-shed tha' that bissch would be tay-ken care of. Ye shed that you would do it for me. You double-crossed me, Cummins. You broke our deal.'

This woman was a mess and she was going to create a much bigger mess if he didn't stop her soon. He couldn't kill her. That would bring too much heat on the situation. The finger would point straight to him and even though there would never be any proof, it would give the filth an excuse to go through his life with a fine-tooth comb and he certainly wasn't having that.

He took her by her jacket collar and effortlessly lifted her off the ground. She looked liked one of the ghosts in a children's horror movie, the ones that float at an angle with chiffon skirts trailing behind them, a bemused look to the face.

She was looking down on him from an angle now, a look of utter confusion on her face. 'Either you're the bravest woman alive, or you're a thick fuckin' bitch,' he said, before letting her drop to the ground with a smack. He heard a crack. It sounded like one of her knees. If Breaker Daly had been there, he could have confirmed the fact. The area of breakages was his speciality. He half-wished that Breaker was with him now, because the bitch deserved to have every bone in her body broken as far as he was concerned. How dare she treat a man of his standing like this?

She was still on the ground and he placed a highly polished Gucci leather loafer on her chest, the toecap touching a nipple which had somehow become exposed through the fall. He pressed the shoe firmly into her chest, moving it around as if stamping out a cigarette end.

He spoke through clenched teeth, and the effects of the alcohol momentarily wore off his victim as he did so: 'FYI – that, for drunken slobs like you, means "for your information" – the fourth woman is being taken care of. We've already got her. OK?

'Now, the next time I see or hear from you, it will be at me funeral. Do ye hear me? Do ye understand? And if I see or hear from you before then, well then it will be your fuckin' funeral you're goin' to. And by the way, I couldn't give a toss who your old man is. You're in this up to your eyeballs, so I suggest you go home, have another bottle of gin and shut the fuck up.'

With that, Cummins made his own way back home, went into his state-of-the-art kitchen and made himself a bag of American-style microwave popcorn. He loved a little snack after roughing up a woman, especially a woman who had no respect for herself . . . Not to mention the law.

50

Timmy was filled with a mixture of emotions. What had his life come to? He was only thirty-eight, young by today's standards. He had a failed marriage, the tragedy of his little daughter's death and he had just ruined his career in a huge way. Despite his earlier contemplation that maybe he should give it another go with Laura, deep down he knew that he would not. He couldn't. He was stupid to have allowed his guilt to fool him into thinking that they could ever make it work. Too much water under the proverbial bridge.

Aside from Kate Waters, policing had been the only good thing in his life. It had given him passion, a reason to get out of bed in the mornings, a drive to feel that although he had screwed up big-time in life, at least there was one thing he could be a success at.

He was not one of those cops who was altruistic about the job. He had not gone into it to become a crusader who thought he could save the world. No, guys like that usually lost the run of themselves and ended up taking a bad fall somewhere along the line.

What gave Timmy faith, and not in the religious sense, was his own self-confidence, the knowledge that he was *good* at what he did, an effective policeman who knew how to spot a con or a scam a mile away and who was pretty much fearless when it came to dealing with the hardest of the hard.

His own motto was: It's a tough job, but somebody has to do it. And he was genuinely of that belief. If there weren't people like Timmy and his colleagues, men and women who were very often required to put their lives on the line for the job, then where would society be? Policing was like any other business, it had its ups and downs. But at the end of the day, only those really passionate about the job made a real difference and Timmy Vaughan was certainly passionate about his work.

Over the years, he had been involved in some pretty hairy situations. He had been kicked, beaten badly, shot at, threatened, held hostage by a heroin-addict bank robber, offered kickbacks from hardened crims, and generally treated like a piece of shit by the scum of the earth who would then, as any seasoned cop would tell you, walk into court and claim all sorts of police abuse, harassment and mistreatment.

He had learned to laugh at the new breed of criminals who thought they could ride roughshod over the police and judicial systems; they might be in a position to spend a fortune challenging the laws of the land, but one by one they were falling and the legislature was constantly putting into place new measures to force these guys to explain their actions. That was all Timmy expected of the system. A fair crack of the whip, for both sides.

But, aside from the death of his adorable little girl, he had never felt so caught out, humiliated and double-crossed as he was feeling now. He was confused and two things were deeply troubling him at the moment.

The first was the disappearance of the three women and Mickser Cummins' involvement in the whole scheme. What really niggled him about it was Kate Waters' earlier assertion that Cummins was doing this for a particular reason, that it was personal. And despite his utter disgust for the woman, he still happened to think that she might be right on that score.

The second area of bother for him was the

issue of Kate Waters herself. He was absolutely shattered beyond belief by her duplicity. Maybe it was a question of personal pride, or maybe it was just the fact that she had actually managed to take him for a ride. He didn't know which was causing him the most grief. All he knew was that if it was the last thing he did, he would bring her down with him. As far as he was concerned, he was going down anyway, professionally speaking.

It all made sense now, of course. The files, *allegedly stolen*, from her office; her stringing him along, just enough to keep him in her clutches, but pushing him away when he got too close. Her so-called *resignation* from the investigation had obviously been intended to force him to bring her even closer to things, to force him to place more trust in her. And then there was the question of her new suitor. What was it she had said about that? She already had somebody to look out for her and protect her. Well, she had certainly been right about that. She had the best in the business on her side.

It was half-past midnight on what had been one of the toughest days of his career. But he was feeling guilty now, guilty that he had crept into the house twenty minutes ago and gone straight to bed. He hadn't even called in on Laura to say goodnight. Things had been better between them these past few weeks, yet, although he had vaguely contemplated a trial reunion with her since she suggested it, he was beginning to take a different view now. His life was too much of a mess. A clean slate was what he needed, not digging up the horrors of the past through some guilt trip.

But he conceded that perhaps Laura had been right all along. Perhaps he had been unfair and let the job take over his life, their lives actually. That was an issue which he would have to address when this was all over. But first, he had to get some sleep. He had a battle to fight, a battle he intended to win.

51

Jenny Smith drove furiously. She was in no rush, but she still could not slow down. She was totally focused on the phone call she had received sitting outside the house in Blackrock the previous night.

She didn't know for sure if the information he intended to pass on to her concerned the missing-women investigation, but he had phrased it in such a way as to entice her into believing that it was.

She had only talked to him once before, when she had quizzed him on the rumours circulating that he was the new kingpin of the underworld, that he was the new baron on the drugs scene, responsible for the importation of millions of pounds' worth of drugs into Ireland each year.

On that occasion, he had smiled a callous smile and made it clear that under absolutely no circumstances did he intend to have any dealings with the media. He had not threatened her, not even so much as pointed a finger at her when he was telling her to sling her hook, but she had left with the very distinct impression that if she ever wrote even a paragraph connecting him by name to drug dealing, she would regret it very dearly indeed.

Jenny had not written about him, but that was more to do with the libel laws than because he had succeeded in intimidating her.

One of the tricks used by crime reporters was to approach a suspect and ask for an opinion on the rumours about a particular crime. Then the journalist could cite the criminal, claiming they were not responsible even while publicly linking them to that crime.

The ploy allowed journalists to describe in great detail the lavish lifestyles enjoyed by the criminals and the horrendous crimes perpetrated to achieve huge wealth. That was what their editors and the public really wanted. As far as Jenny was concerned, her role was not as the public liked to see her – a passionate crusader intent on bringing powerful crime bosses to justice – but merely the painter of a picture that fed the public's desire for voyeurism; and if these guys received more pressure from the cops as a result of her exposés, then so be it.

At any rate, Jenny's attempts to publicly link Spiller Cummins to widespread drug distribution and violence had failed. He was far too savvy to fall for her trick.

But now here she was, driving to his house in Howth, after *he* had telephoned *her* asking for a meet to discuss what he had described as 'details about a high-profile ongoing investigation' which he thought she might find useful. Obviously, whatever he wanted to tell her, it was something that would benefit him. Otherwise, why would a man, so notoriously media-shy, have contacted her? When it came to criminals talking to journalists, there was always a motive.

She spent twenty minutes driving around the picturesque village of Howth before making her way up a narrow, winding road to the cliffside where Cummins resided. It was a huge pile, perched right on the water's edge, with dramatic views over the sweeping coastline. But when he buzzed her through the entrance gates (last time he had come out to her and not even afforded her a glimpse inside) she saw that his house was just like the homes of many of the big-time criminals she had visited over the years: all frills and no substance.

The stunning Victorian house had clearly been

the subject of a very costly renovation programme and the first thing Jenny noticed were the UPVC windows that had been installed in place of the original wooden sashes. Wasn't this a listed building, she wondered. Anyway, she doubted the likes of Cummins – if he had heard of planning permission – would be bothered to apply for such a thing. And she doubted there were too many planning officials willing to sign their names to a letter telling him to comply with the listed building regulations.

Then there was the ornate stained glasswork on the side panels of the front door. They had been left in place, but behind them were steel bars which bastardized the impact. Above the front door had been installed a good replica of the original architrave, but perched smack-bang in the centre of the feature coving was a conspicuous CCTV camera. It totally compromised the quaint Victorian entrance porch.

It was clear that Cummins had spent a fortune on the interior too. In place of what was probably original parquet flooring was a snow-white deep velvet carpet which looked like it had been laid yesterday. Jenny nearly choked when he asked her to remove her shoes. Presumably Cummin's henchmen had to use the service entrance, to wipe the blood from their feet.

A massive Chinese dresser of gleaming ebony and heavily embossed gold trim took pride of place halfway up the huge hallway. Jenny watched the *Antiques Roadshow* whenever she was home on a Sunday evening and she reckoned that this was the real thing, undoubtedly worth a fortune.

He had said nothing more than 'Come in and take your shoes off,' when he opened the front door and he was still silent as he led her down a warren of corridors towards the back of the house.

Everywhere she went she saw expensive paintings, ornate antique vases and gilt-edged frames. She passed a high-tech kitchen with the priciest of German appliances and an open bathroom door revealed Versace tiles, Villeroy and Bosch sanitary ware and Huppe fittings. Her mother worked as an interior designer and Jenny could tell that no expense had been spared. The overall effect was one of absolute opulence, but unlike many of the top-end criminals' homes she had entered, the theme of absolute quality and up-to-the-minute style had been carried on throughout the house.

They entered a tiny little room which was clearly Cummins' office. It was more like a bunker actually, since it was down a small flight of stairs at the back of the property and contained no windows. Jenny's heart skipped when he removed what appeared to be a staple gun from a drawer and swept it over her body. In fact it was the latest in anti-bugging equipment, and he had her remove every piece of her jewellry and even the belt to her Levi's until the gun stopped bleeping.

Mother of God, she thought to herself; John Callaghan would kill me if he knew I was here.

Callaghan was her editor and since the murder of a female journalist from another publication several years earlier, strict regulations regarding crime reporters' activities had been put in place at most newspapers. Jenny had not informed Callaghan of her visit to Cummins because she knew it was more than his job was worth to let her go alone. He would have wanted the police liaison officer – appointed by the Commissioner to consult about her security – to get involved. Somehow, she just could not see Cummins allowing a copper into his mansion as he prepared to divulge sensitive information to one of the best-known investigative journalists in the country.

He didn't so much offer her a seat, as order her to sit and, unlike many other crims she had managed to interview, he made no small talk at all. Instead, he set the rules for their 'interview' to proceed.

'First, I want to make it quite clear that this *is*

not an interview,' Cummins said, his eyes unwavering as he glared at her. Although he was a small man, she could see now why he instilled such fear in people; his eyes were absolutely cold and she had no doubt that he was capable of acting with complete callousness if the situation required it. She wasn't about to provide him with a reason.

'What do you mean, this is not an interview?' she asked, taken aback by his statement. 'Why did you ask me here then?'

Cummins leaned back in his electronically controlled, leather-padded swivel chair. 'Don't come the innocent with me now, love. You and I both know the difference between an interview and a source providing information. The last thing I need is for the cops to put you in the witness box and get evidence about this meeting. Then I would be implicated and I'm not having that.'

Jenny had to hand it to him. He was one smart crook and she knew well what he was getting at. If somebody was acting as a source, then a journalist was obliged to protect that source from identification. But if somebody volunteered as an interviewee – therefore granting an actual interview – then the journalist could publicly acknowledge that this person provided them with information, and could identify them.

In a way, she was flattered. Cummins had clearly been following her career and was aware that she had been called by the State to give evidence in a number of gangland trials following 'interviews' she had conducted with certain criminal figures. Now he was making the very definite distinction that he was a source, as distinct from an interviewee, ensuring he wouldn't find himself in the same position.

And that perturbed Jenny no end. This was the first time that Spiller Cummins had allowed a journalist into his home and she had been so excited about writing chapter and verse for her readers the following Sunday. It was what gave her a fantastic buzz – the knowledge that she could inveigle her way into criminals' homes and get them to open up to her. It took a special talent to achieve such results and Jenny certainly had the knack.

He had his feet crossed on the footstool that matched his chair and he was still smiling at her, clearly enjoying her discomfort. He knew what she was thinking: would she be compromising her integrity as a journalist by agreeing a deal on secrecy with him? Or, more importantly, was there more to be gained by doing it his way?

He could see her mind working overtime as

she weighed up the available options and, magnanimous soul that he was, he decided to help her out a bit.

'Let me put it another way for you. The information I am prepared to provide you with is *so* sensitive that it would leave your fuckin' so-called "colour" stories about me and me criminal lifestyle in the shade. I'm a man of me word and when I tell you that I'm not a patch on the *real story* behind these missing women, I'm not joking, love. One hundred per cent, you won't be disappointed.'

Jenny Smith was hooked.

52

Jenny was in a quandary, a total bind. Never before in her career had she been presented with such a scenario. What he had told her constituted the most earth-shattering and sensational news story of all time. It would rock the police force. Destroy them, in fact.

The story, if Cummins was to be believed, was multifaceted. It contained numerous twists and turns and none of them bode well for the force, particularly for Timmy Vaughan and company. It was very disturbing, particularly if the line about police involvement in the missing-women saga was to be believed.

She didn't want to believe it. After all, she knew Vaughan and she knew several of the men working on the investigating team and, from her experiences, she trusted and respected most of them. But she had to concede that there had been serious allegations of police cover-ups before and she was in no position to let misguided loyalties get in the way. She may have had allegiances to the force – whose members provided her with the bread and butter of her stories – but she also had an obligation to her readers too.

There were several issues to consider.

The first was the assertion by Cummins that the investigating team had 'lost' all of the files regarding the missing-women investigations of the past ten years. Jenny knew that these files would be duplicated elsewhere on the police computer system, but that was not the point. The point was that they had been mislaid and God knew whose hands they may have fallen into.

The second was the claim that the person who lost the files was a civilian, albeit a civilian brought in to work on the case. She now had in her possession photographs of said civilian in a passionate embrace with Timmy Vaughan. Could this be the reason for the cover-up about the missing files? It was enough to lose Vaughan, a married man, his job. It was enough to destroy her working relationship with Kate Waters for good.

The third was the sensational claim that the man murdered less than a week ago on the north side, Martin Tierney, was a police source who was assisting them with their inquiries into the missing women. Tierney had passed information to the police about a notorious criminal gang, but he was not given police protection. In an era when the Witness Protection Programme was being used frequently to apprehend serious crims, this was a major breach of policing protocol. If it was true, it left the team totally exposed.

The fourth was the fact that despite Tierney's murder, Vaughan's team had not revealed their dealings with him to the north side team of detectives who were now investigating his death.

The fifth was the most sensational claim, a suggestion that the police were *actually aware* that two members of the investigating team were involved in the plot to abduct the women, but *no action* had been taken against either member and these details had been concealed from police management, not to mention the media.

Jenny was blown away by the information Cummins had given to her, but she was also extremely concerned about the provisos he had laid down before spilling the beans. He wanted the story handled in a certain way and that most definitely did not involve her going to the police with the information she had. Instead, he wanted her to run it referring to unnamed, but 'highly reliable' sources. In essence, he was insisting that she publish an exposé without checking any of the facts independently. Never before in her career had she run a story like this without verifying the whole thing with another party.

As she contemplated the facts of the case, two things preoccupied her. Were the women still alive? Cummins had claimed he did not know. And what was Cummins' motive and involvement in all of this? He had refused to go into any details, merely pointing out that she was not the only one with police sources – the implication being that *another* member of the team was bent, on the take from Cummins.

Whom could she trust? Jenny simply did not know. With Cummins' claim that he had his own source on the team, she couldn't risk going to any of them to run this thing through. Even Vaughan, a man with a reputation for being one of the toughest and most effective detectives on the force, was involved in the massive cover-up, if Cummins was to be believed. And there was no way that Johnny Callaghan would allow a single sentence of this story to go to print without absolute verification of all of the facts. They would be exposed to a massive libel writ if they got it wrong. Anyway, unless she came up with concrete proof before going to him, he would probably suspend her for breaching security measures in the way she had. So her only possible ally was ruled out too.

Jenny finally concluded that there was one man who might, just might, be prepared to help her. It was a risk, she knew, but her gut told her that he was the most likely – out of all of them – to be on the straight and narrow. It was time to pay a visit to his home.

53

The man the gang knew as Jonathon Hunt was in the house when the doorbell buzzed fiercely. He ignored it. He had no plans to receive visitors and had it been Griffin, he would have received an advance warning, as per their arrangement.

The buzzing would not stop and when his mobile began ringing too, he answered it with a sharp, 'Yes?'

'Open the gate, ye beedin' wus. I want to come in. Now!'

Ken Jones didn't even dare disobey. He was far too frightened of Knocker Griffin following his last encounter to risk any further run-ins with him. The security measures they had used before were obviously out of the window now that things were hotting up. Jones thought Griffin a fool for letting his guard drop and just turning up like this. Jones knew that it was this kind of sloppy behaviour which got criminals fingered.

Knocker laughed when he was met by Jones at the front door. The guy was actually shaking. His entire body seemed to be twitching from head to toe. He loved seeing the fear he instilled in professional types like Jones. He loved humiliating them.

Jones led him into the drawing room, which still looked like the incident room at Blackrock police station. The images of the three women were still on the walls, but a fourth had been added: that of Kate Waters.

Griffin walked over to Kate's photograph on the wall and stood before it. Then he licked his lips and ran his tongue all over her face. 'Jesus, she was a great piece of ass all right. Have ye had a go on her yet?'

Ken Jones recoiled, as if Kate Waters was the last woman on earth he would consider getting it together with. Griffin saw straight through the reaction immediately.

'Jaysus, Hunt, don't tell me you're losin' your bottle. Has the little cow intimidated ye? Is that it? Are ye all upset because she knows who you really are? Because you've been exposed before one of your own sort?'

Griffin was in convulsions of laughter now. He thought the situation was hilarious.

'Enough is enough,' Jones barked. 'I can't take

any more of this! When are you taking them away? That's all I want to know. When do I get rid of them? I want to know. NOW!'

Jones's obvious discomfort drove Griffin into even more fits of laughter. He was falling around the place now, like a deranged madman. If Jones hadn't copped it before, he now knew that he was dealing with a psychopath.

Griffin looked solemnly at Jones, but his eyes seemed to be rolling deliriously in his head. Jones thought he had lost the plot altogether.

'What is it with you? You're a madman. You're totally and utterly mad. Why are you behaving like this?' he shouted at Griffin.

'You call me a madman,' Griffin said, laughing cynically. 'That's the pot callin' the bleedin' kettle black if ever I heard it, ye big prick. Take a look in the fuckin' mirror, buddy. You're the one who is fuckin' stark raving mad. You're a bleeding psychopath. You're off your fuckin' trolley, man.'

Jones paused and took a few steps back. Griffin was up to something. He would have to tread cautiously now. He didn't want to antagonize him further. He had to remember the endgame here, and that endgame was to offload the women. After everything that had happened and with all of the heat coming on from the cops now, the last thing he wanted was to be left with the load.

'Where are ye keepin' them anyways?' Griffin asked.

'Oh, thank God,' Jones said to himself. Griffin had only been winding him up. He was going to get rid of them after all.

He ran to the cellar, with Griffin hot on his heels. When Jones opened the door, the women gasped with the shock of seeing another man. Was he here to hurt them? Was he the one Jonathon had threatened to pass them over to?

'Give me the keys,' he commanded. Jones didn't hesitate to oblige, impatient at the prospect of getting them out of his custody as soon as possible.

Griffin undid all four of the chains and Jones pompously asked if this was not a bit premature, since Griffin still had the task of transporting them to wherever it was he was taking them.

Griffin didn't bother to reply. Instead, he went over to the corner where Kate remained huddled, peered in close to her face and removed his Gucci shades.

Kate gasped out loud. 'Oh my God. Pete! At last. I thought I was going to die. I thought we were all going to die. Oh Christ! Thank God. I knew that one of you would find us. How did you know where to look?' She was smiling at him with relief.

But Knocker Griffin remained silent. He just looked at her impassively, as if he hadn't heard a word she uttered, as if he had never set eyes on her before.

A few seconds passed, with Kate staring wide-eyed into his eyes. She couldn't believe his reaction to finding her. He should have been elated. He should have been busy restraining Jones.

Then reality dawned on her. She retched and vomited violently at his feet. She *could not* believe what was happening.

Kate knew this man, but not as Knocker Griffin, the callous-looking man kneeling before her. She knew him as Pete, her lover, the man to whom she had revealed the sensitive details of the investigation. Step by step, he had been there all along, watching her every move, learning everything about the investigation from her. She'd even told him about Martin Tierney. She retched again, almost choking as she stared at him open-mouthed with disbelief, realizing that it was probably her conversation with 'Pete' about the discovery of the mobile phones which led to Tierney's death. The whole thing was a set-up.

Griffin watched as the reality dawned on Kate.

Then he leaned over, put his tongue in her mouth and licked her face. 'Thanks for the ride, darlin',' he said.

It all made sense now. When she telephoned Timmy on her way to Jones's house that night, Timmy hadn't answered his phone. That was the day he was due to get more of the call records. Obviously her number had come up as one that phoned Cummins' gang. But she had left a message on Timmy's phone, telling him where she was going. Jones had clearly taken care of that end, presumably pretending to Timmy that they had met, but that she had left his house safe and sound. Timmy would have had no reason to disbelieve Jones. None of them would have put Jones in with this lot.

No wonder Timmy hadn't come to rescue her. He obviously thought she was in this thing up to her eyeballs.

When Knocker told Jones to wait in the cellar, Jones didn't protest. He had only one thing on his mind now and that was not antagonizing Griffin. He just wanted to get as far away from him as possible. He watched Griffin walk out of the room, although he was none too pleased about being left in the presence of the four unchained women. Still, he knew that Griffin was only a shout away should any of them try to escape.

He didn't notice, until it was too late, that Griffin had the key to the door in his hand. When the key turned in the big iron lock, Jones could hear Griffin explode into howls of laughter again.

54

She had been sitting outside the house in the car for just fifteen minutes when the gates opened.

Jenny had expected her man to drive out, at which point she intended to block his car, march right up to his window and put the whole scenario to him. She had thought long and hard about it on the drive back from Howth – contemplating how best to approach the only person on the investigating team she felt she could really trust – and figured that the direct approach would probably work best with a guy like him.

When she realized that it was not his car that was emerging from the driveway, she squinted to get a good look at the man at the wheel, whilst trying to duck down behind her own steering wheel to avoid being seen. This thing was becoming far too sinister and dangerous for her and she knew that she should have had some back-up. The least she should do in the absence of any support was to avoid being seen.

She did a double take when she saw who it was.

Cummins had told her that two of the people from the investigation team were involved in the abductions and she had her own ideas about who those individuals might be. But the emergence of Knocker Griffin threw her whole theory into disarray.

Surely the man she had assumed to be the cleanest of them all couldn't be involved in this too? She had never actually met Knocker Griffin, but she had seen his photograph in police circulars. Only last night in fact, after Cummins had phoned her, she had looked at those circulars again to familiarize herself with details of his operations. The photographs were in black and white and printed on matt paper. Perhaps it wasn't him at all?

There was one sure way to find out and that involved a call to one of her contacts in the Crime and Security section at police headquarters.

Any crime journalist worth his or her salt had at least one good contact in C&S, as it was known within the force. It was almost as crucial as owning a mobile phone, because it opened up all sorts of avenues for the inquiring journalist.

The way it worked was simple; a journalist who needed to profile an 'unknown' simply furnished his or her source with that person's car registration details. The C&S contact would input the registration, and this would bring up an address with details of who lived at said address. Then followed a goldmine of information: specifics of convictions held by any of the people who lived at the address, particulars of surveillance carried out, details of other criminals who frequented the address. The possibilities of what a journalist could learn were endless. Police sources were not *supposed* to use the C&S facilities to supply information to journalists, but like most cops, Jenny's source believed that there was no harm in helping to expose the crims who constantly evaded the long arm of the law.

She had not dared follow Griffin. His presence at the house was just too strange. What business would a guy like Griffin have at this house? This thing was getting murkier yet again. Jenny felt a disturbing chill run down her spine and decided that it was time to start taking a few precautions.

Twenty minutes later, she received a phone call from her source. He had been unusually fast in getting back to her, but whatever information he had pulled down from his super computer, she knew that it must be important. He wanted her to meet him urgently at police headquarters. Normally, Jenny would have been happy to oblige, but she didn't want to leave this house.

When her source told her she was about to get the biggest story of her career, she put her foot on the pedal and left.

At police headquarters, she gave her name at the front gate and was astonished when the officer told her to 'go straight up to Superintendent Murphy's office'. Never before had she been welcomed so openly by a police source – usually they were busy breaking their backs trying to distance themselves from journalists, and any contacts that took place were absolutely covert and well out of sight of their colleagues.

She clipped the 'visitor' tag onto her jacket and supposed that Larry Murphy must either be on the way for another promotion (hence the cockiness) or be planning early retirement.

She hopped back into her car, revved up the engine and made her way through the compound. Ironically, police headquarters was the last place she was likely to be arrested for speeding. Everybody around here was always in a hurry.

She screeched to a halt at a stone building at

the back of the compound, where Larry Murphy was already waiting for her.

'God, you're anxious to see me,' Jenny said, her eyes full of the usual sparkle which Murphy admired her for.

But today, he was looking serious, just like a central casting policeman. 'Come this way, Jenny. We've got important business to discuss,' he said, as he ushered her up the tiny stairwell to his office.

She got the shock of her life when she entered the room.

'Now just hang on a minute, Larry, this was supposed to be between you and me. What's all this about? What's *he* doing here?' Jenny said, with suspicion in her voice as she pointed at Timmy Vaughan.

Vaughan was certainly in no mood to be treated disrespectfully by a member of the media, particularly one who was interfering in a high-profile investigation. But Murphy stood between the two, with his back to Vaughan, and he turned to look at Jenny. He had been dealing with her for four years now and he was savvy enough not to antagonize her. The last thing he wanted was for her to storm out of the office and blab whatever it was she knew all over town. He had just learned what was going on himself and he was still in shock. If the details of this case ever got out, the force would take an awful beating from the media, the public and the politicians.

'What's all this about? All I asked you for was the low-down on a car reg, for Chrissake. What's that got to do with Detective Vaughan here?' she asked, full of accusation and resentment.

'Now, Jenny, there's no need to go thinking about conspiracy theories or anything of the sort here,' Murphy said. 'You're quite right, all you asked me for were the details of the owner of the car whose registration you provided me with.' He paused a bit. 'However, the car in question was marked on our flagging system. I, of course, was totally unaware of that until I input the details, and that's why Detective Vaughan has joined us now.'

'You'd no right to tell him,' she spat.

This time, Murphy was not playing Mr Nice Guy: 'No, Jenny, that's where you're wrong, I'm afraid. The detail on the flagging system was very clear. This was a high-priority alert and Detective Vaughan had to be notified the minute anybody, no matter who, requested information about the owner of that car. You know how it works. This is crucial to a major investigation and I know for a fact that I don't need to tell you who owns that car.'

What Murphy did not add was that until ten minutes ago, he had been totally unaware of the significance of Griffin's movements. He still could not quite believe that Vaughan could have been party to such a cover-up, but he had known Vaughan for a long time and he knew that there must be more to this whole thing for Vaughan to have let it spiral so much out of control.

Jenny knew then that she had been rumbled. Obviously they had copped on to what she was at, but she was damned if she was going to be silenced, just because it suited them. Not on a story this big. She was going to hold her ground and let Murphy know that no matter how helpful he had been to her in the past, she *would not be party to a cover-up*.

'So what is it you want from me then?' she asked sarcastically. 'My silence? Because you're not getting it on this one. This is far too big for me to do you all a little favour and forget I ever heard about this story. These women are missing and your people are behind it, Vaughan; at least two of them, for starters.'

Timmy had to hand it to her. It had taken her less than twenty-four hours to figure out something that had taken him weeks. 'You should be on the force, Jenny,' he said. 'You're wasted in journalism. How did you find out about them?'

'I'm not going to tell you that, Vaughan, but I will tell you one thing: I know everything. The lot of it. I know about your girlfriend and the missing documents and I know about her allegiances to the people behind this. And another thing, I know that one of your own men is in this up to his eyeballs too. I even know that you have phone records that prove it and he's still on the job. It's disgusting. Those women are probably dead and you're standing there telling the world that you need help in locating them. The reality is, Vaughan, that they are probably in the same place as poor Martin Tierney. He was helping you too.'

What she didn't say was that Kate was the one who had initially tipped her off, because she still couldn't figure out – in light of the conversation with Cummins – why Kate had telephoned her in the first place, since she was actually involved in the cover-up. That would have to wait until she figured out what Kate Waters was up to.

Vaughan was shocked at the depth of her knowledge about the details of the case. Obviously, somebody had given her a full briefing. But that could only have been himself or Paddy Daly and he knew for certain that Daly would never talk. He valued his career too much.

'You've got some of the picture there all right, but I'm telling you, Jenny, somebody is using you. This is not how it seems at all. There's a lot more to this case than meets the eye. You've got to keep this quiet for the time being,' he said.

'Oh don't come the guilt trip with me, Detective,' Jenny scowled. 'I'm not falling for that one. This is the story of the century and I intend to run with it. There's absolutely nothing you can do to stop me. Even a call from management won't stop this one. It's too big to ignore.'

'OK,' Timmy said, 'I'll do a deal with you. Kate Waters – and I assume that's who you're talking about as being one of the two people involved – has gone to ground, but we were just about to move on the officer who, as you rightly said, has been in contact with the people behind this thing. You can come and witness it first-hand. I'll give you the exclusive on the whole thing, so long as you give us just a bit more time to figure this mess out.'

Jenny bit her bottom lip. It was a tempting offer. She was being invited to be part of a sensational 'bust'. It would make for fabulous copy. What the heck, she thought; if they didn't give her chapter and verse she had enough to expose the whole sordid mess anyway. Either way, she couldn't lose.

55

They drove across the city at great speed. Jenny in the back with Vaughan quizzing her, and Murphy at the wheel like a madman.

It took them twenty minutes with the siren blaring and when they pulled up at the house, Jenny tried to ask Vaughan some questions, but he abruptly told her to 'shut up' and yelled that he would deal with her later.

Paddy Daly was already waiting for them. He had been at Blackrock police station and the house was only a short drive from there. With all the drama of a Starsky and Hutch film, Vaughan raced dramatically from the car to the front door, banging and shouting his officer's name until the man came to the front door.

'Out here now and explain yourself, Farrelly. We know you're in this up to your eyeballs. It's time to do a deal or you're going down, for a very long time.'

It certainly wasn't Vaughan's normal style, but three women's lives were at stake and his career was riding on this. Add to that the fact that this had become personal on a number of levels and all rational behaviour went out of the window.

Jenny took in the scene from the back of the unmarked car. It was truly bizarre. This was yet another twist to the saga.

Jack Farrelly was up in arms, shouting his head off and threatening all sorts against Vaughan and Daly: 'What in the hell are you talking about, Vaughan? I'm an officer on the team, for God's sake. What is it that you're trying to pin on me? I'll sue you and I'll sue the force for this. I'll see that you never work a case again.'

Vaughan had had enough. He took Farrelly by the back of his sweater and roughly pushed him towards the car, jamming his head in through the back window which Jenny had opened to hear the commotion.

'See this woman?' he said, shaking Farrelly's head into the opening in the window with each word he uttered. 'She saw Griffin leaving your house. We have a witness. There's no use pretending. Do the decent thing, you miserable bastard, and tell us where they are.'

Farrelly looked at Jenny, who in turn looked at

Vaughan. Then it registered on his face. She was shaking her head slowly, indicating that no, Farrelly was not the person she had been referring to when she had told them that she saw Griffin leaving the home of one of Vaughan's officers.

Vaughan let Farrelly go, pushing him aside like a used rag. 'What are you talking about, woman? We have details of telephone contacts between him and the gang. You said that you knew the identity of the officer concerned. This is him. This is our man.' Even as he uttered them, he didn't quite believe the words any more.

'This is not the house I saw Griffin coming out of. It was a different house, not here in Dun Laoghaire,' she said.

Farrelly stood in a daze as the officers got into the car and Jenny provided the address. Within ten minutes, they were at the home of the computer specialist, the man who had, it seemed, single-handedly abducted the missing women.

56

This time, they had a rational talk outside the house before Vaughan burst in. Paddy Daly, never having been quite able to believe that Farrelly had the nous in the first place to become involved with the likes of Cummins and his crew, wanted to be sure they were making the right move.

'Is this the house?' he asked Jenny, still not exactly sure why she was in the car with them.

'Absolutely,' she said. 'I've been here twice. I followed him home here yesterday. I saw him drive in.'

'What were you doing following a member of the investigating team?' Timmy blazed at her.

Jenny just looked at him disbelievingly. 'Well, it's a good job somebody did, Detective. Otherwise where would you all be now?' she said. Touché.

'Seriously though, Jenny, what led you here?' Daly asked her, trying to make the peace and get a lead on the latest development.

'Well, the first time, just after the press conference, I figured that he was the one who was most likely to talk to me. The rest of you all seemed to be battening down the hatches, but he seemed quite distanced from everyone else. He looked pissed. I thought that was as good a reason as any.'

'And the second time? Why did you come back here earlier today? What was it that led you here again?' Daly prodded.

'I got some information, information regarding all of the cock-ups in the case, including Martin Tierney, and suspicions that some of your own were involved in the abductions. I wanted to come back and check it. I was just about to confront him.' The shock of her near meet with him seemed to register with her now. Had she not seen Griffin, she probably would have confronted her man and she would almost certainly have ended up in the same boat as the three missing women.

Daly and Vaughan still didn't know for certain that the man she was referring to was definitely responsible for the abductions. They didn't know who she was talking about because she hadn't been able to provide a name and Vaughan, for his part, still wondered if it wasn't Kate Waters who had played a central role in the disappearances.

After all, he had not yet figured out how she fit into this whole thing.

'Anyway,' Jenny continued, 'I saw Griffin coming out of the driveway and I *thought* it was him, but I wasn't absolutely sure. I've only ever seen his photograph in those police circulars you guys issue and that's when I rang my friend Superintendent Murphy. I just wanted to run a check on his car details to be sure.'

Then it hit Vaughan like a bolt out of the blue. He grabbed Jenny by the shoulders, turning her to face him. His face was redder than usual and his eyes were wild. 'Jesus Christ! You said the man you followed was at the press conference, looking a bit pissed off, looking distant.'

'That's right. That's why I followed him. I thought he didn't quite fit in and would be my best bet. He looked disgruntled.'

'Christ, Jenny, what did he look like? Nobody on our team could afford to live in a house like this. What did he look like? Come on. Think, woman. Think!'

Jenny was still in shock from the way Vaughan had grabbed at her so violently. She was slow in getting her thoughts together. 'Well, he was kind of – how do I put it? A bit inconsequential-looking, I'd say. He looked *normal*. That's how I would describe him. I wouldn't have him down as a crim, if that's what you're asking.'

Vaughan was bursting with impatience now. Daly intervened to calm him down. The last thing any of them wanted was a replay of the scene they had just had with Farrelly. He removed Vaughan's hands from Jenny's sweater.

'Jenny, I know you're in a bit of shock here. Just calm down. Just think clearly for a minute.'

Jenny looked appreciatively at Daly.

'Christ, I was so focused on getting him to talk to me, I didn't take down his particulars. But I remember he was wearing glasses. He had dark hair. He looked a bit nerdy. Yeah, that's how I would describe him, dark-haired, about five eleven and nerdy-looking.'

'The bastard!' Vaughan shouted. 'The bastard. It's *him*,' Timmy said to Daly, knowing that his young colleague had just drawn the same conclusion based on Jenny's description.

'Just hold on a minute, boss. We don't know for sure that it's Jones. We can't just rush in there. What if it's somebody else? Somebody more prepared for our arrival?' Daly cautioned.

Vaughan was wild with fury. 'No, Daly, I'm telling you, it's Jones. The last time I heard from Kate was when she left a message on my mobile telling me that she was going to see Jones, that he had *called* her and asked for a meet. Jones told me that they had met and she had been all inquisitive about what he knew, and he felt she was asking some inappropriate questions. But I haven't heard from her since. I thought she was in on it, Daly. Jesus Christ, Paddy, he's got Kate too.'

Murphy, hardly understanding any of it at this stage, and Daly and Vaughan made to jump out of the car. It was only Jenny who was thinking straight now.

'Wait!' she shouted.

All three policemen looked at her like she was crazy.

'You won't get in. The gates are too high.'

In unison, all three turned to look at the huge electric gates. They looked around in confused panic.

'You can't exactly buzz the intercom and announce your presence, lads, now can you?'

'Jesus, she's right,' Vaughan said, reason slowly coming back into his voice. 'What the hell are we going to do? We've got to get in there pronto. This is literally life and death.'

'I should be the one', Jenny said.

'No way,' Vaughan shouted back. 'No way. If we're right, we already have four missing women in there. I'm not sending a fifth one in, just so as you can make your name as the heroine and win another award.'

Jenny slapped him in the face. 'Kate's been good to me. If she's in there, I want to ensure she gets out safely.'

'So that's how you got tipped off in the first place, through Kate?' Vaughan asked.

Jenny was in no mood for playing games. 'If Kate hadn't called me – and she told me little of what was going on, she just wanted some info on Cummins – none of us would be here now. She just helped me put two and two together. I knew nothing until your press conference, Detective Vaughan.'

'I think she's right, Timmy. She should ring the intercom. He won't let us in, but he'll probably let Jenny in, especially if he thinks she's uncovered his involvement,' Daly reasoned.

When the intercom buzzed, Jones ran over to it, complimenting himself on his foresight in installing one in his dungeon. The women in the room didn't attempt to scream. They assumed it was Griffin back to cause havoc.

Jones assumed the same and activated the gate button. He had no reason to assume it was anybody else. In all the time he'd been renting the house, only invited guests had ever called.

Then they heard a commotion upstairs. There seemed to be people running everywhere. The women could hear men's voices, at least two of them. Kate was not sure, but she thought she recognized Timmy's booming voice. She prayed to God that she was right. She also prayed that it was not Knocker Griffin back again. How could she have been such a fool?

They heard footsteps on the stairs and then banging on the door of the cellar. At first they all remained silent, wary of who was on the other side. So many bizarre twists had occurred that Kate didn't know who she could trust any more.

But the banging persisted and then a man's voice called out to them: 'This is the police. Who is in there? Identify yourselves.'

Kate could hardly believe it. 'We're in here. We're in here,' she screamed. Nikki and Andrina screamed too. Sophie looked like she was on her last legs. She didn't have an ounce of energy left.

'Is that you, Kate? Is that you?' Timmy shouted as he ran at the door and tried to break it down.

'Yes, Timmy, it is me. I'm here with the other women. Hurry, Timmy, get us out of here, for God's sake,' she shouted.

Daly arrived with an axe he'd found outside and warned them to stand clear of the door.

'Call an ambulance, Timmy,' Kate shouted between the bangs. 'Sophie needs serious help. She's in a bad way.'

Kate could hear Timmy making the call on his mobile, then the door began to give way.

When the door finally gave, Vaughan, Daly, Larry Murphy and Jenny all burst into the room. Each recoiled at the sight of the four women. And then they saw Jones, huddled in the corner, just as he had years ago when he knew his father was on the way.

'The animal! I'll kill him. I'll kill him,' Timmy shouted, when he took in Jones's pathetic figure.

Murphy, Daly and Jenny each consoled one of the missing women, whilst Timmy cradled Kate in his arms.

'Leave it be,' she said. 'He's a sick man, Timmy. Besides, I think he was set up. We all were, even me too.'

57

Despite the media furore which surrounded the case, Timmy got the backing of his superiors *not* to tell them yet that the women had been found safe. That would give them time to begin to recover and to be united privately with their families.

It was also Saturday – the day following the dramatic rescue operation – so Jenny Smith would have an opportunity to write up her story for Sunday's newspaper. She would get her 'exclusive', just as Vaughan had promised. After all, were it not for her nous and diligence, they probably would never have found the women, not alive at any rate.

Timmy had not been home yet. He had spent the rest of last evening reuniting the three women with their families, and then attending a series of conferences with his superiors, outlining most, but not all, of what had happened in the investigation. That was another reason they were happy to keep quiet about the rescues; they wanted time to put a damage-limitation spin on the whole affair.

Despite the heroic rescue of the women, the top brass were none too pleased when they learned the full details, especially the bit about Martin Tierney. The withholding of information regarding the man's death was a serious breach of professional conduct which merited severe disciplinary action, they warned him. Timmy knew the score about the veiled threat: if this information got out, they would make him the fall guy and if it remained secret, he would escape with a scolding.

Kate had refused to go to the hospital for a check-up. She was badly bruised, but had insisted it was more psychological than physical. She had returned home to Killiney, where Timmy had joined her at eleven o'clock.

'I feel such a fool, Timmy,' she told him as they sat by the fire. 'They set us up. The whole thing was a set-up and I was central to it. I can't believe I was so naïve.'

'So when did you meet Griffin?' Timmy asked gently, not wanting to put too much pressure on her, but wanting to put a picture together in his head as to how this thing had all come together for the gang.

'Just over five months ago, just before Sophie Andrews went missing, in Doheny's, my regular watering hole with the girls. I can hardly believe it.'

Timmy could hardly believe it himself. Pete Connors, it sounded like such an unassuming name. A HR specialist, he had said he was. He had to hand it to Griffin, the man had balls.

Kate continued, her voice quivering as she told him the rest of the story. 'When he was describing himself as a Human Resources consultant, he left out the word "gangland". Oh my God, Timmy, to think that I fell for it hook, line and sinker.'

Timmy said nothing, just let her take her time explaining. She curled up in a ball on the armchair, hugging her knees protectively to her body. 'Timmy,' she began.

'It's all right, Kate. You don't have to apologize for getting involved with him. The guy is a professional of the highest calibre. How were you to know? Even I would never have suspected that a guy like him would have the balls to do what he did to you. You couldn't have been expected to think he was part of anything. Sure you met him before any of this even began – as far as we were concerned anyway.'

Kate looked him full on in the face now, her

big eyes wide with despair and filled with grief: 'I know it wasn't my fault, Timmy, but God, oh my God, we –' she hesitated and then spat it out – 'we did things together. It's disgusting. I call myself a good judge of character. It's what I do for a living and look how I misjudged him. Christ, Timmy, I confided in him when we learned about the purchase of the mobile phones. It's my fault that Martin Tierney was murdered.'

She was wide-eyed with disbelief. Timmy was too. By way of explanation, she told him: 'We were out in Greystones, at the Hungry Monk.' Timmy looked shocked. The Hungry Monk had always been *their* special place. He went to say so, but left it. He understood now why she had confided in Griffin. She had obviously felt herself opening up to him. She must have been giving things a chance if she brought him there . . . to their special place, he thought resentfully.

He kept quiet. He could see she was devastated. She had been used in the worst way.

'He began asking me about my job and I told him about some of the breaks we were getting. But I swear to you, Timmy, I never named Cummins, or Tierney.'

His look said it all. She hadn't needed to. The minute Kate mentioned the development regarding the mobile phones, Griffin would have known immediately that it was Tierney who spilled the beans.

Kate knew what he was thinking now. She bowed her head in shame, couldn't believe she had been so unprofessional, so gullible.

He allowed her a few minutes and when she seemed calmer, he ventured further: 'What about the so-called Jonathon Hunt, Kate? How on earth did you end up there?' he asked.

'How was I to know that our computer wizard, Ken Jones, was the one behind the actual abductions? I mean he was so *helpful* throughout the course of the investigation. I know you didn't like him, but he was so thorough, always offering a different point of view. He telephoned me that night and said that there was an important development he wanted to discuss, but not over the telephone. Because of what was going on with the phones, I bought that. So I went to his house in Blackrock. Then when I got there, he had the whole place set up like a monument to these missing women and then he offered me a glass of wine, and obviously, he drugged me. The last thing I remember is feeling drowsy and then I woke up in the cellar. He told me they wanted me. To hurt you.'

She paused and then looked at him accusingly. 'Why didn't you follow up on it when I phoned you, Timmy? Why did you believe him?'

Timmy bowed his head. He felt so stupid, so guilty too. 'We had just received details of phone records showing that Jack Farrelly had been in touch with the gang. We were monitoring that and then I discovered that *your* number popped up too. Fifteen calls to one of the gang's phones, Kate. What was I supposed to think?'

'But why didn't you come after me when I left the message saying that I was meeting Jones?'

'I'll never forgive myself for that. I went to Jones and quizzed him about your whereabouts and he scoffed at the suggestion, told me that you left his house after an hour. He said that you must be in it with Farrelly and that we should accept what the information he was collating from the phone print-outs was telling us, and follow you and Farrelly. It turns out that he'd planted Farrelly's number in the call record sheet to make the scenario involving *you* look more plausible.'

'So how did the irrepressible Jenny Smith become involved then? She's the one who really led you to us in the end, is she not?'

Timmy didn't want Kate to know that Jenny had revealed Kate's call to her. He knew that Kate would feel even worse if she sensed that he thought she'd been unprofessional.

He told her he strongly suspected that Cummins had tipped Jenny off, in an effort to expose the shambles of an investigation. 'After all, all of the information she had when she came to us was fairly accurate. Had it gone to print, it would also have been extremely damning for our investigation team. That's why I think she got it all from him.'

Kate was confused. 'Why can't you just put pressure on her and find out for certain who she got the information from? Surely in a case this important, she should tell you that?'

Then Kate stopped dead in her tracks as she recalled her own telephone call to Jenny. That, she realized, was how Jenny got on to this thing in the first place. She gave Timmy all of the sordid details about her late-night phone call to Jenny, inquiring about Mickser Cummins and his crew.

'That's how she got on to it, Timmy. Oh God, that was my fault too,' she said, expecting to be admonished.

'So what, Kate? You rang a journalist for a bit of help. That's no big deal. It's not like her lot don't ring us often enough, now is it? Besides, if you *hadn't* called her, she would never have put things together so quickly. The outcome could have been very different.'

Then he added: 'And another thing; the files that were stolen from your office, he gave them to Jenny, just to embarrass the team, especially me, no doubt. He wanted her to print all of the details, to embarrass us.'

Kate tensed up. She knew that this would discredit Timmy and his team, not just her. 'It's OK, Kate. She's not going to do anything with them – although knowing Smith, she has probably already photocopied them; she's agreed to return them.'

Kate relaxed her shoulders a little bit. She was grateful that he wasn't giving her a hard time.

'The fact is, if you hadn't called her, you probably wouldn't be sitting here now. And those women would probably be dead by now.'

58

Timmy felt a twinge of guilt. He hadn't been home in two days, nor had he heard a word from his wife. He knew she wanted him to come back to their marriage. In theory, he had not left it, but in practice, he had.

He intended to go back to the house in Monkstown and talk to Laura soon, but first, he had an important meeting. The person he was meeting was not expecting him, but Timmy had no doubt that he would get an appointment nonetheless.

He was exhausted after a night on Kate's couch, but nothing was going to prevent him from going to see Cummins. He called Paddy Daly in to sit it out at Kate's house – despite her protestations that she would be fine alone – before heading off at high speed to the other side of the city. He wanted answers and he wanted them now.

He pulled up outside the house in Howth, but

did not bother ringing the intercom. Instead, he used the number Kate had given him for Griffin, for he knew that Griffin would be with Cummins now, lording it over the whole mess they had created, especially for Timmy Vaughan.

The phone was answered after just two rings and Griffin went silent when he heard Vaughan on the other end of the line: 'It's Timmy Vaughan here, Griffin. Tell that wanker of a boss of yours to open the gates immediately. I'm outside. But I'm sure you can see that from the camera on the gatepost anyway.'

Griffin began to spout about search warrants and the like, but Vaughan could hear Cummins beside him, instructing Griffin to let him in. 'He's got nothing on us, Griffin. Whatever it is he's here about, it will be beyond physical evidence,' the gruff voice said. Vaughan heard the smug laughter that followed the words and wanted to take Cummins by the scruff of the neck and beat him to within an inch of his life.

The gates swung open and Vaughan drove slowly up the imposing driveway. He was intent on taking in his surroundings. He intended to return here one day, with the Criminal Assets Bureau in tow, to seize every last possession Cummins owned. But not today, today was a day for learning all about the motive for the set-up. As Kate had said early on, this thing was personal.

Cummins opened the front door and signalled to Timmy to follow him. Timmy stopped when they got to the kitchen and took a high stool without being invited.

'What can I do you for, Detective?' Cummins asked. 'To what do I owe the pleasure of your esteemed company?'

Cummins was sneering. He knew that Vaughan had nothing on him. He had distanced himself from any crime. He had been very clever about that indeed. It had always been his policy and it had certainly worked for him to date.

Timmy got right to the point: 'Cut the crap, Mickser, and give me a few straight answers. Then I'll be out of your hair for good.'

Cummins was all wide-eyed innocence. 'What answers could I possibly give you, Detective? What exactly is the nature of your inquiry?' he asked. His voice was drenched in smugness with every word he uttered.

'Let's get something straight here, Mickser. I am not here in a policing capacity. This is personal. I think we both know that. I just want some answers and then I will be gone.'

Mickser Cummins knew that Vaughan meant

business. Cops and criminals frequently had off-the-record chats like this. It was merely a question of straightening things out in a situation where no guilt was admitted, although it was certainly implied.

'Shoot,' Cummins said, a blasé tone to his rough voice.

'Why, do you suppose, would a member of the force get hooked up with the likes of you?' Timmy asked. 'I'm just speaking hypothetically, of course. I'm curious to know.'

Mickser relaxed on his high stool, clearly enjoying being called upon for his opinion on such a matter.

'Well, now, I suppose if that member was deeply unpopular and didn't have any friends within the ranks, it might be very easy to manipulate him, to make him feel like a part of the family. But that's only my theory, of course.'

Timmy knew that it stood to reason. Kate had pretty much said the same when she was profiling the abductor at the outset of the investigation.

'And, of course, if that person felt totally undervalued by his colleagues, he might have good reason to jump to the other side of the fence – so to speak – to show those same colleagues just how clever he was,' Cummins added.

A good point again, Timmy conceded privately and Cummins had just put the blame squarely on Timmy for causing Ken Jones to behave in the way he had.

'OK,' Timmy said, 'that's good enough for me. But tell me this then: why would a criminal, generally involved in more profitable activities, mastermind such a scheme? Where would the benefit lie in that, do you know?'

Cummins was smirking now. 'Well, I couldn't say for definite, Detective, but I imagine it would be a question of revenge. I imagine that could be a motive.'

Timmy regarded him silently for a few minutes, marvelling at the lengths Cummins had gone to in taking revenge against him. It all seemed so elaborate – all for a measly drugs bust which had probably cost Cummins only a million quid, chicken-feed to the likes of him.

'Tell me this then: why would a person orchestrating such a ruse go to such pains to involve a totally innocent woman? Why would the likes of Kate Waters be brought into this?'

Cummins swung his legs from the stool and looked Vaughan straight in the eye. He wanted to explain this bit. It would be such fun to watch Vaughan's reaction to what he was about to learn.

'Well, I don't know anything about this Kate Waters person, Detective. But I can tell you something interesting.' He paused, took a breath to emphasize the significance of what he had to say. Timmy's gut wrenched as he awaited what he was sure would be a real blow. It was just gut instinct.

Cummins looked at him innocently. 'Perhaps the starting game never included this woman, Waters. But things change, don't they? And you know what they say, don't you? Hell hath no fury like a woman scorned. Have you ever scorned a woman close to you?'

With that, Cummins patted Vaughan on the shoulder, almost sympathetically. The colour drained from Timmy's face. His own wife, Laura . . . surely she was not the person behind all of this?

59

Timmy took in the grotesque image of his battered and drunken wife. Her face had been beaten to a pulp and she seemed to be having trouble breathing. From the way she was tenderly touching her rib cage and wincing, he reckoned she had suffered several punches to that area too.

Laura was pissed again, just like in the old days after their daughter died. This time he couldn't blame her though. From the sight of her, he reckoned she needed something strong to anaesthetize the pain.

'He did this to you. Didn't he?' he asked, an hour after leaving Mickser Cummins' palatial pile.

Laura looked at her husband defiantly now. 'So what if he did? I'll never tell you who *he* is, anyway. I don't care. It was worth it. I hope she rots in hell.'

Timmy put his head in his hands. He felt like shit, because he knew that at the end of the day, his actions had driven his wife to go so far. He had confirmation now. Laura was behind this whole thing and her primary motivation had been to hurt him and Kate, in particular. Her overtures about them getting back together had just been part of the set-up.

He sat across from her in the cold kitchen, staring incredulously at her drink-ravaged face. It defied belief. A copper's wife. It could never get out. She would be crucified if it did.

'You'd be furious if you knew it was all my idea, wouldn't you?' She sniggered. 'Well, it was,' she boasted, 'the bit about your girlfriend. All of that was down to me. They had other ideas but I persuaded them that I meant nothing to you and that they would be better off dragging her into it. They wanted to let the underworld know that you don't mess with their business and get away with it. So there you go, the finer points were definitely down to me.'

Timmy was repelled. She was even talking like a criminal now. He was shocked to learn her perception of him, to hear that she thought he wouldn't care if the likes of Cummins injured her. It was the first time he realized that he had damaged her self-confidence so badly.

'Of course you mean something to me. Of course I would have cared,' he offered.

She raised her drunken voice now: 'Yeah. Sure, Timmy. Just like you cared for me the night our daughter died. Only it wasn't me who you were caring for when I went looking for you that night, was it? Oh no, it was *her. That bitch. I hate her. I hate her so much. I wished they'd killed her. I wish she was dead.*'

Laura was hell-bent on continuing now. 'They came here to this house, him and that Knocker Griffin fella. They tied me up, they were real professional about it. They meant business. They said that you had made a laughing-stock of Cummins and that you were going to pay for it, but I had photographs of you and your lady friend and I convinced them that they would be much better off going after you and her. Then they had to devise a big scheme to get her involved. That's where the missing women came in. I told them they needed to create a crime which would involve her working with you.'

Timmy was appalled.

'But those women could have been killed, Laura. One of the gang wanted them murdered. He was in so deep that he needed them dead.'

She levelled a cold, blank stare right at him and began a long, low laugh which developed into a callous crescendo of madness. 'That was the whole point, you fool,' she said contemptuously. '*I wanted your woman killed. I wanted her off the face of this earth. I wanted her to suffer for what she did to me, to my baby.*'

'But there were other women involved in this who had nothing to do with what happened to our family, Laura. Didn't you care about them?'

He knew even as he asked the question that it was a futile one. Laura had lost it years ago and she was beyond caring. She had been driven to all of this by grief.

'The only person I cared about, Timmy, was killed a long time ago. Who suffered for that, Timmy? Who suffered for my Kyra?'

There was nothing more to be said. He left the room and made a phone call. His wife needed medical attention and as he waited on the line for the family doctor to take his call, he realized that she had given him all the answers he needed. The whole thing had been a set-up, designed to extract maximum revenge – for Cummins and for Laura.

Cummins had been right. 'Hell hath no fury like a woman scorned.'

60

South Dublin, 2001

Laura opened the door to the private detective. He handed her an envelope. It contained the details of four weeks' work. She handed him two thousand pounds.

She had told him to call after eight o'clock, when Kyra would be safely tucked up in bed. She expected to be reading bad news and she had not wanted to let her precious little girl see her upset. She would never do anything to hurt little Kyra. They loved her so dearly.

She sat in the sitting room. It had once been homely, full of love and happiness, shared by the three of them. Now it felt empty. She was not really a drinker, but she had taken a bottle of gin from the drinks cabinet because the look on the private detective's face had signalled she might need one.

Slowly, she inched open the brown envelope.
There, in full technicolor, were the images she
had prayed she would not see: her husband, childhood sweetheart, the father of their adored child,
in a passionate embrace with another woman. A
stunning-looking woman too. And clearly younger.
That had hurt her even more.

There was a print-out containing details of
telephone calls and meetings, fifteen such meetings in total over the past month. The dates of
the meetings were printed clearly for Laura to
see. She checked the diary she had been keeping.
They corresponded precisely with the evenings
when Timmy had been on night duty.

She read the profile the detective had prepared
on the woman. She was a committed professional,
full of life and clearly full of passion. Everything
that Laura Vaughan had once been. Her name
was Kate Waters.

All of the information she needed about the
woman was on the neatly typed A4 biography.
Laura was on her third large gin by the time she
made up her mind.

It was bitterly cold, the rain lashing out of the
heavens. She bundled little Kyra up in a sleeping
bag and put her in the back of the car. She let
the seatbelt hang loose for the trip. They were not

going far and she would have to wake the child and force her to sit up if she was to use the seat-belt. It wasn't worth the bother. She merely wanted to visit the woman's house, to let her see that she was destroying a family.

She drove slowly up the coast road from Monkstown, the car weaving in the blustery winds as the sea howled to her left. With the rain teeming down, she didn't see the cyclist who was walking along the coast road with his bike. She hit him, sent him tumbling in the air, and swerved as he came down on the bonnet of the car. She braked hard with the impact, but the sudden manoeuvre sent her spinning into a frenzied skid. The car spun into the boundary railings that separated the beginning of Dun Laoghaire pier from the road. That was all she could remember.

Timmy's phone rang at half-past ten. He had been half-tempted to ignore it, but Laura's number had flashed up. He always answered her calls, no matter what, just in case it was something to do with Kyra.

The first police officer to attend at the scene had found the phone buried beneath the passenger seat. He was an eager new recruit and figured that rather than wait for the station computer to identify the driver of the car, he would scroll down the phone until he reached the first number on the speed dial'. That one was usually the partner, the parent or the spouse.

The young recruit described the vehicle to Timmy and Timmy said that yes, it was his wife's car. Could Timmy please meet them at St Michael's Hospital in Dun Laoghaire?

Laura remained unconscious for two days. When it was learned that she was the wife of a detective, the investigating police officer 'forgot' to get the hospital to take a blood sample to test her alcohol level.

Only Timmy was present when Kyra died. He thanked God that Laura had not seen her face as she weakly attempted to fight death. The little girl's eyes had opened briefly, more a flicker really, just before she died. Timmy knew that nothing could ever torture him as much as that memory.

61

Dublin, May 2004

The police-appointed psychologist sat across the table from Timmy and Paddy Daly in the Law Library. They were there with the State solicitors and barristers who were running the case, a case which was looking less and less likely to get into court as the days went by.

'He's a very sick man, you know. I am acting for the State in this case and even *I* could not say that he is fit to stand trial.'

Professor Mark Browne was the most eminent clinical psychologist in the State and when he spoke, people listened. The State used him a lot because juries almost invariably were persuaded by what he said.

'Are you saying that this is a complete plea of mitigating circumstances, that we would at best do him on insanity?' Finbar Charles, the lead prosecution barrister asked.

'I'm saying more than that to counsel, actually. I am telling you that the man is not fit to stand trial. I don't think he ever will be,' the professor replied.

'But how is it that he was able to hold down a responsible job, a job he was exceptionally good at, as it turns out, and at the same time, he can be deemed unfit to stand trial? Where's the logic in that?' Timmy asked.

'The man had an horrific life. He was mistreated, belittled, abused and psychologically tortured by his father for the entirety of his adolescence. Even the school records prove it. He was never afforded even a modicum of respect. In fact he was tortured for not having any friends.'

Browne looked at Timmy now. 'Your profiler, Miss Waters, had the right read on him all along. He was somebody who looked like he fitted in, but who didn't. That was why it was so easy for these criminals to target him. They offered him respect, friendship, the trappings of success, a private jet no less . . . All of the things he had never had. He was totally deluded by them. They gave him what he *craved* all of his life. No self-respecting expert in the field, having read these

files, could fault him for going along with them.
I don't know what else to tell you, Detective. But
this case should not go to trial.'

'I think he is right, I'm afraid,' Finbar Charles
said.

Timmy had to stifle a snort of disbelief. It was
the first time he had ever heard a senior counsel
turn down the opportunity of a long trial in court.
And the thousands to be earned from it.

He knew that the one person Jones could identify in relation to the whole thing was Griffin,
but there were two reasons – one of them very
dear to Timmy's heart – why this would never
happen.

The first reason was that Jones could not be
regarded as a credible witness, and the second
was that if Griffin was put on trial, the whole
messy business involving his so-called relationship with Kate would emerge and she would end
up being totally discredited. Her career and life
would be in ruins.

The senior counsel added: 'The ironic thing is,
your man Jones is the only person against whom
there is any real evidence. He did everything. There
is nothing to link your gang to it, I'm afraid.
Nothing that we can credibly take into court at
any rate. The whole thing was a set-up.'

Vaughan stood, dug his hands into his pockets and left the room. He was sick of being told about the set-up.

62

'So, Kate, what lies ahead for you in the next few months?' Jenny asked as they sat on the deck at the back of Kate's coach house. They could see the mist settling on the sea below them. 'Any good cases coming up that I should know about?' Jenny quipped, knowing the answer before she even got one.

'As if I would tell you if I did!' Kate retorted good-naturedly. 'If I told you that, then you might go and save my life again and I couldn't have that now. I don't want to be indebted to you again, Jen. Once was enough, thanks very much.'

Both women laughed. They had become good friends since the conclusion of the case and Jenny, true to her word, had left all of the seedier details out of her exclusive story on the heroic rescue of the missing women. She had all but named Cummins and his crew as being the criminals behind the abductions and the whole country was now aware that the police knew – once again in the case of gangland criminals – who was behind the crime. It had caused uproar in political circles because the opposition were playing tough and demanding to know why the police – if they knew who was to blame – had failed to bring anybody to justice in the case. It was the usual political shenanigans that surrounded high-profile crimes and everybody knew that it would be forgotten as soon as the next big gangland crime made it into the headlines.

Jenny had even admitted to Kate that she knew the whole story about Kate and Timmy's past relationship and Kate in turn had admitted to Jenny that she still loved Timmy, that she couldn't get him out from under her skin.

'So what are you going to do about Timmy then?' Jenny asked in her usual upfront fashion.

'To be honest, Jen, I really haven't decided that yet. I don't know that we can ever have a future together, not after everything we put his wife through. I don't know if I could have it on my conscience, to hurt her all over again,' Kate said.

Jenny, as Kate was learning fast, was a pragmatist. She wasn't a girl to beat about the bush.

'Look, Kate, everybody makes mistakes in life and lots of relationships don't work out. But do you know who the brave people are? They are the ones who have the guts to get out when there's no going back. They are the ones who have the courage to say they failed, and take the big steps and try again.'

Kate was hesitant to accept Jenny's advice. Emotions weren't as cut and dried as Jenny portrayed them.

'There are more complex issues at stake here, Jen. It's not as simple as deciding I fancy him and giving it a go. We have a whole history together and some of it isn't very nice.'

But Jenny was not to be deterred. 'That's true, Kate, but you've just said yourself that you can't get him out from under your skin. What's the harm in giving it one last shot? All it can do is help you make up your mind one way or the other.'

What Kate had not told Jenny was that Timmy was calling at her home later that evening, after his visit at the hospital with Laura.

'So how is she?' Kate asked, as soon as he walked in the door.

'The same as last night. The same as the night before, and the night before that. She's responding to the drugs but they reckon that she has been suffering from depression for the past ten years. They are doing some regression therapy with her and it appears the problems in our marriage may go back to her childhood. They think she may have suffered some trauma which came back to haunt her when she formed her first adult relationship – with me,' Timmy said.

That sounded about right to Kate. Adults who repressed early childhood traumas often only allowed those traumas to manifest when they formed deep relationships with other adults.

'That would certainly explain why she became so introverted after Kyra was born. She may have felt that now she had security, she could let her true feelings come out. It's not uncommon, Timmy.'

He felt like a traitor, but he had to ask her this next question: 'So where does that leave us then? The ball is in your court, Kate. You know how I feel about you.'

Kate hugged him close to her. 'It leaves us as very good friends, Timmy, that's the first and foremost thing for us. After that?' She paused, not wanting to give him false hope, but not wanting to crush any future either. 'Well, after that, we will just have to take it one day at a time. I'm not going anywhere, Timmy, but who knows what the future will bring?'

63

Three months later

Knocker Griffin, former alias Pete Connors, shifted anxiously from foot to foot at the Aer Lingus reservations desk at Dublin Airport. He wished the girl would ever hurry the fuck up with his first-class ticket to Malaga. He had a few drugs contacts there and he intended to start afresh. But he needed to get out fast before Cummins noticed he was fleeing the nest.

'If you could just bear with me a minute, sir, I'll go and authorize your gold card. We've got to seek telephone authorization for last-minute bookings, Mr Griffin,' the snooty ground hostess told him.

A seasoned criminal of Griffin's calibre should have known full well that the young woman was, in fact, going off to telephone the airport police to let them know that the man they wished to

439

apprehend had just attempted to buy a ticket to the Costa del Crime.

Five minutes went by before Griffin started to get seriously antsy. He figured that something was afoot and made to turn around and leave the queue.

'Ah for fuck's sakes,' he said, as he found himself face to face with Detective Timmy Vaughan.

Standing either side of Vaughan were two officers from the Criminal Assets Bureau. Vaughan smiled broadly as the younger of the two read the criminal his rights: 'Mr Griffin, I am arresting you under the Proceeds of Crime Act. We have information to suggest that you have been living off the proceeds of crime. As we speak, our officers are executing warrants for the seizure of your Mercedes car and the three apartments owned by you in Dublin city . . .'

Knocker was by no means a quitter, but he knew that the game was up for him now. When Mickser Cummins got wind of the fact that he had been doing a runner when apprehended – and Knocker knew that the cops would be more than happy to tell him this fact – he would be up the creek without a paddle. Because Knocker certainly did not have the legal or financial back-up to fight the avalanche of charges he knew were coming his way.

He walked quietly away with the officers.

No Knickers Grimes and Breaker Daly sauntered into Mickser Cummins' palatial home. They didn't bother with the service entrance and planted massive muddy footprints on the pristine carpet as they entered.

They walked casually to the back of the mansion, where the gym and sauna were located. No Knickers called out Mickser's name.

'In here, lads,' he said, his voice muffled from the insulation of the sunbed he was lying on.

He was furious with them though. They'd been out of contact the night before and he had needed them to run a few jobs. Now that Griffin was out of the picture, he needed the pair of dozy plonkers more than ever.

Knocker had only gone and gotten himself arrested two weeks earlier by the filth. Heading off to the Costa del Crime he was!

'Fucking gobshite,' Cummins had said to the police tout who called him to inform him of the arrest. 'Fleeing the scene of the crime to the second biggest hang-out in the universe for Irish crims. He's bleedin' dozier than I thought he was. Does he not know that all of those flights to Malaga are monitored by your lot? I'll have the bastard if he so much as breathes my name to those pigs.'

Cummins' police tout had duly, and of course subtly, informed Griffin of Cummins' instructions. Needless to say, Griffin kept schtum when the lads at Store Street station – to which Griffin had been transported after his arrest – passed him on to Timmy for interrogation. It had only been a shot in the dark anyway. Timmy knew that hardened crims rarely ratted each other out. They usually left it to take revenge at a later stage, when nobody was looking.

When No Knickers and Breaker entered the room, Cummins let out a roar at them. He'd been watching them walk their filthy boots onto his beautiful white carpet. 'You stupid pricks!' he shouted. 'I told yez to use the back way. Get those bleedin' filthy shoes off yez now.'

'Ah shut the fuck up, ye big wanker. I won't be wearin' them after today anyway,' No Knickers said. He'd always hated the way Cummins talked to him and he was relishing the thought of being able to get away with treating the man like dirt. All the years of insults and abuse he'd taken from Cummins had been worth it – just to see the look on his face now.

Just as Cummins made to jump from the bed and lunge at No Knickers, Breaker Daly took out a handgun and pointed it directly at Cummins' temple. 'This is from Hacker Hanley,' Breaker said, referring to the new drugs baron who was recruiting from all of the big camps in town.

There was a loud bang, followed by another, then another. And Mickser Cummins went to meet his maker. For the first and last time, he had been set up.